Jack looked at Artie. But Artie wasn't looking at him. Fear rolled off the ghost like ripples of heat off the summer blacktop, and it was infectious.

The long jog up here had already gotten Jack's heart pounding, but now something seemed to clutch at it, a tightness in his chest. It was at least eighty degrees despite the lengthening shadows, but he still felt cold.

Jack turned to see what Artie was staring at.

His mouth dropped open.

The Ravenous.

The thing was huge, eight, maybe nine feet, but it was hard to tell because it was crouched over its victims, a homeless guy with silver hair and dark, leathery skin, and a skinny goth girl with too-black hair who looked like a junkie runaway.

They were nothing. Spirits. Wisps of intelligence and imagination, the essence of people long dead. But here in the Ghostlands, the realm of the spirits, they were more than tangible. The world of the living was all gray and washed out, but the ghosts were real and solid . . . and screaming.

It tore them apart.

Prowlers Series
by Christopher Golden

Available from Pocket Books

PROWLERS

predator
and prey

CHRISTOPHER GOLDEN

POCKET
BOOKS

LONDON • SYDNEY • NEW YORK • TOKYO • SINGAPORE • TORONTO

An *Original* Publication of POCKET BOOKS
a division of Simon & Schuster UK Ltd.
64–78 Kingsway
London
WC1B 6AH

www.simonsays.co.uk

ISBN: 0-7434-4016-1

First Pocket Books UK printing January 2003

10 9 8 7 6 5 4 3 2 1

POCKET BOOKS and colophon are trademarks of
Simon & Schuster

A CIP catalogue record for this book is available from
the British Library

Printed and bound in Great Britain by
Bookmarque Ltd, Croydon, Surrey

For Amber

acknowledgments

Thanks, as always, to Connie and my boys, to Lori Perkins, Lisa Clancy, Micol Ostow, Tom Sniegoski, and Rick Hautala. Special thanks to Pete Donaldson and Brian Gilbert.

PROLOGUE

There were sharks in the water.

Not literal sharks, of course. Not literal water, either. It was more a sort of lesson on life, an observation Kenny Boone had heard a thousand times without ever really listening. Probably because he always figured he was one of the sharks.

But the truth was out today, friends and neighbors.

Kenny was a fish.

And there were sharks in the water.

It was a Wednesday night in the middle of August. The day had been hot as hell, but in the long afternoon shadows it started to cool off, and when night finally fell, it was almost liveable. Enough so that South Street Seaport, tourist mecca on the tip of lower Manhattan Island, was swarming with people looking to let off some steam. A night like this in New York City brought out more than just the tourists. Locals left the office as early as they could to find a watering hole to cool down in, maybe head out with some friends.

That was the kind of night Kenny needed. But it isn't what he got.

Three years he had spent in sales for Signature Software. In that time he put every other member of the sales team to shame, burned past them so fast their faces were charred. Kenny Boone had set the damn bar, raising corporate expectations for everyone else by exceeding his quotas by such huge margins every quarter.

A week ago the VP of sales had died of a heart attack. The job should have been Kenny's for the taking, but the CEO had hired from outside, an old friend he'd worked with at another corporation a decade before.

First thing the new VP did was announce layoffs. Kenny Boone was the first to go.

All his life he had been convinced he was a shark. It hurt so much to discover he was wrong. Kenny had packed a box with his things and then, just before he got on the elevator, realised that the last thing he wanted to do was go home. Instead, he had asked Kayla Frigerio to let him store the stuff in her office until he could get back to pick it up, and then he hopped on the subway and headed down to South Street Seaport.

In his custom Italian suit, creases so sharp they could cut, he sat at an outdoor table at Moreno's Bistro and ordered a beer even as he pulled out his cell phone. A little company was all he wanted. He had called Bart Tapply first, a friend from Signature. Then other friends and acquaintances in the city, co-workers and clients mostly, for he didn't really know too many people away from the job.

Come meet me for a beer. I'm buying.

Everyone had something else to do. Everyone but Kenny. Or maybe it was just that they sensed he was wounded, that his ego was bleeding. And only a fool would go anywhere near blood in the water. Blood in the water would draw the sharks. They would sense his weakness, and he figured most people were smart enough to realise that if they hung around with him, they might look weak by association.

Assholes, Kenny thought.

Hours passed and like a fool he kept trying. He had a nice dinner at Moreno's, but he hated to eat alone. Did enough of that on business trips. So he had to rely on the beer to keep him company. By seven o'clock he knew from the look on the waiter's face that he had worn out his welcome at Moreno's so he started to wander the Seaport. There were other restaurants, other bars.

A couple of guys—Chaz Wexler and Rob Gonci—had said to call them back, that they'd try to meet him if he was still around later. So he made it a point to be around, knowing how much of a loser that made him, but not caring at this point. All he wanted was contact with someone who wasn't interested in sharks and fish, someone who would laugh at a bad joke or shoot the breeze about the Mets with him.

The river slapped the wooden pilings that held up the pier. Sea gulls fluttered nearby, picking up scraps of everything from curly fries to cotton candy. A little after nine he finally decided to head home. With his now wrinkled jacket slung over his shoulder and his briefcase dangling from his other hand, he set off across the cobblestones. Having the cobblestones was good 'cause it kept the inline skaters and skateboarders off the main Seaport area and bad because he was considerably drunker now, and it made him sway even more than he normally would have.

But being drunk was not all bad. It blurred the world for him, and he needed that. People stared at him; a forty-ish mother with two small children who had no business still being awake chided him aloud. Disgusting, she clearly thought he was. Kenny smiled at her, then flipped her the middle finger. Her husband began to move toward him angrily but the wife held him back.

Kenny laughed.

As he headed for the subway, his attention was drawn to music—sweet, heart-wrenching blues. Curious, his thinking fuzzy, he pushed through a constant flux of humanity to have a look at a cute brunette girl singing blues tunes older than her grandfather. It was incongruous, sure, but the girl sounded sweet and earnest and she was easy on the eyes, and so she drew even more people than the juggling clowns and fire swallowers and soapbox prophets.

"Been downhearted," the girl sang, an old one Kenny remembered hearing on his father's turntable back when people knew what vinyl records looked like. He'd been a kid then, and there was always someone there to pick him up if he fell down.

Not anymore.

Yet somehow, all of a sudden, as he stood and listened to the young girl playing the blues for whatever coins and dollars people would toss into her guitar case, he began to feel a little bit better. Kenny had been screwed, no question. And nobody had wanted to come down and join him for his personal pity party. Not that he could blame them. Most of them probably had real excuses anyway but even if they didn't, who would choose to sit around and get all maudlin with him when he was in this sort of mood?

You're drunk, you loser, he told himself. *Stumble home, sleep it off, then start again.* After all, it was not like a head-hunter would have a hard time finding him another position. It was just that he was so close to that VP spot he could almost taste it.

There'll be another, he thought. And as he watched the pretty girl with the painfully earnest face and the weary voice, it occurred to him that everybody sings the blues sometimes.

Kenny laughed softly to himself. The sentiment was true, but even in his head it sounded corny as hell.

Exhausted from his own self-pity, too drunk for his own good but just sober enough to get on the right sub-way train home, Kenny turned away from the blues girl and bumped through the crowd, using his briefcase to help clear a path. He had not gone five steps before his bleary gaze focused on a woman perhaps ten feet away. Under his breath—but probably a little louder than Kenny realized—he said, "Whoa."

She wasn't the most beautiful woman he had ever seen

but she was certainly the most striking. Her skin was the color of caramel and her hair was died a deep blood red. In a white, belly-baring tank top with spaghetti straps and a pair of dark blue jeans, she looked like a goddess.

Yet her appearance was not the most incredible thing about her. Kenny blinked a few times to clear his vision and gazed at her more closely. The girl stood there at the edge of the crowd listening to the blues, and no one went near her. She was not just alone, but the crowd seemed almost unconsciously to have given her a wide berth. For a moment he only stood and watched her, aware of how odd he must look with his jacket over his shoulder, briefcase at his side, swaying and staring. Aware of it, but not caring.

Then she looked at him. Kenny blinked and rocked back a bit as though her gaze were enough to knock him down. The woman smiled slightly and turned her attention back to the music. Kenny shook his head in amazement, took one more look around for a boyfriend or anyone else she might be with, but no, the girl was alone.

And that seemed like a sin to him.

Kenny ran a hand through his hair but didn't bother with any other attempts to improve his appearance. He was drunk. There wasn't a damn thing he could do to hide it. He just hoped it wasn't obvious *how* drunk.

"Excuse me?" he said as he stepped up beside her.

Her eyes were orange. Kenny was speechless for a second. Then he realized they had to be contact lenses and he felt foolish. What was he supposed to say to a woman like this?

"Yes?" she asked, one eyebrow raised, as if she were amused by the interruption.

He wasn't sure if that was good or bad.

Kenny smiled, hoping he didn't completely reek of beer. "Sorry. Not real good with the native tongue tonight. It's just that I couldn't let myself go home unless I talked to you first. I saw you standing here by yourself and, well, there's something wrong with that picture. I thought I'd at least introduce myself, ask you if you wanted to go for a cup of coffee, and then you could tell me to go away."

With a toss of her bright red hair, she laughed throatily, almost nastily. Her teeth showed with that laugh and Kenny flinched when he saw her wide smile. There was something wrong with her teeth. Too many of them, too sharp, as though they'd been filed down to points. He blinked, glanced away a second as he shifted the briefcase from one hand to the other, draping his coat over it. When he looked back at her, he saw that it had only been in his mind. She had a beautiful smile.

"That's how you think it will go, hmm?" she said.

"Pretty much," he confessed, still troubled by the hallucination he had just had. He had no idea he was that drunk.

"Give it a try," the girl said defiantly. She thrust her hands into the pockets of her jeans and regarded him curiously.

Self-conscious now, he hesitated. But there was nothing to lose here. At worst, he was killing a few more minutes before he went home to his apartment alone.

"Hi. I'm Kenny," he said, sticking out his hand. "Kenny Boone."

She shook his hand, and he was surprised at the strength in her grip. Her skin was hot to the touch.

"My name is Jasmine."

Kenny swallowed nervously. "Would you like to go and get a . . . a cup of coffee or something, Jasmine?"

Again she smiled. Again, for just a moment, he had the sense that there was something wrong with her teeth.

"Sorry, Kenny. I'm waiting for someone. But thanks for asking."

He fell apart inside, like his soul was made of glass and she had just shattered it. After the day he'd had, the last thing he needed was this arrogant, beautiful woman playing games with him. Kenny didn't even have the energy to tell her off.

With a shake of his head, he turned to leave. "Thanks for nothing, you bitch," he muttered.

Kenny bumped full on into a lanky guy who stared at him with eyes the color of polished brass. Contacts again. Had to be. The guy had blond hair, too long but it hung on him well, and a two-day stubble on his chin. There was something about him, not just his look but the way he carried himself, that reminded Kenny of a gunfighter.

A smile flickered across the guy's face for just a second, and then he was all business. "You probably shouldn't have said that," the gunfighter said.

"Yeah?" Kenny replied, angry now, letting the beer do the work his brain ought to have been doing. Instinct told him to walk away but alcohol and pride wouldn't let him.

"Yeah," the guy said sadly. Then he glanced over Kenny's shoulder at Jasmine. "We're gonna have to go somewhere else to talk, aren't we?"

"Hello, Dallas," Jasmine said, greeting the man warmly. "It does look like we'll have to relocate. You know how the cattle can be. Don't want a stampede."

Kenny was slow catching on, but now he got it. This was the guy she was waiting for. And now they were having this conversation around him, like he wasn't even there. He thought again about fish and sharks, and for just a second he felt good about himself. As down and dirty as he had gotten to play the game of software sales over the years, he had never been as casually cruel as these two.

"Excuse me," he said dismissively, trying to push past the guy she'd called Dallas.

"Too late for that, partner," Dallas replied.

He grabbed Kenny by the arm, spun him around to face Jasmine and led him into the shadows. Kenny tried to pull away, but he could not. They were strong, these two. Jasmine slid up to him, taller than he was. Her arms went around him, and then her hands were on his throat.

She smiled as she broke his neck. Her orange eyes and her impossibly sharp teeth were the last things he saw as they let him slip slowly to the pavement to die.

Kenny's eyes were open.

He stared up at the night sky; stars washed out by the lights of the Seaport and of Manhattan itself. Voices drifted to him. Someone called out in alarm. With a roll of his eyes he could see

Jasmine and Dallas walking away from him, calmly speaking to each other as though nothing had happened, as though he had been forgotten.

Forgotten.

But not forgotten, because now there came more shouts of alarm. Someone nearly stumbled over him, a teenage girl. She glanced down at him and winced, then looked around for someone else to join her in her staring. Then there were others . . . so many others . . . voices shouting . . . staring eyes . . . heads bent over to study him . . . who did it? . . . how'd it happen . . . he was talking with some girl, where'd she go?

Sirens. He heard sirens. The rumble of gathered voices like thunder, a storm not far off. Ominous. Threatening. More faces above him, police officers pushing people back, EMTs. But all of them look strange, now, like shadows of people, like two-dimensional gray things he had to blink to see.

He didn't feel drunk anymore.

Words echoed. Dead. He's dead. You're dead. I'm dead.

I'm dead.

Another face above him, suddenly, but this one isn't a shadow. A young guy, Latino maybe, with a goatee and a cigarette burning. He's real, this one. Full color, 3-D, like Kenny could reach out and touch him. So he tried. At first it was like his hand was underwater. But then his fingers broke the surface and he stretched an arm out, up . . . and the goateed guy grabbed his hand and hauled him up onto his feet.

Kenny's stomach convulsed and he felt like he was going to puke. But not from the beer. He wasn't drunk anymore. Not at all.

He leaned on the guy for balance and the smoke got in his eyes, but the weirdest thing was he couldn't smell it. Couldn't *smell the smoke at all, and usually the acrid odor of cigarettes made him nauseous.*

"Hey," said the smoking man. "Hey. What's your name?"

Kenny opened his mouth. Wasn't sure if anything would come out. He glanced around him and saw that the people, the buildings, South Street Seaport itself . . . everything looked as though he were watching it on an old black-and-white TV with bad reception. Everything except the river, and the guy with the cigarette and the goatee. Those were real.

"I'm Kenny," he said. "Kenny Boone." *And the introduction reminded him of Jasmine and her sharp teeth. Jasmine who had . . .*

"Call me Rafe," the guy said. "Don't worry, Kenny. You're off balance right now, but you'll be feeling better soon. Get your bearings and stuff, y'know?"

"I'm dead," *Kenny told Rafe.*

Rafe smiled and nodded kindly. "Sí, amigo. You got it in one. Better than most."

Kenny wanted to cry, wanted to scream, but all he felt was a kind of numb resignation. He turned around and there, on the ghost-gray pavement, he saw a pair of expensive Italian leather shoes sticking out from between the two EMTs who crouched there. Me, *he thought.* But how could it be? I'm here.

Forlorn, he turned to look at Rafe again, thinking this was just the perfect end to the perfect day. Smoke from Rafe's cigarette curled in the air but Kenny still couldn't smell it.

But he smelled something. Something . . . what was that smell? Like skunk and burning rubber.

Rafe's eyes went wide. "Oh, no!"

"What?" *Kenny demanded.* "What is it?"

"Run, man! Just run!"

With that, Rafe took off, running flat out across the gray cobblestones as though he were in the final stretch of a marathon. As Rafe ran, the shadows of the living seemed to swirl and undulate around him like thick fog. Kenny knew that wasn't possible, that in the flesh and blood world it was still a hot August night where something awful had happened, but that everyone would go home to their lives. Not Rafe, though. Not Kenny. Not anyone over here, 'cause this wasn't the flesh-and-blood world.

There were only ghosts here.

Slowly, hesitant in his confusion, Kenny started to run after Rafe. It didn't feel like running, though. More like falling. Simple as that, really. He tried to follow Rafe through the smog-shapes of the living, of the flesh world, but the man was gone.

Somewhere far off he heard shouts of alarm and knew somehow that they were cries of the dead, the shouts of ghosts, not voices from the flesh world.

"Rafe?" Kenny called.

No, no, he thought. Not going to be alone again. Not here.

He ran faster, the shadows of life all around him, obfuscating his vision for a moment so he had to wave his hands in front of his face to brush them away, push the life away.

Please, no, Kenny thought.

Then he slowed. Frowned. There was that smell again.

He paused, began to turn. "What is that?" he whispered into the land of the dead. There are only ghosts here, he thought again.

But he was wrong.

As he turned, it lunged from the flesh-shadows with a roar that washed away the gray all around him, silenced the voices in the distance for just an instant until, somewhere, ghosts began to scream. Soul-sucking eyes big as half-dollars burned with hunger as it stared at him. A thick, green, leathery tongue slid out over a mouthful of teeth like razor blades, viscous drool dripping from its snout.

"Only ghosts," Kenny whispered. He began to back up, hands raised. "Not fair. It isn't fair. What . . . what happens now? After this?"

Its claws lashed out, tore Kenny open, then hauled him up and began to eat.

"Not fair," Kenny moaned again.

Then he was no more.

CHAPTER 1

Like a ghost, the framed photo of Jack Dwyer's mother seemed to stare at him from atop his bureau. He caught a glimpse of it out of the corner of his eye and grinned, feeling foolish. On his bed lay several T-shirts and two pairs of denim shorts he had discarded. Jack ran a hand through his unruly hair and then reached up into his closet for a gray Boston Red Sox shirt he had only worn a couple of times. He wasn't a big sports fan, so he always felt like a poseur when he wore it, but he figured it was more interesting than a plain Gap T-shirt and slightly more subdued than the one with the big Batman logo on the front.

Plus the clock was ticking.

From a chair in the corner of the room, he picked up the blue jeans he had tossed there moments before and put them on. Belt, wallet, car keys, then socks and sneakers. As he sat on the bed, lacing up his sneakers, he

15

glanced up again at the picture of his mother, Bridget. She had died when Jack was nine years old, and he wondered if that was why just looking at the photo could make him feel like a child.

He bounced up off the bed and paused briefly in front of the bureau to gently touch the corner of the frame. Though he had few strong memories of his mother, he clearly recalled her standing in his bedroom doorway so many times, trying to get him to hurry and decide what to wear to school that day. More often than not, she had had to decide for him.

It was a rare day off for Jack. Along with his older sister Courtney, he owned and managed Bridget's Irish Rose Pub, their inheritance from their mother. When he was working, the only thing he had to decide was what color his shirt was going to be, for every day he wore one embroidered with Bridget's logo on the breast.

That was simpler, and Jack liked things simple.

At the door, he paused and glanced around the room, feeling as though he had forgotten something. His gaze settled on his nightstand, and he strode quickly back to snatch up the book that lay there, *Journal of the Gun Years,* a western by Richard Matheson. One last time he patted his pockets to confirm the presence of his wallet and keys, then he strode out of the room.

The Dwyer siblings owned the whole building, and their apartment above the pub consisted of two bedrooms, a kitchen, a bathroom, and a living room that doubled as a guest room. Lately the "guest room" had become a semi-permanent third bedroom for Molly

Hatcher, a friend of the family, though her relationship to Jack and Courtney was far more complicated than that.

Jack poked his head into what had become Molly's room, but she wasn't there.

"Mol?" he said, glancing about the hallway.

"In here."

Her voice had come from Courtney's room. Curious, Jack went across the hall and stood in the open door. Courtney lived a pretty Spartan life, and what she had she kept neat. A bed, a desk and chair, a computer, a bureau. Yet while once her room had looked so empty as to make one wonder if anyone actually lived there, in the past month it had acquired a new sort of clutter in the form of newspaper clippings and internet articles that were pinned on the walls all about the room.

Molly stood beside Courtney's desk and stared at one of the articles. She wore cutoffs that drew attention to her long legs and a light cotton shirt unbuttoned over the green tankini top she wore. Her usually unruly red hair was tied back in a ponytail and she held her hands on her hips as though what she read had made her angry.

"Hey," Jack said. "You ready?"

When she turned, a hint of that anger and frustration remained on her face. Then Molly saw him, and smiled happily.

"Are you sure jeans are the most comfortable beach wear?" she teased.

He shrugged. "I look stupid in shorts."

"You're going to look stupid in jeans. Tell me you at

17

least own a bathing suit. I mean, I know you don't get out much, but—"

"I haven't been to the beach in a year," Jack confirmed. "But I do own a bathing suit, thank you very much. I'm wearing it under my jeans."

"Good," she said. "Now all we need are beach towels and we can get out of here."

But they both hesitated a moment, the brightness of their conversation dimming somewhat. Jack glanced at the articles on the wall again, and Molly turned to follow his gaze.

"Courtney find something new?" he asked.

Molly studied the wall, hugging herself now. "A lot of little things. Suspicious things in Wisconsin, Louisiana, Quebec . . . let me see . . . Arizona, L.A. Mutilation murders mostly, though the Wisconsin one was some builders who found some remains while digging a foundation for a house. Yeah, I'd want my house built there now. Might be Prowler killings or they might be something else."

Jack stepped up behind her and examined the print-outs and clippings, the grisly headlines, photographs of the victims alive and well and smiling.

"Chances are, most of them are human killers, and the FBI or the local cops will catch up to them," he reminded her. "But we can't go running around the country every time there's some nasty murder. We're not detectives. If a pattern shows up, or if somebody says they saw a monster, then we'll look into it. We'll fight them when we can find them. But there's only the four of us, Molly, and it's a big country."

Grim-faced, she turned to him. "What makes you think it's just this country?"

Jack nodded. "A big world out there, exactly. We can't be the only people who know the Prowlers exist. There must be others out there who are fighting them."

"We should find those people, then," Molly said, her eyes searching his.

"You're probably right." Jack glanced away a moment, then he studied her curiously. "There's only so much we can do. We have lives to lead. Responsibilities. You're going away to Yale in less than two weeks, Molly. It isn't like you can take off on some hunting trip to Arizona after that."

For a long moment she stared at him and Jack wanted to turn away from the intensity of her gaze, but would not. Molly hated the Prowlers as much as he did, probably more. They had discovered the monsters' existence several months before, when a pack had come to Boston, and Artie Carroll had been one of the first to die.

Jack's best friend.

Molly's boyfriend.

Jack and Molly had always been close, but Artie's death created a new intimacy for them, both in their need to grieve together, and, after the discovery of the Prowlers' existence, in their need to destroy the creatures. Over the ensuing months they had done both, and during that time Molly had left the home of her brutal, alcoholic mother and moved in with the Dwyers.

It simplified things and complicated them all at once. Molly started to work in the pub, they focused their efforts on tracking news stories that might lead them to new Prowlers, and they tried to pretend that their intimacy was not on the verge of becoming something more than friendship. Not that it was a bad thing, these feelings they clearly had for each other, the single kiss they had shared in Vermont a month earlier when they had almost died.

It would have been nice, but Artie had been dead only a few months and Molly was obviously still haunted by his memory.

Jack, on the other hand, was haunted by his ghost.

Shortly after Artie's murder, the ghost had appeared to Jack in the pub after hours, and had touched him somehow, pried open a place in his mind that would allow Jack to see other spirits as well. Lost souls. A spirit world Artie called the Ghostlands. Among those lost and wandering phantoms were many of the victims of the Prowlers. With their help, Jack and Molly had survived, had destroyed a lot of monsters. Molly knew about the Ghostlands, but at Artie's request Jack had never told her that her dead boyfriend's ghost still hung around. He thought she suspected, but she didn't *know*.

Complicated.

The silence between them lingered too long.

"Yeah," Molly said at last, her voice a hush. "Two weeks and I'll be gone. Then you can have your living room back."

Jack didn't know what to say to that. He clutched the book in his hand and shifted uncomfortably, gave her a little half-smile without knowing what it was for.

"We should go," Molly said at last.

"I'll get the towels," Jack replied. "You've got the radio?"

"In my room. I'll grab it."

They met up again moments later at the door that led down into the restaurant. It was not quite nine o'clock in the morning, two hours before they would open for the lunch crowd. The kitchen staff would begin arriving any minute, and the waiters in less than an hour, but for the moment, Courtney Dwyer was the only other person in the place.

When Jack and Molly went down the stairs, Courtney was sitting at one of the round tables in the restaurant section of the pub. The place was all dark wood and brass rails and Chieftains on the sound system overhead, a quintessential Irish pub, but a little bigger, a little brighter, a little cleaner. *Boston* magazine had singled them out twice in the past three years, which was good for business.

"Everything under control?" Jack asked as they walked over to the table.

Courtney glanced up at them, a strand of her chestnut hair falling across the freckled bridge of her nose. She blew at it, but then had to brush it back with her hands. She wore a dark green shirt with the pub's logo across the breast, khaki pants, and white tennis shoes. It was a more casual look than she usually wore on the job, but Jack thought it suited her. When his sister dressed more stylishly, it seemed to drain some of the humor out of her.

"I think we're good," she replied. "They cleaned up

pretty well last night. Kitchen's stocked, I've already done the ordering. I'm just trying to get next week's schedule out of the way."

Jack laughed. "So what you're saying is, we're not needed at all."

A sly grin spread across Courtney's face. "I won't even notice you're gone."

"I'm deeply wounded," Jack replied, holding a hand over his heart.

Courtney began to rise from the table. She was twenty-nine years old, but with the light spray of freckles across the bridge of her nose and the mischief that sparkled in her blue eyes, she looked younger. At least until she stood and had to put some of her weight on the lion's-head cane she had inherited from their grandfather. She was young and smart and vivacious, but the accident that had killed their mother had left Courtney reliant upon that cane for the rest of her life, and Jack often wondered if people could see past that.

"Get going already," she told them. "When you come back you can remind me what a beach looks like."

"We'll be back by five or so if you end up needing help on the dinner shift," Jack said.

With a wild grin, Courtney lifted her cane and held it like a baseball bat. "Do I have to chase you two out of here?"

Molly clapped a hand on Jack's back and propelled him toward the door. "Nope," she said. "We're going. The world might crack in two if Jack has a little fun, but we'll risk the apocalypse."

preDatoR anD pRey

As Jack held the door for Molly, ready with keys in hand to lock it behind them, Courtney called to them from inside.

"Thanks for the warning. You two have fun on your date!"

Jack gaped at her. He saw Molly stiffen a little beside him. For a moment, he fumbled for the words, then yelled back to his sister.

"It's not a date, Courtney. We're just going to the beach."

Courtney stood in the middle of the restaurant, leaning on her cane, her smile insinuating that she knew better. "Whatever you say."

Jack considered protesting again, but didn't want to make too much of it. He locked the doors and then he and Molly walked over to the lot where his old Jeep was parked, Courtney's words hanging awkwardly between them.

The Mustang's engine purred as Dallas guided it up and down the streets of Newton, Massachusetts. On the CD player was a bootleg live recording of the Clash he had taped himself in an earlier era. He'd burned the CD himself, but the quality was crap given the source. Dallas didn't mind the hiss and pop at all.

Seven years had passed since the last time he had been by to visit Valerie and it was going to take him a few minutes to get his bearings. Up in this part of Newton, all the streets pretty much looked the same; huge old Colonials and Victorians were set back from the tree-shaded road.

The homes were kept up perfectly, BMWs and Benzes in the driveways, trophy wives walking the dogs or landscaping the gardens for pleasure rather than necessity.

A redhead in a half-tee jogged by with her retriever on a leash and smiled at Dallas as he passed in the restored, blue '67 convertible. He shot her a pleasant grin but kept his attention on the road, looking up and down the streets he passed for Valerie's house.

He sniffed the air as he drove.

His foot tapped the brake and Dallas gazed down one side street. The trees were old and leaned in over the pavement, creating a tunnel of leaves, the road below dappled by shafts of sunlight that slipped through the canopy overhead. Five houses down was a hundred-and-fifty-year-old Victorian painted a sort of rust color, its shutters and trim the hue of brick.

Dallas turned the volume down a couple of decibels and took the right onto Ashtree Lane. He slowed in front of the house, then pulled into the driveway behind a little red MG. There was a recent model Honda next to it. Past the cars he could see the carriage house that was attached to the main structure. Valerie had gutted the place and put a swimming pool inside, but externally the house looked just as it had when it was built. She had owned it once before, in the twenties, and when she bought it again she restored it completely.

Keys jangling in his hand, he popped the trunk and grabbed the single, large suitcase he had brought with him. He whistled as he went up the walk and the stone steps and knocked on the door. A minute passed and he was about to knock again when he caught the scent of Valerie inside, moving toward the door.

It opened, and Dallas grinned. She stood there in a white cotton tank undershirt and matching French-cut panties. Her black hair was cut short and was such a just-rolled-out-of-bed mess that she looked almost punk. Valerie's face was lined and angular, her nose straight and thin, her lips perfect. She smiled at Dallas as though she might like to have him for dinner.

"What the hell are you doing here?" she asked.

Dallas shook his too-long blond hair back and hefted his suitcase in his hand. "Visiting."

"You have just totally made my week," she said, then punctuated the sentence with a feline yawn and stretch. "Get in here," she said with a toss of her head.

Valerie shut the door behind him. The second Dallas put his suitcase down she threw her arms around him and gave him a quick, sweet kiss before laying her head on his chest. Dallas kissed her forehead and ran his hands over her well-muscled back.

"So what are you really doing here?" Valerie asked.

"Got a local gig," he replied. "In Boston. But I couldn't swing back up this way and not see you."

She drew back and stared up at him, one eyebrow arched. "Cheaper than a hotel."

"There's that," he confessed.

Valerie knew better, of course, well enough that Dallas did not even have to argue the point. They went back a very long way, had shared a great deal. Decades might go by without their speaking, but when they saw each other it always seemed as if only a week had passed.

"Val?"

Dallas looked up at the voice. He had scented the human in the house the second he stepped inside. While he and Valerie were talking, the guy had come softly down the stairs and now stood just across the foyer. He was young, twenty-two maybe, with a severe cut to his dark hair and the kind of strong jaw and facial structure that you usually only saw in old war movies. The guy wore beige cotton pants and buttoned up his shirt as he stared expectantly at them.

"What the hell is going on here?" he demanded.

After the first glance, Dallas did not look at him again. "Still bringing home strays, I see."

Valerie tried to stifle a naughty giggle. "You're awful."

"I just know you," Dallas replied. "You always keep a house pet or two around."

The boy toy with the military jaw had heard enough. He marched across the hardwood floor. "Hey, pretty boy, maybe you oughta let go of her now," he snapped. "Val, who the hell is this guy?"

Valerie ignored him. Instead, she gazed up at Dallas and rolled her eyes. "His name's Paul," she said in a stage whisper. "He's grown a little attached."

"What . . . what the hell is with you, Val?" Paul stammered, unsure now.

"They always do with you, sweetheart. You're irresistible."

"Flatterer."

"Truthsayer," Dallas replied, shooting her a wounded expression.

"Look, I don't know what this is supposed to be, but I am about through with it," Paul said, his anger returning full force. "I'm talking to you, man." He tapped Dallas hard on the shoulder. "Hey!"

Dallas made a face. "He's really gonna cramp our style."

Valerie took a step back from him, glanced at Paul, then back at Dallas. "No he's not."

"Damn it, Val, do not talk about me like I'm not here! I swear to God you don't want to cross me."

Dallas couldn't help laughing at that one. Valerie held up a hand to cover her own grin, but her face reddened. He loved that little girl quality about her.

"He's funny, I'll give him that," Dallas told her. "Is he traceable?"

"Not really," she replied.

With a nod, Dallas turned toward the fuming man again. Paul puffed up his chest, fists balled in rage, but he had the scent of fear on him, too. Apparently he was bright enough to have realized that there was something going on here other than losing his girlfriend.

"Hi, Paul!" Dallas said brightly.

The guy blinked, startled.

"What're you, an actor?"

Confused, Paul glanced at Valerie and then nodded.

"What is it with you and actors?" Dallas asked her.

"Maybe I just need a little drama in my life."

Dallas sighed. That had always been the issue with

Valerie. He was methodical, finding order in things, and she was always the chaos girl. He shrugged and looked at Paul again. The guy had deflated somewhat, thrown completely off track by this new turn in the conversation.

"I've got a new role for you," Dallas told him. "You get to be bait."

Then Dallas began to change, skin tearing and flaking away as the thick coat of fur sprouted from within, muscles swelled, bones popped and realigned. His snout stretched and he bared his gleaming fangs in an amused, savage grin that Paul would undoubtedly see as a snarl.

Paul began to scream.

Valerie only laughed and watched as Dallas lunged at him, claws slashing down, blood spraying the hardwood.

Ogunquit, Maine, was an hour and a half from Boston but worth the drive. Jack had not been to the little seaside village in several years, but it had not changed very much. There were plenty of clothing stores and gift shops in the tiny downtown area, but Ogunquit had none of the crass, jaded atmosphere of Hampton and Salisbury to the south or Old Orchard Beach to the north.

As far as Jack was concerned, the only unpleasant thing about Ogunquit was trying to find parking at the beach. Eventually he had solved the problem by parking in the dirt and gravel lot behind the Betty Doon motel near the center of town and hoping the Jeep wouldn't get towed. He and Molly had walked down to the beach from there.

It was a unique beach, accessible only by a small

bridge that crossed a river that ran parallel to the shore and then curved out into the ocean, so that the beach area was shaped like an enormous letter J. The riverside was calm, and there were a lot of families with small children there, a rainbow of umbrellas scattered across the sand.

Jack and Molly had settled on the other side, where the surf was high and the water was almost always cold. The beach was crowded, but they had managed to find a decent spot.

That had been four hours ago.

Now he lay on his stomach on a towel in the shade of the umbrella and enjoyed the heat and the almost tropical breeze. Voices shouted nearby, children screeching as they splashed. Where the tide had receded and left the sand damp, teenagers played Frisbee and fathers flew kites with their children.

Jack had not been so relaxed in what seemed like forever. He was dimly aware of his book still clutched in one hand. Molly lay on her towel only a few feet away. With his eyes slitted open he could see her propped up on her side, facing him, watching the people on the beach, a bottle of cold spring water in her hand. Molly seemed pensive.

"Surrender," Jack said, his voice raspy from lack of use.

She glanced over, obviously surprised to hear from him. "What?"

"Surrender," he repeated. "How often do we get to do something like this? Just relax and do nothing at all? But at the moment your mind is somewhere else. I've gotta say, that seems pretty criminal to me."

A lopsided grin spread across her features. "Sorry. I'll try to reach the nirvana that you're in."

"You'd love it here," Jack told her, his smile a mirror of hers. "So you going to tell me what's on your mind?"

"College."

"Ah," Jack said with a tiny, sage nod. "A lot of new responsibilities. Big changes. Not that I have any idea what I'm talking about. I'm just repeating what I've heard."

"Do you ever regret not going?"

He rolled over on his side. "Never thought about it much, to be honest. I know, that's weird, right? Maybe I should. But I guess I always figured I shouldn't lose any sleep over something that was so out of my control. The pub's a lot of work."

"Courtney would have managed," Molly reasoned. "Hired more staff. I'm sure she would have done whatever it took to make it happen if you had wanted to go."

"I guess," Jack allowed. "But maybe I really didn't want to go. She's the only family I've got, you know? She always stuck by me so I did the same for her. Plus, it was my mother's place." He paused and studied her. "You're lucky, y'know? Okay, it sucks that you don't have any financial support from family, but you can go as far as that brain'll take you. Nothing holding you back."

"You think of the pub as having held you back?"

Jack shook his head. "No. Of course not. It just narrowed my options, that's all. It was my decision. I just had to figure out what my real priorities were. You know what I mean?"

"I think I do," she said, and a thin smile appeared on her face. "You make it sound so easy."

Jack frowned and studied her. "You're not having second thoughts, are you?"

"Me? No," Molly replied, dismissing the question out of hand.

Though he wanted only the best for her, Jack could not help being a bit disappointed. The truth was, he wanted her to have second thoughts.

Again, Molly seemed to drift off, lost in thought. She tipped her water bottle up and took a long swig. A radio played an ancient Eagles song a couple of encampments away.

"Want to go in for another swim?" Molly asked.

"Maybe in a little bit." He closed his eyes and lay his head down again, enjoying the breeze and the shouts and the comfort of the heat and sand. Which was when Molly poured the cold water all over his back. Jack let out a shout as he leaped up.

"You're evil!"

"Well, come and get me, then!" she said, and took off down the sand toward the water.

Jack gave chase, and though he fully intended to get her back for the shock of that cold water, he was happy to see that she had shaken loose whatever thoughts had been bothering her.

Molly ran into the water, hurdling waves as it grew deeper, and then dove right in, unmindful of the cold temperature of the ocean. Jack followed, his momentum nearly causing him to trip, but he took a few last long

PROWLERS

steps and then plunged into the water after her. Molly was maybe six feet away, and he lunged at her. She shrieked almost giddily and tried to dodge him, but was not fast enough. Jack grabbed her by the shoulder, put his other hand on top of her head, and dunked her into the Atlantic even as they were both battered by a high wave.

He barely kept his footing, but he lost hold of her. As he glanced around to search for her again, something tugged on his legs and he went under, sputtering and choking on salt water. Jack scrambled to get his feet beneath him again, and when he stood up, he saw Molly close by. Her grin was even wider as she pushed her wet hair away from her face. The bathing suit clung damply to her in a way that made him want to look again and yet made him feel as though he ought to look away, all at the same time.

Molly tensed as though she had seen that reaction on his face. Her smile faltered and the energy seemed to go out of her.

"Can I ask you a question?" she asked.

"Yeah."

Molly ran both hands through her water-darkened hair, straightening it out. "Is this a date?"

Jack blinked, his mouth slightly parted. He started to speak, then stopped, unsure how to reply. Her eyes searched his for an answer. After a few seconds of fumbling, he slid down into the water and allowed himself to float as he regarded her.

"Do . . . I mean, do you want it to be?" he asked at last.

"I'm not sure," she said, slipping down into the water

32

just as he had, swimming just a bit to keep afloat. "We never talked about what happened in Vermont, when we . . . I mean, I think I do, want it to be. But wanting that makes me feel like I'm betraying something."

"Betraying Artie," Jack said.

She nodded.

"I can't help you with that," he went on. Though there were so many things he wished he could say, that he ought to say, for Molly's sake. "Maybe if we had time, that would change things. But I don't want to confuse you, or myself, and you're going away in a couple of weeks."

For a second he thought she was going to argue. Wanted her to argue. But then Molly just started to swim, no longer meeting his gaze.

"Where do you want to have dinner?" she asked.

But Jack did not answer. His attention was riveted on a spot just past her, where a thirtyish man with a toddler on his shoulders waded into the waves. And where the ghost of Artie Carroll, in jeans and a torn sweatshirt, hung above the ocean and beckoned to Jack.

"Artie," Jack whispered.

Molly flinched at the name, then turned to see exactly what Jack was staring at.

CHAPTER 2

Artie.

For a moment Molly simply drifted there in the water, letting it tug at her and rock her with its inexorable power. She tasted salt on her lips, felt the cold of the ocean seep into her bones, turning her numb. But she knew that it was not truly the water that had done that. A wave rolled past, lifting her up and then gently lowering her again, and she stared first at Jack and then at the distant spot along the beach where he stared at a place just above the waves.

A sea gull flew past.

Children chased one another in the sand just along the shore where the waves rippled like little bits of magic. A gray-haired man—an older father or young grandfather—directed a trio of girls in the construction of a sand castle of extraordinary proportions.

The gull must have cawed. The surf must have whispered on the sand. The children must have shrieked with pleasure. Molly could hear none of it. She found herself suddenly deaf. Deaf save for the single word that Jack had spoken.

Artie.

Molly had suspected, but she had not known. Even now, Jack would doubtless try to explain it away. But it wouldn't work anymore. Now she knew.

Slowly, she rose up from the water and stared at that spot where she thought the ghost must be.

Jack touched her arm and she flinched.

"Molly. I . . . I need to . . ."

She turned away from him and waded through the low waves toward the shore. As though she had broken through some barrier, the moment she set foot on the dry sand the world seemed to rush back in all around her. The flap of the wind against an umbrella. Splashing and laughter and voices.

But even out of the water, beneath the sun, she still felt cold.

The ghost shimmered above the water like heat rising off pavement. As Jack swam parallel to the shore, there were moments when the sun shone down at a strange angle that made the spectre seem to disappear completely for just a moment before reappearing. Artie's too-long hair had been blond in life, but with the halo effect of the sun shining through it—through him—it looked almost white.

Though he knew how foolish the thought was, Jack

could not help but imagine that everyone on the beach was staring at him. Self-conscious, he swam a little farther out from shore, past a pair of twelve- or thirteen-year-old boys who were bodysurfing.

Waves rolled by underneath the hovering spirit, their tips just cresting white, and the higher ones almost seemed to blend with the strange vapour that comprised the ghost from the knees on down. Jack glanced back to the shore and saw Molly sitting on her towel, knees drawn up in front of her, hugging herself and staring at him. A sickly sort of flutter began in his stomach, and he forced himself to turn away, to look back at the ghost.

"What the hell are you doing here?" Jack asked.

Artie was not looking at him, however. The ghost's black eyes, like holes torn in some endless night, were instead turned toward the beach.

"Why did Molly take off like that?" Artie asked, and his voice had a tinny echo, as though he were speaking through some cheap microphone.

"I said your name."

Those black eyes turned upon him now, and though Jack knew that this dead soul was his friend, for the first time since the night the ghost had first appeared, Jack was a little bit afraid of Artie.

"Whaddaya mean, you said my name?"

Jack glanced around to make sure there were no swimmers nearby, and he shot an angry look up at the hovering phantom.

"Don't blame me, Artie. You were the last thing I expected to see today. You show up like this, in the middle of the day, when I'm on the beach with a couple thousand of my closest friends, and you expect me not to be a little surprised? It just came out, man. Besides, I think she probably caught on a long time ago."

The ethereal substance that comprised the ghost wavered. Artie seemed about to chastise Jack again, but then he just lowered his head, a sad expression on his face.

"It wasn't supposed to be like this," Artie said, and he began to sink down into the water, parts of him disappearing as they touched the waves. "She wasn't ever supposed to know, Jack. I don't want her looking over her shoulder for me the rest of her life. That's not fair."

"There's a lot that isn't fair," Jack replied, keeping his voice low. "You're dead, for starters. And you know what else isn't fair? Having you around, talking to you, knowing that Molly might have been able to get some closure if you'd just *talk* to her, through me. I've gotta wonder, Artie, if you're avoiding adding to her pain, or your own. 'Cause Molly? She can live, start again. But you're done. That's not fair, is it?"

"But if she's in pain now, don't blame *me*, all right? I don't think I can take that."

Dark shadows spilled from Artie's empty eyes, and Jack wondered if that was what the tears of ghosts looked like. For a long moment Artie said nothing more, and Jack just floated there, feet extended toward the bottom, rising and falling with the waves.

"You're sure she heard you?"

"Take another look at her," Jack said. "What do you think?"

Though he had meant the comment to be sarcastic, Artie did glance over to the shore again. He slipped lower in the water and Jack was unnerved at the way the portions of him below the surface just seemed to dissipate. Only Artie's head and shoulders were above the waves now.

"What are you going to do?" Artie asked.

"I don't know." Jack studied the ghost and wondered if the despair he saw in its features was genuine or something he had projected there.

"Look, Artie, I should get back to her. I assume you didn't show up to get some sun. What's so urgent?"

Artie flinched, his ghostly form shuddering again. A wave washed up and over him, momentarily erasing everything below his nose. Jack turned away, unsettled by the sight, but when he turned back the ghost's countenance had begun to coalesce again.

"I'm sorry," Artie said.

"For what?"

"Everything, I guess. Just try not to forget who the dead guy is, okay?"

Jack smiled thinly. "That's low. Playing my grief for sympathy."

Artie reached up and, pushing a hand through his long blond hair, he shifted back and forth somehow, as though he were standing. It was eerie to see him behaving in ways that were so familiar. In those moments it became hard to remember that he was dead.

"Seeing Molly like that threw me off," Artie explained. "But I really did need to talk to you. Need your help. I guess it could have waited until later, but the more time that goes by for me here in the Ghostlands, the less I think about what's proper there, with the living. All I could think was that we needed to talk and then I was here and I saw you and . . . Do you want me to come see you later?"

Again, Jack was chilled by the familiar. In life, Artie had had an excitable way of talking, of running his words together in a rush of enthusiasm or anger. That had changed some, since his death. But here was the old Artie again.

"I should go see what's up with her," Jack agreed. "But you're here. At least tell me what's got you so worked up. More Prowlers in Boston?"

One last time, Artie cast a regretful glance up at the shore. "It isn't Prowlers," the ghost said, and again his voice had that odd static, that hollow echo. "You have to understand, Jack, that I thought it was over, now. I'm dead. There isn't supposed to be anything left for me to be afraid of, yeah? But turns out there is. Big freakin' joke on me. Apparently there's something here, in the Ghostlands, and it's been here for a while only nobody bothered to tell me that. They must have left it out of all the guidebooks.

"The dead just call it the Ravenous, Jack, but from what I've been able to figure out so far, it eats souls. It cruises the Ghostlands like some kind of animal, a lion or something, and it eats the spirits of the dead."

Jack stared at Artie in horror, for once barely noticing the way the light shone right through him. On the shore nearby, a fortyish couple began to wade into the water side by side, so when he spoke again, Jack dropped his voice even further.

"So . . . so what happens then?" he asked. "If a ghost is eaten, what happens to it then? I mean, a soul is immortal, right?"

Reluctantly, he looked into Artie's eyes. In the depths of the darkness there he could see a distant nightscape, something that might have been stars, rolling shapes that might have been black waves on some eternal ocean.

"No one knows for sure. But the whispers say that's it, Jack. That's the real end. Nothing's supposed to be able to touch us over here. Even the most desperate and lost spirits only have themselves to fear until they get where they're going. But the Ravenous gets you? You'll never get there."

Jack shook his head in frustration. "I don't get it. What am I supposed to do?"

Hushed laughter came from nearby and he turned to see the couple who had just entered the water doing their best not to look at him. They were too close. Jack felt foolish for a second, but then he just couldn't bring himself to care.

"Talk to people on your side. A priest, maybe a medium. Turns out some of them are actually for real. Somebody's got to know something about this thing, where it came from, how to hurt it. But we've got to stop it, Jack."

With a kick of his feet, Jack swam a short way from the couple, and Artie followed.

"Absolutely," he told the ghost. "Before it gets you."

Artie only stared at him. "If we don't destroy this thing, it's going to be waiting for all of us eventually." The ghost began to rise up from the water again. Through his gossamer form, Jack could see a sailboat out on the ocean. "I'm sorry I startled you. I know it's my fault. If she really does know, and you think it would help her to talk to me . . ."

Then Artie wasn't there anymore. He disappeared like the spray from the breaking waves. Jack turned and rode the next one in, bodysurfing until he found himself on his knees in six inches of water.

It wasn't anger. At least, not entirely. But the chaos of clashing emotions inside Molly could not be calmed, could not be made sense of. So though anger wasn't really what it was all about, that was how it came out, as a bitter, cold rage at the only person close enough for her to hurt.

Jack stayed down in the water for several minutes, swimming a little, talking to the air.

Not the air. She knew that. But that was how it looked.

When he dove into the water and then swam for shore, Molly stood and picked up her towel. She had the urge to hit someone. Or cry. But crying would just have pissed her off even more.

By the time Jack jogged over to her, she was taking apart the two pieces of the rented umbrella. He stood behind her and said her name, soft and with great tenderness. The same voice that had caused so much confusion for her of late.

"Molly," he said again.

41

She bent and picked up his towel with one hand, the pieces of the umbrella under her arm. She shook the towel once and thrust it at him without meeting his gaze. Jack took it, threw it over his shoulder.

"Don't you think we should talk?"

Her lips pressed together and she cringed, shook her head slowly. Forced the tears to stay away.

"No. I've got nothing to say to you right now."

"You must have a ton of questions."

At last she turned to glare up at him, the hurt so deep in her that it felt as though it was almost blocking the words from coming out. She swallowed and her stomach hurt. "Not now, Jack. I can't talk to you right now."

He shook his head, lifted his hands as if they might heal her. "You knew. You can't tell me you didn't."

Molly glanced away. "Maybe I suspected. But I asked you, Jack. And you put me off. You told me no. You said he was gone! Then . . . we kissed. I feel things I already felt horrible for feeling, but now . . . what am I supposed to do now, Jack?"

She spun away from him and stormed away up the sand toward the pavement and the shops and restaurants. People stared openly, but Molly didn't care. Who were these people anyway? Certainly no one she would ever see again. She didn't know them.

At the moment she wondered if there was anyone she really knew.

The long August day was only beginning to wane, dusk still several hours off. The sun angled down with a golden hue only found this time of day, this time of year. Arm in arm, Dallas and Valerie wandered through Quincy Market, suffused with the good feeling of the people all around them. Balloon sellers in clownface did a stellar business. In the Cityside restaurant, its patio open to the cobblestone walk, a lanky scarecrow of a man played Billy Joel songs on the piano.

Dallas knew that his current employer, Jasmine, had been part of Owen Tanzer's movement to draw together the scattered Prowlers of the world, to try to take over. He thought it was pretty funny, actually, the idea that a tribal culture whose members were disseminated across the face of the earth could come together and usurp the planet's dominant species, a species with a sense of unity the Prowlers lacked, a species that outnumbered them twenty-five thousand to one.

Tanzer had been a zealot, and zealots always ended up dead.

For his part, Dallas liked the world just the way it was. He enjoyed the company of humans, particularly females. He loved the music of humans, their food, and their literature. When he killed them, it was rarely out of bloodlust. Most of the time, in fact, it was for money. Jasmine was only the latest in a long line of employers, including various governments and corporations, who had utilized his skills. He was always up to a challenge. But it wasn't often he was hired to kill one of his own.

As they turned down a side street and began to move away from Quincy Market, past a bistro and a gourmet coffee shop, Valerie bumped him to get his attention.

"Hey. You're so far away. What's on your mind?"

Dallas smiled. She really was beautiful in her human face, with that rich lipstick the color of dried blood. He suspected he was one of few among his kind who could have appreciated the beauty of her façade as well as that of her true countenance.

"Just thinking how much I missed you," he said. "I stayed away too long."

Almost demure, she glanced away. The reaction made the lie worthwhile.

At the end of the street, on the corner, stood a three-story building whose architecture was an elegant testament to the Boston of a bygone age. The sign on the front of the building identified it as Bridget's Irish Rose Pub. Dallas paused, touched Valerie on the arm and nodded toward the restaurant.

"That's the place."

She glanced at it. "Looks nice. Too bad we can't eat dinner there."

He laughed. "Maybe when this is all over, if I do my job right. It looks busy, too, which is helpful."

Valerie turned into him, pressed herself against him, kissed his bristly jaw, then his throat, nipped him there with her teeth.

"When you do it, I want to be there."

"Of course," Dallas promised easily.

But she stared at him then, expecting some other response from him.

"What?" he asked.

Her hand tightened on his arm. "I missed you, too,

Dallas. Don't let it go to your head. I let you in. I gave up my toy for you. And, yes, I'm hoping we can have some fun, add a little spice to my life. As long as you realize that I'm not going to be *your* toy. If you want to play with me, that's all right, but if I'm with you, I'm in it. I've never been any good at being a bystander."

A thrill went through Dallas. The truth was, he had forgotten just what it was about Valerie that had entranced him all along. Beauty was hardly sufficient. Now he remembered. Charm didn't work on her.

"No argument," he replied.

Valerie nodded once, then glanced at the pub again. "The bartender?"

"If it's the right one. He's supposed to be big, broad-shouldered, with a graying beard. Cantwell is the name he uses."

One corner of her mouth lifted in a lopsided, mischievous grin and she crossed the street between cars. As Dallas watched, she went into the pub after a quartet of humans. Though many people did not eat until later when the summer days were so long, Bridget's seemed quite busy. Dallas turned and went back up the sidewalk to a pair of pay phones. He picked one up, leaned against the kiosk, and watched the front door without even pretending to speak.

Perhaps three minutes after she had entered, Valerie pushed out the front door of the pub and darted across the street and into the flower shop. Seconds later the door opened again and a big, bearded man stepped out. *Cantwell*, Dallas thought. It had to be, though he could not see the man's face. The bartender tilted his head back slightly and sniffed at the air. For a full minute he lingered on the sidewalk in front of the pub, and then his gaze settled upon the flower shop.

Dallas stiffened.

Then the door to Bridget's swung open again and a waitress stuck her head out, said something to Cantwell. The bartender nodded and grabbed the open door. Before going inside, he looked around one last time, and Dallas got a good look at his face.

"Aw, no," he whispered.

The door closed behind him. A minute or so later Valerie appeared on the sidewalk beside Dallas.

"He caught my scent right off," she said excitedly. "But there were so many people in there, I don't think he got a look at me. So what do you think?"

Dallas shook his head and started walking away from the pub. Valerie sniffed in annoyance and followed.

"Don't give me attitude, now, Dallas. I did exactly what you asked me to do. You wanted to size up your target, now you've had your chance."

"You did great," he said flatly.

"So when are you going to do it?"

Dallas paused, but did not look up at her. His thoughts were astir. "I'm not," he admitted.

"What do you mean? Why not?" Valerie asked.

He looked up at her with a smile that had no humor in it. "His name isn't Cantwell. Or it wasn't always."

Valerie gaped at him. "You know him?"

Images flashed in the assassin's mind of his daughter, Olivia, whom he had not seen in years. After her mother's death—or truth be told, since long before then—he had made no effort to connect with her. Yet when word reached him from her pack that she had not been heard of in quite some time, he had begun to poke around. Olivia had last been seen in the New York area, where Jasmine was forming her new pack in the aftermath of Tanzer's death. Dallas had known her since before the dawn of the twentieth century, and so it was only natural that he should ask for her help in locating the girl.

But Jasmine had never been one for sentiment. She agreed to help find Olivia but only if Dallas would take this job. In addition, she would pay him his usual fee. In the end, he really had no choice. While he harbored some resentment toward Jasmine for capitalizing on his daughter's disappearance, he had begun to get carried away, as he always did, with the stalking of his prey.

Now, though?

"Hell," Dallas muttered. "Small world, huh? Cruel irony. I can't kill him."

Silence descended between them, and both of them turned to look back along the street at the pub in the distance.

"So, what are you going to do, then?" she asked.

Dallas thought about it, then ran his hands through his long hair, pushed it away from his face.

"Well, the whole point of killing him, drawing him out, is to make sure he can't protect the others. I get the feeling it's them, this Dwyer guy and his girlfriend, that Jasmine really wants dead. So I guess I'll just have to find another way to get Cantwell out of the picture."

CHAPTER 3

The music seemed loud in Bridget's Irish Rose, though the volume had not been turned up. It was simply that the pub was quiet and almost empty save for the staff, and so Sarah Mclachlan's voice filled the restaurant and bar areas as though she were standing in the middle of the room.

Courtney Dwyer loved this time of day at Bridget's. It was just after four o'clock, half an hour or so before the early dinner crowd would begin to trickle in. The wait staff pulled double duty between three and five o'clock, polishing the brass handrails, vacuuming, wiping down seats and tabletops. The same sort of thing was going on back in the kitchen, where the cooks were preparing for the evening onslaught, during which they would not have a moment to spare. Anything they could do now to cut down on the amount of cleanup at the end of the night would get them off work that much sooner.

Most days Courtney used the time to make certain the kitchen was properly stocked and to figure out what she would need from the fish market the following morning. But that was second nature to her now, and no real effort. The rest of the time was spent eating an early dinner—something she would not have time to do once the crowd began to roll in.

That afternoon she sat at a table at the back of the restaurant, not far from the kitchen, and worked in a small notebook on the food orders and inventory. Courtney never looked at receipts until after Bridget's was closed for the night.

Her dinner, lamb tips with mashed potatoes and mixed vegetables, cooled half-eaten on a plate she had shoved aside. It was not uncommon for her to become distracted by work and drift away from her meal, and she had grown used to eating cold food.

Gazing at the inventory in her notebook, she nibbled the top of her pen and then set it down. Courtney scanned the restaurant and was pleased to see that six tables were taken, even at this time of day. Up at the bar, a few regulars hovered, eyes on the television bolted to the back wall. Bill was the head bartender, and he looked good back there, confident. *Master of all he surveys,* she thought, and allowed herself a small chuckle.

Her guy saw her looking at him and smiled, and Courtney lifted her hand in a small wave that was uncommonly girly and coquettish for her. His hair and beard were sprayed with white, but she found that salt-and-pepper look to be very dignified and handsome.

"Courtney? You got a second?"

She glanced up to find Janis Kelso standing on the other side of the table, fidgeting with her hands. Courtney could not remember if Janis was twenty or twenty-one, but it always amazed her that the girl was even that old, given that she looked about fifteen. She had black hair that fell in a stylish swoop down across one side of her face, a tiny waist, and a brightness to her features that only added to the teenage aura that always surrounded her. Or almost always, because at the moment, flush with emotion, the enthusiasm that usually emanated from the girl was gone.

Courtney was concerned, but she forced a benevolent smile onto her face. "Sure. Do you want to sit down?"

Janis hesitated, then shook her head. "No, no, that's all right. Look, I just wanted to tell you I'm . . . I know I was on from two to close, but I've got to go home now."

"What do you mean?" Courtney asked, growing annoyed. "Are you sick?"

The waitress nervously smoothed down the front of her blouse and glanced away, unwilling to meet Courtney's gaze. "No, no. I'm all right. I just . . . I can't work with Dougie anymore."

Courtney frowned. Where her employees were concerned, she did not like to pry unless they had problems that were work related. If Janis was seeing Dougie Roos, one of the cooks, and things had gone sour, Courtney just did not want to know. On the other hand, if there was some other reason, she certainly could not ignore that.

"What's the issue between you two?"

Janis shifted uncomfortably and put her hands on the back of one of the chairs as if to keep her balance. "He's been . . . he's just all over me. Every time I go in the kitchen, it's like he's waiting for me. Telling me how good I look, asking me to go home with him. Last night, a couple of times he started feeling me up and I had to send one of the other waitresses back to pick up my orders. And now he just did it again, like ten minutes ago."

Courtney stared at her. She could feel the heat of her anger burning on her face, and a tightening in her chest. With a sigh she shook her head and started toward the kitchen.

"Anybody see Dougie do this?"

Janis stiffened, drawing Courtney's attention again.

"It happened," the waitress said, an edge to her voice.

Now Courtney softened. She realized that the girl might have misunderstood her anger, and she met Janis's gaze evenly. "I believe you. I just want to know if anyone else saw it. Anyone who did should have stepped in."

A shudder of relief went through Janis and she smiled before shaking her head. "Pretty much everybody's heard the things he's said to me. But I don't know for sure if anybody saw him grabbing at me."

Courtney closed her notebook and stood up, reaching for her cane. Her fingers closed on the silver lion's head that topped the walking stick, and she squeezed tight, its contours jutting into the soft skin of her hand. The urge to hit someone with it was strong.

"When are you scheduled to work again?" she asked, standing face to face with Janis.

"Not until Wednesday."

"All right," Courtney said. "I'll see you on Wednesday. You won't have to work with Dougie anymore."

"Oh," Janis replied in a small voice. "Well, but what are you going to do tonight? I hate to leave you shorthanded."

"Jack and Molly will probably be back by six or so. They're not on the schedule, but I'm sure I can shanghai one of them."

"Okay," Janis said quickly. "Well, thank you. Really, Courtney. Thanks."

Touched by the gratitude in the girl's voice, Courtney grew even angrier. The idea that Janis could be driven out of Bridget's, made to risk her job by bailing in the middle of a shift because some jerk was harassing her . . . it stoked a fire in her that Courtney usually held a pretty tight rein on. Her mother would have called it an Irish temper. Courtney just thought of it as human nature.

"Go on," Courtney said, mustering a kind smile for Janis. "Go home."

Janis thanked her again and double-timed it into the back to get her things. Her half-eaten meal forgotten, Courtney went to the hostess stand by the front door. Wendy Bartlett sat at a table to the right of the door, beneath the windows that looked out on Nelson Street, and rolled sets of clean silverware up into green cloth napkins, something useful to kill the time before the dinner rush began.

"Hey," Courtney said.

The second she saw the look on Courtney's face, Wendy tensed up. "What is it?"

Courtney shook her head. "I'll tell you later. I may need you to wait tables once the rush starts."

Wendy shrugged. "You've got it."

That taken care of, Courtney hustled back toward the kitchen. She was such an expert with her cane after nearly a decade using it that her gait barely qualified as a hobble. She passed Janis on the way, who thanked her quietly one final time before leaving.

When she pushed through the doors into the kitchen, Courtney spotted a pair of waitresses—Kiera Dunphy and Jenny Boyce—at the counter waiting to pick up dinner orders for their customers. They turned around the second she came in, and something in her expression wiped the smiles off their faces.

"Kiera. Jenny. Give me a minute with the guys, will you?" Courtney asked.

The waitresses exchanged a glance, then agreed quickly and went out into the dining room. A radio played WZLX somewhere back in the kitchen, and steam rose all around. The temperature was twenty or thirty degrees hotter back there, even with the air conditioner pumping, and when Tim Dunphy appeared behind the counter, his face was damp with perspiration and the tattoos on his arms gleamed. Tim was Kiera's brother, a good guy from a rough South Boston neighbourhood, and he ran the kitchen nine nights out of ten.

"What's up?" Tim asked, his Southie accent thick.

"Can you come around here?" Courtney asked.

Tim frowned. He ran a hand over the stubble on his shaved head. "Sure. How come?"

Courtney didn't respond, but she let him know with a look that she needed him to comply. She did not want to say it out loud, but it was important for the other kitchen staff to see Tim as being on her side, rather than on theirs. There were eight people on in the kitchen at the moment, five cooks and three dishwashers. Another cook would come on at five. But when she was done, they were going to be one man down for the shift, and that never made them happy.

Tim came around the counter to stand next to her. He wiped his hands on a dishrag and glanced at her oddly, but said nothing.

"Guys!" she called. "Can I have your attention please?"

Dougie and another cook had already wandered over to where they could see her from behind the counter, and now the dishwashers dropped what they were doing as well. The other two cooks had food on the grill and on the stove, and so they kept working, though they were clearly listening.

"I've had complaints from members of the wait staff about harassment," Courtney began. Then she glared at Dougie, searing him with her eyes. "One of them claims that she was groped back here."

Tim swore, shaking his head angrily. "By who?"

"Dougie."

The others all turned to look at Dougie, some with disdain but most with curiosity. Dougie sneered and threw his hands up.

"Janis. I can't believe that bitch. I never touched her."

Courtney laughed, though not in amusement. "Really?

Then what makes you think it was Janis?" She looked around at the others. "I just wanted to make sure you all heard this, so I didn't have to say it more than once. We don't put up with that kind of crap here. Not ever."

Then she turned to Tim. "You're going to be short a body tonight."

"We'll manage," he assured her, his anger perhaps even greater than her own.

"Good," Courtney said. Then she looked at Dougie. "You're fired. Go. Now."

With that, she glanced again at Tim, who nodded once in assent and support. Then Courtney walked out of the kitchen, a strange sort of exhilaration crackling in her like an electric charge. She had walked with a cane since she was nineteen years old and she did not get to kick ass very often.

It felt good.

But all that good feeling drained out of her when she looked across the pub and saw Jack and Molly coming through the front door. Both of them wore expressions of such despair that Courtney immediately wanted to reach out to them, and there was a kind of dark energy between them that told her they were at odds without a single word being exchanged. It looked as though their day off had not gone as well as she had hoped it would.

Jack turned toward Molly as though he wanted to say something but she only shook her head and kept walking. He watched as she made a beeline for the stairs that led to the apartment above the pub. Molly passed right by Courtney without even acknowledging her and went up the steps as though she were running away from something.

In the middle of the restaurant, with fans turning lazily overhead and heartbreak music on the sound system, Jack watched her go until the door at the top of the stairs closed. Then he shook his head and walked over to the bar. He sat at the far end, away from the small group of regulars, and Bill slid a Coke across the bar to him.

Courtney recalled having thought of this time of day as peaceful only minutes before. Now she hurried across the restaurant and up the step into the bar area, worried about Molly, but mostly concerned about her brother.

"What's that all about?" she asked as she slid onto a stool beside him.

Jack smiled thinly. "Well, at least you guys are talking to me."

Behind the bar, Bill crossed his arms and frowned. "She looked pretty pissed, Jack."

Courtney's little brother pushed his hands through his hair and groaned. "Yep."

"It's okay if you don't want to talk about it," Courtney told him.

"No. It's all right." He looked over at Bill, then at her, an expression so innocent on his face that he looked like a little kid to her again.

"While we were on the beach, I saw . . . a ghost. It was Artie. Something important came up and he just appeared there, hanging out over the water. I was surprised, you know? Who wouldn't be? And I . . . I said his name."

At first Courtney didn't understand. She was surprised, of course, because Jack had not mentioned seeing Artie's ghost for a very long time, so she had thought his friend's spirit had gone on to wherever lost souls went when they weren't "lost" anymore.

Bill got it immediately, though. "You said his name. And she heard you," the bartender said.

Jack nodded.

Then Courtney understood. "It had to happen eventually, Jack. I don't know why you had to keep it from her in the first place. Sure, it would have been hard for her, but this has to be even harder."

"It wasn't my call," Jack told her, throwing up his hands. "Artie didn't want me to tell her."

For long, drawn-out seconds the three of them stewed with their thoughts on the matter. Down the bar one of the regulars was trying to flag Bill down, but he ignored the guy. Normally Courtney would have chided him, but not right now. Jack needed them and the old barfly, Rollie McKeckern, was not going anywhere.

"What was so important?" Bill asked.

Jack raised his eyebrows. "Huh?"

"Artie had something urgent to tell you. What's the crisis?"

As he explained it to them, Courtney shifted uncomfortably on her stool. Any time Jack talked about the spirits he saw, this Ghostlands, it gave her a chill. She thought of her mother and other people she knew who had died and wondered where their souls were.

Now, though, with this other thing, a monster in the

Ghostlands, stalking the phantoms of people who were already dead . . . in some ways it was even more awful than the Prowlers. From the quaver in his voice, she could see that it was unnerving her brother as well, and why shouldn't it? Jack had grieved for Artie once, and the idea that they still had to be afraid for him, for anyone who had already died, was horrifying. Courtney shuddered as Jack told them its name: the Ravenous.

"Artie wants me to look into it, talk to a priest or, I don't know, a psychic or something, and see if anyone knows anything about this thing. How to kill it, or at least stop it." Jack looked at Bill. "You ever heard of anything like this?"

Bill shook his head. "Sorry. My . . . my kind of people aren't much into spirituality. Even the nonviolent ones are usually involved in more . . . physical pursuits."

Courtney knew he was talking about other Prowlers who lived secretly among humans, just as Bill did. And what he said made sense. Prowlers were monsters in a way, yes, and directly linked to a lot of old myths and legends. But they were physical creatures, not supernatural beings.

"You could talk to Father Mike," she suggested.

Jack perked up. "Y'know, I never even thought of him. Is he still at St. Mary's?"

"I think he's at St. Anthony's now."

St. Anthony's was in the North End, a ten-minute walk from the pub.

"I'm going to go up and take a shower," Jack said, deep in thought. "Then I think I'll take a walk over there."

Rollie McKeckern was getting agitated down the bar. Bill scowled at the man and went down to get him another beer. When Courtney glanced at her brother again, he was staring at something in the restaurant. She followed the line of his gaze and saw Molly coming down the stairs. Her unruly red hair was tied back in a thick ponytail and she had changed her clothes.

Courtney started to rise to go over to her. She had no idea what she would say, what she *could* say that would make Molly feel any better, but she had to try.

Or she would have, if the girl had even looked her way. Instead, Molly went across the pub and out the door without so much as a glance toward the bar. The sad cast of her features, her face pale and drawn, her eyes hollow, would linger with Courtney for hours.

The long summer afternoon seemed to stretch the sunlight so that it reached out across the sky and down into the city with a strength and tenacity it lacked any other time of year. The light was golden and perfect, and its warmth ought to have settled into her flesh, making her feel more alive.

But Molly did not feel warm at all. She felt cold and numb and somehow set apart from the rest of the world, held at a distance almost as though she herself was a lost soul wandering the Ghostlands, watching people pass by laughing and holding hands and knowing that those things were forever out of reach.

Oh, for God's sake, she chided herself as the thought crossed her mind. *Stop being so dramatic.*

But she could not help how she felt, could not shake that feeling. It was ironic, yes, but it was real. Her junior year she got mono, and she remembered what it had been like the day she checked herself into the hospital. Her mother had been off with her boyfriend of the week, probably nursing a two-day drunk, and Molly had come home from school in a kind of haze where everything around her was a blur. By the time she got off the T near the hospital, she had no idea how she managed to get that far.

It was like that now.

One minute she was in front of Bridget's and the next she was meandering her way in a fugue state through Boston traffic and tourists and employees who dared leave a few minutes before five, and found herself on Long Wharf, between the Marriott and the New England Aquarium, staring down at the dirty water where the sight-seeing boats bumped against one another in the dock.

Once upon a time, Artie had bought fresh-squeezed lemonade from a vendor right at this spot, and then accidentally spilled it all over himself in the midst of a rant about the state of the American prison system. Artie Carroll had felt everything passionately, and that was one of his greatest assets. He was also a guy with absolutely no control over his surroundings, and no faith that he could ever exert any. But that never stopped him from speaking his mind, and Molly had always admired that.

Jack was something else entirely. Passionate, yes. In some ways, just as passionate as Artie. Unlike Artie, though, Jack believed with all his heart that he could force his environment to behave the way he believed it should. That attitude—as naïve as Artie's in its way—had kept Molly alive more than once, and she admired it. But there had been an innocence in Artie's surrender to the world around him that Jack did not have . . . might never have had at all. Though Molly wondered if it had just been stolen from him the night a drunk driver killed his mother and crippled his sister, if Jack's insistence upon controlling his world came from that one awful example of how uncontrollable it was.

As angry as she was now at Jack, she knew that she was just as mad at Artie. It made her head spin. How could she be so angry at a . . . a ghost. Artie was dead, and she missed him every day. But she had been trying her best to move on, to seal off the wound his death had left in her, knowing it would never heal but thinking that she could survive it.

And Jack . . . she felt something for Jack, something that neither one of them had expected, but that maybe they ought to have. They had been close, the best of friends, and shared so much. And they both had loved Artie. After his death, that shared emotion brought them closer than ever.

Then, a month ago, in Vermont, she kissed Jack. It would be easier for her to tell herself she knew she was going to do it, but the truth was she had been thinking about it for days by the time she finally did it. And it was not as though Jack had fought it.

They had not talked about that kiss in the weeks since they returned from Vermont, but silently, they had begun to dance around the realization that something was happening with them. Artie's death still echoed in their lives, and so neither of them wanted to broach the subject of the growing affection between them.

Then today, the conversation. *Is this a date?*

Molly leaned on a wooden post that jutted up from the wharf and stared out at what she could see of the ocean between the tour boats. All that she felt for Artie, and for Jack, surged up in her and seemed to be tainted now, like the water that lapped against the pilings below, greasy with leaked fuel.

A pleasant ripple went up the back of her neck, like fingers stroking her there. Molly stiffened, images of Artie in her head. Could he touch her now? Was he there, watching her? How often had he been there in the months since his death? Had he seen her cry for him, stood over her while she slept, watched her with Jack? Had he seen them kiss?

Though she knew it was foolish, she stared around, twirling in circles, wondering if she might catch a trace of him out of the corner of her eye. But only Jack could see the ghosts. That was his curse, not hers. People glanced at her oddly as they walked on past her, on their way to the Aquarium or the Chart House restaurant, or to the hotel. Molly ignored them. She wrapped her arms around herself and finally felt the sun begin to soak into her, warming her at last.

As she stared out past the boats to where the water was clean and deep, she wished she could see the harbor islands.

"How am I supposed to feel now?" she whispered, pretending it was to herself but knowing that it was really to him.

Just in case.

"I can talk to you now. Jack can help with that. And you can speak to me. But you've been here all this time, and you never have. So what are we supposed to say?"

Her eyes were dry, but she felt as though she ought to be crying.

"I'm so angry at you. I have things I want to say. But the worst part of it all, the thing that hurts me most, is that now that I know you're here, I'm not sure if I want you to be. Maybe that makes me a terrible person. I miss you so much. I loved you. But . . . nothing can change what happened to you, and just thinking about it makes all the pain I felt when you died come back fresh."

She raised her hands up and stared at a spot on the water as though it was really him she was talking to.

"What am I supposed to do now?" she asked, her voice breaking.

Still she could not cry, and somehow that hurt even more.

At her side, ethereal, invisible to the world around him, Artie reached out and ached to touch her, to comfort her. His fingers passed right through her as though *she* were the phantom. He pulled his hands back quickly, shoved them in the pockets of his sweatshirt and just stared at her, hating himself for being so helpless.

He wept, but real as they felt, he knew they were only the ghosts of tears.

CHAPTER 4

St. Anthony's was on the corner of Prince and Hanover in the North End, a neighborhood that Jack imagined looked pretty much the same as it had a century or more before, only with more restaurants. His own allegiance to Bridget's notwithstanding, Jack knew that to be guaranteed a decent meal, the North End was the safest bet in Boston. Its narrow streets were lined with dozens of restaurants from tiny, inexpensive holes-in-the-wall to airy, trendy bistros. Competition between bakeries was intense down that way as well.

Once upon a time, the entire neighborhood was occupied by Italians from the old country, and the restaurants and businesses still reflected that influence. But as the property values had gone up, a younger, hipper, more generic crowd had begun to move in. The North End still had its Italian identity and heritage, with parades through the streets on all the major feast days, but Jack had watched over the years as the locals struggled to avoid becoming some sort of attraction, Walt Disney's version of what an Italian neighborhood should be.

So far, they were succeeding, but the line was a thin one.

As he walked down Hanover Street, he rolled all that over in his head for the thousandth time, mainly to avoid thinking about Molly. He could not get her out of his mind completely, but until she was willing to talk to him, there wasn't anything he could do except stew about it.

St. Anthony's was a beautiful old domed church on a piece of property the size of a postage stamp. Jack had been by it hundreds of times but had never been inside. Now he went up the short walk to the front doors, pulled them open, and stepped inside. The place was vast and empty, the echo of the squeaking door still resounding inside. Jack went through the foyer and into the church, feeling a bit self-conscious about being in there alone until he spotted a man snuffing candles up on the altar.

Jack strode up the aisle, torn for a moment as he wondered if he ought to kneel or something. Then the man—a deacon or lector or something—turned and saw him.

"Can I help you?" the man said amiably.

"Yeah. Sorry to—" Jack gestured back toward the doors, then shrugged lightly. "Anyway, I'm looking for Father Logan. Is he available?"

With the metal instrument in his hand, the man snuffed two more candles even as he replied. "Mass ended just a few minutes ago. You can probably catch Father Logan in the sacristy still."

PROWLERS

Sacristy, Jack thought. He hadn't been to mass regularly since before his mother died. He had no idea what a sacristy was. When the deacon or whoever turned around again, that fact must have been plain on Jack's face, for the man sniffed imperiously and pointed off to the left of the altar.

"The first door on the left. Just knock."

Jack thanked him, though reluctantly given the man's attitude. Before turning away from the altar, he seemed to recall some ritual whereby he was supposed to cross himself or kneel, but since he was not sure and did not want to look the fool in front of this man, he just walked off. Once he had left the main hall of the church, he found the sacristy easily enough, a tall wooden door with iron straps across it that made it look medieval. With only a moment's pause, he knocked.

"Come in," a voice called from within.

As he pushed the door open, Jack had a moment of panic. Father Mike had been a comfort to his mother when Jack was very small, after she had been abandoned by his father and was striving to create something out of the pub. He had performed her funeral mass, and had checked on Jack and Courtney from time to time for years. He and Courtney still talked a couple of times a year, but Jack had never felt as close to the priest as his sister did. Not close enough to have this conversation.

But it was too late to stop now.

Father Mike was hanging his priestly vestments in a closet on the other side of the room, but turned as Jack walked in. He was perhaps an inch shorter than Jack, with thinning hair that had once been a rich brown but was now mostly gray. He wore round glasses that made him look a bit more dignified, but even with the spectacles and the black clothes and white collar, he still had a broad Irish face, pale skin with a flush to his cheeks.

The priest smiled as he looked at Jack, but it was just Father Mike's benevolent grin, with no trace of recognition in it.

"Hello," he said. "What can I do for you?"

"Father, hi. I'm Jack Dwyer. Courtney's brother?"

Father Mike's face lit up. "You're not."

Jack laughed. "I am."

The priest studied him. "Good Lord, Jack. I'm sorry, it's only that we haven't seen each in four or five years and, well, you're not a boy anymore, are you? I might've passed you on the street and not known you. How old are you now?"

"Nineteen."

"Nineteen," Father Mike repeated. Then he stepped forward and they shook hands. "You make me feel old, Jack."

"Well, we're even then, Father. You make me feel like I'm still ten."

"Good one, lad," the priest said. "What brings you down to see me? Now don't tell me something's happened to our dear Courtney?"

Jack smiled. Father Mike was in his early fifties, as best he could remember, and had grown up in South Boston. His parents were from County Cork in Ireland, but he himself had not visited Ireland until he was in the seminary. Still, there were times when he slipped into the vocal cadence and inflection of the Irish. It wasn't quite a brogue, but a hint of one, picked up from his parents. Something else that seemed out of place in the North End.

"Courtney's doing all right," he assured the priest.

"Good, good," Father Mike replied. "I'm pleased to see you, Jack. It's been far too long. I don't imagine you've come just to make a social call, though. How can I help?"

It was silent in the room save for the loud ticking of the clock on the wall. Out in the church the candle-snuffer was probably still going about his business, maybe locking up the place until the next mass; if they locked the church between services. Otherwise it was just the two of them, back in that very plain room with a crucifix on the wall, a table with four chairs, and a small sofa against the far wall.

Backstage, Jack thought.

Father Mike gazed patiently at him.

"Maybe we should sit down," Jack suggested.

"All right."

They moved to the table. Jack pulled a chair out and slid into it. Father Mike turned his chair backward and straddled it much as a much younger man would. It was a habit Jack remembered from years before. The priest leaned on the back of the chair and studied him, a frown of concern etching lines in his forehead.

Something fluttered in Jack's stomach. He uttered a nervous laugh. Father Mike sat up a little straighter, his expression serious.

"Just talk to me, Jack. It's all right," the priest said.

And, oddly enough, it was.

"No matter how I say this, it's going to come off strange," Jack said. "But I don't know how else to talk to you about it. I guess the way to start is just to ask you if you believe in ghosts."

Father Mike blinked. "Well, now. Of all the things I might have expected to come out of your mouth next, that one wasn't even on the list."

Jack stared at him. "That isn't an answer."

The priest nodded grimly. "Right enough. The answer is I'm not sure. I've never seen a ghost myself, but the core of our faith is the belief in the everlasting soul, that heaven awaits those who follow the word of God, and damnation those who spurn him."

"But some of them get lost along the way," Jack muttered to himself as much as to the priest.

Father Mike nodded. "That may well be. Though you sound fairly certain. You've had some experience in the matter, then? Something that convinced you?"

Jack splayed his fingers across the oak table and gazed down at them, feeling the grain of the wood, solid and real. He nodded.

"A lot of somethings. I guess you find that pretty hard to believe."

"Let's say I try to keep an open mind," Father Mike replied. "I said I've not had any experience in that area myself, but I've heard stories, Jack. Many, many of them, and some from sources I trust a great deal. I'm not ready to discount anything at this point."

For a long moment Jack let that sink in. Then he took a deep breath and let it out, and at length, he glanced up at the priest again. "Some souls get . . . they get lost, Father. On the way to wherever they're going. For whatever reason, they stick around. Confused or angry or what have you. That's what ghosts are."

Father Mike crossed his arms on the back of the chair and propped his chin on top of them. Behind his glasses, his eyes looked too large. "If you say so. You sound like an expert."

Frustrated, Jack sat back in his chair. He studied the priest, clock ticking seconds away. Then he shook his head. "I've seen a lot of things, Father. I won't try to convince you. That's not why I'm here."

"I never said I didn't believe you, Jack." Father Mike acted concerned that he had said the wrong thing, and his tone was placating now. "Catholic doctrine believes in purgatory, a place where those sinners who have offended God with their actions but not enough to deserve damnation might suffer a kind of aloneness and despair for their sins. That might account for stories of ghosts, or it might not. The church hasn't a formal position on the matter, and frankly neither do I."

Jack was disappointed, but he tried to mask his feelings. "I understand," he said. "Just . . . you said you'd heard a lot of stories. Have you ever heard of anything that—that *eats* ghosts? Something that attacks people who are already dead?"

"Wow," Father Mike said, sitting up straight and taking off his glasses. "And wow again. Maybe we *should* talk more about this, Jack. It sounds like you're really going through something here."

When Jack did not respond to that, Father Mike went on. "The answer's no. Of course there are demons, the fallen angels of prehistory, whose work it is to tempt mankind to sin. But our belief is that they prey upon the living, and upon those already damned."

Not long into the conversation, Jack had gotten a feeling it was going nowhere. Now his instinct was confirmed. He slid back his chair and stood up. "Thanks for your time, Father. Sorry if this was all too weird for you."

"Jack," the priest said kindly, also rising. "Are you sure you don't want to talk about this some more? I think it might do you some good."

"Maybe another time," Jack replied, offering a smile that felt hollow to him. "I'll come back and see you."

"All right," Father Mike said reluctantly. "Make it sooner than five years this time."

"I will."

The conversation with Father Mike had Jack frustrated and at a loss as to what to do next. It wasn't as though he could just flip open the Yellow Pages and find a medium, and calling the Psychic Hotline wasn't going to get him anywhere. The only good thing about the visit was that he could now scratch the Roman Catholic clergy off his list of possible information sources . . . and being so perturbed had distracted him from thinking about Molly for a while.

Now, though, as he walked up Nelson Street toward Bridget's, he could not help but let his mind stray to her again. He wondered if she was back, and hoped that she would be willing to talk, but dreaded it at the same time.

He was two doors away from the pub, passing in front of Skouras Travel Agency, when Artie shimmered into existence in front of him. It was nearly six o'clock and the shadows were lengthening enough that they lent the ghost a substance and texture that he usually lacked. In that moment, with the tarnished, diffused daylight hazing the air, Artie looked almost alive.

But he looked terrified as well. His black eyes, like pin-prick holes in the universe, were wide and somehow still able to communicate emotion. Particularly now. Artie hung in the air, the laces of his high-top sneakers dangling, untied, and he rushed toward Jack as though he might attack him.

"Come on!" Artie said. "Right now!"

"What?" Jack asked, stumbling back a step. "What's going on?"

Across the street, two fortyish women glanced at him, then picked up their pace to get away from him.

"The Ravenous is nearby. You should see it. You should know what you're up against. Come on!"

With that, Artie turned and ran off. Though Jack knew that he wasn't really running, that he went through the motions, it was easier to see that than only see his friend just floating along. For a moment, he hesitated, glancing at the front door of the pub. Then he swore under his breath and took off after Artie.

They ran west, up side streets, and Jack's chest started to burn. He wanted to stop Artie, to ask him how much farther, but the ghost kept ahead of him, glancing back now and again to be sure that Jack had not collapsed. Finally, panting, he began to pass more and more people, and then he ran into Downtown Crossing, with its department stores and jewellery shops and cobblestones. The area was jammed with people making their daily exodus from work, jockeying for the entrances to the T. Others were shopping, swarming in and out the storefronts like ants.

A slim, sort of prissy-looking guy in a suit bumped Jack into an obese woman who scowled at him without even meeting his eye.

" 'Scuse me," Jack muttered.

No cars were allowed on the section of the street that was cobblestoned, so there were plenty of people on the road. Still, it was not quite as congested as the sidewalk so he stepped off the curb and dodged between people laden with packages and briefcases. They brushed by without a glance. Jack did all he could to weave among them, but Artie was well ahead of him now. He craned his neck to try to see the ghost, caught sight of his gossamer form for just a second, but then lost him again. Artie did not have to go around the people; he simply passed through them as though they were the ones who were not really there.

Jack wanted to shout for him to slow down, but even though no one would likely have noticed, he was too self-conscious to do so.

"Damn it," he cursed under his breath.

Then he slipped past a woman in a power suit, and spotted Artie maybe thirty feet ahead. The ghost seemed almost frozen, his spectral form shimmering as though buffeted by some ethereal wind. The shadows of the buildings on either side of the street had created a valley of twilight gray where everyone seemed suddenly insubstantial.

Jack caught up to Artie, went around in front of him, and flinched when he saw the look of utter horror on his best friend's face.

"Artie?" Jack said, voice a quiet rasp, trying not to draw too much attention.

"It's here," the ghost replied, without even glancing at him.

"It's . . . you mean the Ravenous?"

"Look," Artie instructed.

Jack spun around, but all he could see was the crowd, already thinning as the last of the major commuter rush filtered out of Downtown Crossing. There were still people going into Macy's, and a kid tricked out in punk styles ten years older than he was walked out of the Barnes & Noble on the other side of the street.

"I don't—" he began.

"No. *Look*," Artie said again.

Jack felt stupid. He knew what Artie had brought him here for, but was still so unused to seeing the Ghostlands that it was not yet second nature to him. The truth was, he sort of hoped it never was. Maybe there was some switch inside him that he could turn on and off, where he could see the spirit world and then not see it. But it didn't feel that simple. It was a lot more like lighting a candle than it was turning on a lamp.

Still, in that moment, he did it. He blinked, took a moment with his eyes closed to clear his mind, and when he opened them again, the world had changed. It was as though everything around him had been shot as negative film, the flesh-and-blood people seemed ghostly to him now, as did the buildings. As the people moved, there was almost a strobe effect, as though they trailed some of their life energy after them.

He looked at Artie. Solid. His shaggy blond mane of hair seemed to have life now, his sweatshirt with the rip at the neck had texture. But Artie still wasn't looking at him. Fear rolled off the ghost like ripples of heat off the summer blacktop, and it was infectious. The long jog to Downtown Crossing had already gotten Jack's heart pounding, but now something seemed to clutch at it, a tightness in his chest. It was at least eighty degrees despite the lengthening shadows, but he still felt cold.

Jack turned to see what Artie was staring at.

His mouth dropped open.

He whispered: "Oh, shit."

"I can't get any closer, Jack," Artie said, voice so near, all the other noise around them slipping away. "If it sees me . . ."

The Ravenous.

The thing was huge, eight, maybe nine feet, but it was hard to tell because the thing was crouched over its victims, a homeless guy with silver hair and dark, leathery skin and a skinny goth girl with too-black hair who looked like a junkie runaway.

In the midst of the afterimages, the mirages of the living, the real people that swept around them, there were only these two ghosts. Probably this part of town was swarming with lost souls on a regular basis, wandering through the commutes and regular schedules they'd had when they were alive. But right now, it was just these two. The others had all been faster or smarter or just more awake. The others had gotten away.

They were nothing. Spirits. Wisps of intelligence and imagination, the essence of people long dead. But here in the Ghostlands, the realm of the spirits, they were more than tangible. The world of the living was all gray and washed out, but the ghosts were real and solid . . . and screaming.

It tore them apart.

As Jack watched, unable to tear his eyes away, this obscenity clutched at them with enormous paws, its claws gleaming silver. Its matted fur squirmed with life; things like maggots crawled through the thick black coat. It opened its massive jaws and ripped and tore chunk after chunk out of the dead souls. It was eating them, their essence, all that made them human.

"We have to stop it. Help them," Jack said, his voice a rasp. "And you, man, you've gotta go! Get out of here!"

At last Artie looked away from the thing, and then it seemed as though he could not look back. He shied from it as though he could pretend it was not real.

"You can't help them. We don't know yet how to stop it."

"We'll figure out a way," Jack said. "For now, just get the hell out of here."

predator and prey

Artie gave a reluctant nod and rushed off in the other direction, not even pretending to walk now. He simply floated off until, maybe twenty yards away, he seemed to dissipate in a kind of mist. Jack thought for a second that meant that his connection to the Ghostlands was severed, but then he saw that the living people around him were still phantom images, the city like a shadow of itself.

But Artie was safe, at least for the moment. Right now that was all he could wish. When he turned to look up the street again, the thing was snuffling its black muzzle in the last bits of the old homeless man, in the ectoplasm or whatever it was that made up his ghost. The Ravenous snatched a piece of the old man up in its jaws, tossed it in the air, and scarfed it down in one gulp. Tiny shreds of the man's soul fell onto its filthy fur, still moving, squirming, and Jack realized with deepening horror that the things in its coat were not maggots at all, but remnants of its victims. He had seen monsters before, up close, but the Ravenous made him hold his breath, made icy shudders run through him.

"God," he whispered.

The Ravenous paused. Then it turned around and *looked* at him. Jack's mouth opened but nothing came out. His chest hurt, his throat was dry, his bladder felt too full. He could hear the echo of his heartbeat in his head; too loud, too fast.

It saw him.

Jack Dwyer was alive, not a ghost, but when he was looking into the Ghostlands, the Ravenous could see him.

A growl like thunder shook the ground under his feet.

The Ravenous whipped its scorpion tail back and forth, bared its fangs like gleaming scalpels, and started toward him.

Jack stumbled backward. He held his hands up. Then it hit him. He had to stop seeing. He closed his eyes tightly, pressed the palms of his hands against his face, and then opened his eyes again.

Still the Ghostlands, gray fog and the monster coming for him. It roared, loud enough to hurt his ears.

"No!" Jack shouted. "No! Make it stop! Stop seeing!"

Again he squeezed his eyes shut, slapped himself in the temples, and began to stagger away, then to run, eyes closed. He slammed into someone and went down hard on the cobblestones. Voices shouted obscenities at him.

He heard the snarl of the Ravenous, could practically smell its stink. In his mind's eye, he could still see the soul-maggots in its fur, and the way it had torn apart the spirits of the dead.

"No!" Jack shouted again, and he opened his eyes.

Business suits. Briefcases. A couple of teenagers gawking at him, and an elderly couple with shopping bags scowling in his direction. The crowd on the streets had thinned, but the people that were still there cast him disgusted glances, this guy who had been shouting and slapping at his head and covering his eyes. He knew what they must think, and didn't care.

He couldn't see the Ghostlands anymore, could not see the Ravenous. But even as he rose, quivering, to his feet and began to walk out of Downtown Crossing, he was certain he could feel it there, its presence, stalking back and forth across the spirit world, just out of sight. It was searching for him now, Jack knew.

It had his scent.

Courtney had invited him to stay, but Bill had opted to go home. The last thing he wanted to do was overstay his welcome. He slept at her apartment a few nights a week as it was, but he did not live there, and he did not want to make any assumptions. Besides, the mornings after the nights he stayed over she usually slept later than usual, and it added stress to her life to have to rush through her usual ritual to prepare for the pub to open.

So he didn't stay. But every time he had to go home, when he kissed her good night and let himself out the rear door at the back of the kitchen, he regretted it. Tonight was no exception.

When he had set the alarm on the kitchen door and locked it tight, he slid the pub keys into his pocket and walked down the alley that ran behind all the buildings on Nelson Street. It was used for deliveries and trash pickup, mostly, but it was also the easiest way to get to the small open lot where he, Courtney, and Jack all parked their cars.

The attendant was long gone for the night but he always left Bill's car where it could be retrieved. It was an Oldsmobile Delta 88, a boat of an automobile he had acquired back when he was playing professional football and held onto ever since. The Olds had its share of dents and rust, but he kept it up pretty well. It was familiar, nicely broken in, and in some ways was just as much a home to him as his apartment.

Bill glanced up at the stars and began to whistle as he strode across the lot to his car. He reached for the door handle, and froze.

Twitching, he stepped back and sniffed the air. A low growl began to build in his chest and he glanced quickly around. He edged along the car, watching the shadows. When he reached the trunk, he saw that someone had popped it with a crowbar or something. His nostrils were filled with conflicting odors, but the stench from the car was clear above all the others.

Bill opened the trunk.

In it lay a human corpse that had been torn apart.

CHAPTER 5

Bill slammed the trunk.

He started to change, could feel the bones shifting in him, the fur beginning to shoot like needles out from under his false skin, but he took a breath and composed himself. Bill raised his chin and sniffed at the air again, caught the scent right away.

A Prowler scent.

Not that he was surprised. The corpse in the trunk had been torn up by two of his kind; their scents were still on the dead man. But only one of them was on the car. Again, Bill inhaled that odor. It was male . . . and there was something familiar about it. He couldn't place it, but whoever had left the little present in the trunk of his car was someone he had met before.

His head whipped to the left and another growl, softer this time, escaped his lips. Without a glance back, he sprinted down the alley, all of his senses attuned to his surroundings. The pavement was littered with decaying garbage and oil stains and he avoided them without even glancing down.

The body had been dead a day or more, in his trunk no more than half an hour. But the scent was fresher than that. Minutes.

Whatever had left it there had lingered to watch.

His muscles rippled under the masque of human flesh he wore and he yearned to let the beast out, but not yet. For in seconds he had reached the end of the alley, where it spilled out between two trendy boutiques right in the middle of Quincy Market.

There were no street performers now, no tourists, no balloons or flower vendors. Only the rustle of overfilled garbage cans in the summer breeze off the harbor, and the cooing of pigeons, and the forlorn forms of one or two homeless people who had found shelter on benches or in doorways.

And across the wide promenade that separated one long building from another, through the trees that had been planted in the midst of the concrete jungle there, Bill saw him. Just a silhouette, the shape of a man that was a false shape, his outline on the far side of a glass-enclosed restaurant, perhaps a hundred yards away.

Across the open concourse, even with the flutter of pigeons and the distant sound of car engines, he heard a low laugh.

With a snarl, Bill ran. Too swiftly to be human, but he didn't care now. He dared not risk being seen in his true form out here in the open like this, but was not going to worry about some street drifter talking about some guy who moved too fast to be a man.

The air made a hushed sound as he sliced through it. A long iron and wood bench was in his way, and Bill cleared it in a single hurdle. This place, usually teeming with life, was like some post-apocalyptic landscape now and there was nothing to slow his pace. He reached the spot where the watcher had stood but of course he was gone. Bill raced around in front of the main structure of Quincy Market, the marketplace's granite steps on the right and the brick colonial grandeur of Faneuil Hall to his left.

No sign of anyone.

But the scent lingered.

And from not far off, the sound of running feet.

Another growl came, and this time he did not swallow it, but let it out in a rolling thunder that echoed off the buildings around him. His legs pumped beneath him, muscles rippling, and yet still he fought the change. All the questions that rose up in him at the thought of the corpse in his trunk were pushed away. *Why* would have to wait until he had in his hands the one being who could answer that question.

He breathed in the Prowler's scent, and he *knew* it, but still could not place it.

Around the corner of Faneuil Hall, he ran past a glass structure that housed a small florist and then he came in sight of Congress Street, the wide avenue that separated the Quincy Market area from Government Center and the ominous concrete behemoth that looked more like a prison than City Hall.

A lone figure, crouched low, ran in a diagonal line toward the road. Lean and quick, but Bill couldn't tell any more than that in the dark, from this distance. Despite the lateness of the hour, cars raced by on both sides of Congress Street. Bill swore loudly and kept up his pursuit, though a feeling of dread began to build in him.

No, no, no, he thought, anger boiling up along with the dread.

He leaned into the wind, gaining momentum, aware that at his obvious age and size, anyone who spotted him from a passing car would have to remark on his speed, but not caring. He couldn't be arrested for being fast.

Fast, he thought, and grunted. *Not fast enough.*

For up ahead, a convertible charged through a red light and squealed to a halt at the curb. From that distance, Bill could see that the driver had blond hair, but no more. The Prowler—the creature that had planted that corpse in his trunk—leaped into the passenger seat without opening the door. The tires shrieked as the car accelerated out of there, shooting up Congress Street in the opposite direction.

"Damn," Bill whispered as he came to a halt, watching the car disappear. The word came out as a snarl.

Now he would have to find the answers to his questions on his own. He turned to walk back toward the parking lot where he had left his car. When he reached the alley, the police were waiting for him.

Only a few blocks from where she had picked Dallas up, Valerie slowed the Mustang down. Not only did she not want to attract the attention of the police, she was just plain nervous about driving his car. It was pristine, absolutely perfect, and just the thought of how crushed he would be if she wrecked it was enough for her to want to pull over right then and switch with him.

Dallas didn't seem to notice. He had been laughing even as he leaped into the car, barely able to catch his breath. It was infectious, and Valerie had laughed right along with him. This was a part of Dallas that rarely surfaced. Each new challenge, each hunt, brought out a grim determination in him, so these moments of reckless abandon were precious to her. Over the years their relationship had been a sort of revolving door; for a time she would be his mate, and then one of them would grow bored and leave.

Whenever Dallas came back into her life, Valerie would learn all over again just what it was that made her miss him so much.

"Whooo!" he said happily, slouching down in the Mustang's passenger seat. "He's fast for a big one, isn't he?"

A devilish grin split his features, and it made Valerie laugh again.

"I don't get you," she said. "You know him well enough not to want to kill him, but you'll torment him mercilessly?"

Dallas shot her a blank look. "Well, yeah! I said I knew him. I didn't say I liked him a hell of a lot."

Valerie shook her head, still smiling. "You're not going to tell me any more than that, are you? How you know him? What it's all about?"

He slid over beside her in the seat and put a hand on her leg, suddenly intimate. "That's on a need to know basis, darlin'. And you do not need to know."

Which was what made Valerie think that whatever Dallas's connection to Cantwell was, it involved a woman.

"What do you think is going to happen with Paul's body?" she asked.

They sped beneath streetlights and she turned left, planning to double back to where they had started. The engine hummed smoothly, making her think of the constant low drone from a beehive. Dallas turned sideways and looked back the way they had come as though he thought Bill Cantwell might still be chasing them. His grin evaporated.

"If the police respond as quickly to my phone call as I expect them to, it won't be up to him. Just in case, though, we're going to go back and keep an eye on him."

A tiny alarm went off in Valerie's mind. "Let's just be careful, all right? He's got your scent now, maybe mine, too."

Dallas stroked her leg suggestively. "We'll stay downwind. Once it all plays out, we can hunt the other three together, make a party of it, just you and me and the prey."

A shiver of pleasure went through Valerie. Together would be nice. And the feast they would have . . . her mouth had begun to water just from his words. She reached out and ran her hand through his beautiful hair.

"How I've missed you," she whispered.

A horn blared. Valerie looked back at the road to find that she let the car drift into the opposite lane. She jerked the wheel back just before she would have collided with a pickup truck. Both hands on the wheel, she held tight and slowed the car even further, her chest heaving with panic.

After a long moment, Dallas began to laugh again, though softly this time.

"Keep your eyes on the road."

The front door to Bridget's was locked when Molly finally returned to the pub. It was one-thirty in the morning and she felt as though she had been through the longest day of her life. A trip to the beach always left her exhausted and the long drive back and forth had not helped, but she knew that she was more emotionally drained than plain tired. She had her keys in her pocket, but when she reached the pub she saw Courtney inside, shutting off some of the lights.

Molly rapped on the window and Courtney looked up quickly. When she saw who it was, she smiled, but there was something bittersweet about it. Courtney hobbled to the door, punched in the numbers that would deactivate the burglar alarm, and unlocked it.

"Hey," Molly said.

"I wasn't sure you were coming back tonight," Courtney told her.

"Neither was I." Molly shrugged a bit and then slipped past her, waiting while Courtney locked up again. "But I have to work tomorrow, and I didn't think it would be fair to you to just disappear."

PROWLERS

Courtney rested her weight on her cane and regarded her closely. Molly thought the woman looked like she had a lot to say, like she might be about to launch into some kind of lecture or begin to philosophise. Instead, she simply nodded.

"I appreciate it. I'm sorry about all this, Molly."

"Me, too."

After a moment's pause, Courtney stepped up and gave her a small hug made awkward by the cane. "I'll be up in just a minute."

Molly nodded and headed for the stairs at the back of the restaurant.

"He's probably waiting up for you," Courtney said from behind her.

"Good," Molly grunted. "He and I need to have a talk."

Many of the stairs creaked, something she only noticed when the pub was empty and quiet. Fans rotated lazily on the ceiling; Courtney would leave them on low all night to keep the place from heating up early. Molly had never realized how many steps there were to the apartment.

The door was unlocked. It was almost always unlocked, even when the pub was open, a fact that Molly had chided Courtney and Jack for many times. Eventually, she was sure, some drunk was going to find his way up from the bar. But the Dwyer siblings were both stubborn and hardheaded, and getting them to change their behavior was even more difficult a task than Molly would have guessed.

She pushed the door open and stepped into the apartment. It was mostly dark, save for a small light in the bathroom that was always on and the pale blue flicker of the television in Jack's room. His bedroom door was wide open. The air conditioner in Courtney's room hummed quietly. It was turned up high enough that it was almost cold in the apartment, and Molly shivered. She went down the hall and stood in the doorway to Jack's room.

He was sitting up on the bed, and when he saw her he froze as though he had been caught doing something awful.

"Hey," he said softly.

Molly swallowed hard. "You're up late."

Jack glanced away nervously, but only once. After that he kept his gaze steady on her, as if he thought it would prove something to her.

"I was worried about you."

"I'm fine," she said. "Or as fine as I can be. I walked around a lot, went over to Helen Darcy's for a while. It was . . . I hadn't seen her in weeks, so it was good, just to be with someone else. Someone who doesn't know . . . what we know."

There was a pause then. It felt to her as though they were not people but actors on a stage and the audience was all around them. Jack sat on the bed in his underwear and a Boston Red Sox shirt, and Molly stood a few feet away with her unruly hair spilling all around her and the distance between them felt full, almost pregnant with expectation.

The audience, she thought, and a chill went through her.

"Are we alone?" she asked suddenly.

Jack blinked. "How do you mean?"

She stared at him. "Are we . . . alone?"

Understanding dawned on his face with a comical expression. "Oh. Well, yeah. As far as I know. But I can't always tell."

Molly glanced at the television, where an ancient western in black and white flickered on the screen. "Do you have any idea how pissed off at you I am?"

"Kinda," he replied.

She shot him a withering glance.

"Okay, maybe not," he allowed. "But you didn't even give me a chance to explain. It wasn't up to me, y'know? I wanted to tell you. It was—"

"No!" she said quickly, and held up a hand. "I'm pissed at him, too, but don't lay this off on Artie. You felt something happening, the same way I did. Something between us. As . . . as wrong as that would be, for it to happen so soon, only a few months after he was murdered . . . it was happening." Molly forced herself to stare at him, snapping off every word now as though it tasted vile to her. *"You should have said something."*

For a moment, she thought he was going to defend himself. But then Jack just nodded.

"You're right. I should have. And I'm sorry."

The anger was rolling out of her now, and it felt good. All the emotions that she had caged within her all through that day and night could finally be set free.

"It's like this big joke on Molly, now. Courtney obviously knew, otherwise she would have brought it up to me just now. I'm assuming Bill knows, too."

Jack glanced away, and she knew it was true.

"So it's just me. Do you have any idea how much that makes me feel like an outsider? With all I've been through, even with the awful things we've seen together, I felt like, for a little while, I had a family. As long as we stayed here, working the pub, hunting these monsters together, I was a part of something. I was even thinking that maybe it was a bad idea for me to leave for Yale right now, that maybe I should put it off or even go somewhere else, somewhere closer, because someone has to fight this fight, and it's *us*. We're already in it. It's something we share.

"I felt like I had a family, Jack," Molly said, calmer now, anger all used up, only the sadness remaining. "But then I found out I was just a stray you'd taken in. You and Artie plotting to protect me from myself. Well that just sucks, Jack! It isn't fair. What would have happened if we *had* started to get . . . closer?"

Some flicker of recognition went through him then, and Molly stared at him.

"Let me guess," she said slowly. "You talked about it, didn't you? With him? You couldn't talk about it with me after we kissed in Vermont, but you talked about it with him?"

Jack let out a small, defeated sigh. "Yes, we talked about it. To tell you the truth, Artie's been pushing for us to get together for a while."

Her mouth hung open, and she just stared at him.

"He . . . how could he want that?" she asked in a tiny voice, feeling as though she had withdrawn to some place deep inside herself. "If he loved me so much, how could . . ."

She could not finish, and only stared at Jack, distraught and hoping for some sort of explanation that would make sense of it all.

"Artie loves us both," he said gently. "But he's gone, Molly. I can talk to him sometimes, but he isn't really here. Artie thought that if you knew, you'd never really be able to put it in the past. As for us . . ."

The pause brought her attention and Molly stared at him, still thunderstruck. Jack shrugged.

"I've always loved you as a friend. I care about you so much, and Artie knew that. Knows that. He said he hoped something would happen with us because he knew I would take care of you."

The words were like a door slamming shut in her mind. Molly stiffened, stood up straight, and glared at him with all the venom she could muster.

"I don't need you to take care of me, Jack Dwyer," she said bitterly. Then she stared around the room, wondering if Artie could hear her, hoping that he could.

"I don't need you to take care of me!" she repeated.

But this time, she wasn't talking to Jack.

With that, she turned and stormed to her room and slammed the door.

Only seconds after Molly went into her room, Artie appeared at the end of the bed. Jack flinched, startled, then sighed as he put one hand over his heart.

"So that went well, didn't you think?" Artie asked.

Jack gave him the finger.

Frustrated, but knowing they needed to talk, he

padded barefoot out into the hall. He jumped back slightly when the door opened and Courtney entered. Jack's gaze ticked toward Artie, who made faces behind his sister's back.

"Did you talk to Molly?" Courtney asked.

Jack smiled, tried not to look at Artie, and nodded. "Yeah. She's still pretty pissed, though."

"Can't blame her," his sister said. "I have no idea what you're gonna do about this, Jack, but maybe you should have a talk with Artie. Maybe it's time for him to move on, y'know? Spare the girl."

Behind her, Artie's expression went slack. No more funny faces. No more kidding around. Jack noticed that in that moment Artie's body seemed to waver, even to fade somewhat. When he had first appeared—though of course transparent—he had been completely visible right down to his high tops. Now his spectral form seemed less defined, his body ending just below the knees in a swirl of mist.

"I'll . . . I'll talk to him," Jack replied.

Courtney touched his arm. "Hey. I can't even imagine how hard this all is for you. But I just think you need to think about what's best for everyone. If Artie really loves you guys, I think the best thing might be for him to just leave you alone. There's got to be something better waiting for him somewhere, right?"

Jack glanced at the ghost of his best friend. Artie wore a small, sad smile.

"I'll talk to him," Jack said softly. "I'm gonna go downstairs and sit for a bit. Just take some time to think."

PROWLERS

Courtney touched her brother's face and smiled the big sister smile she had been giving him all his life. Then she turned away, headed for the kitchen. She liked to keep a glass of water beside her bed during the night, Jack knew. He watched her pull a cup down from the cabinet in the darkened kitchen, then he headed out the door and down the stairs into the pub.

Jack went to the bar and poured himself a 7-Up from the tap, then sat on a stool. Artie settled down on the seat beside him, as though he actually needed its support. But the stool did not move, did not slide out from the bar even an inch. He wasn't really there.

"I wanted to talk where Molly wouldn't hear me," Jack explained.

"I got it, Jack. I'm not slow."

There was a bitterness in the ghost's tone that Jack wished he could find surprising, but did not. Courtney had expressed thoughts that Jack had not even allowed into his own head.

"She didn't know you were there."

Artie would not look at him. "I know. But maybe she's right."

Jack exhaled slowly, staring at Artie. Staring through him. He could see the four beer taps beyond the ghost, and the rest of the bar beyond that. Could see right out to the street. But if he focused on Artie, right there in front of him, he could almost make himself *not* see all of that, could almost make himself believe Artie was really there.

"Maybe," Jack allowed. "Maybe so. But that's not a conversation for right now. Later, we oughta talk. For now, though, that thing saw me, man. The Ravenous absolutely *saw* me. I'm not gonna pretend I wasn't scared. I want to destroy the thing just as badly as you do, but I talked to Father Mike, Artie, and he has no idea what I'm even talking about."

Artie turned toward him then and Jack had to look away from those black eyes. He could never look at those eyes for long.

"We just have to keep trying, bro. You saw what that thing does. All right, yeah, I was always pretty dubious about psychics and mediums and that sort of thing when I was alive, but at this point I'm pretty much convinced ghosts are real."

Jack smiled and shook his head. Artie grinned as well and his body became more solid, the outline of his form better defined.

"Not that I'm suggesting you call some infomercial hotline or something," Artie went on. "But if you and me can talk, there've gotta be other people who can do the same thing. Maybe people who've been doing it a lot longer and know more about it. *Someone* on your side has to know something about the Ravenous."

Jack frowned. "I don't get it. Nobody over there can tell you anything useful?"

Artie shrugged, put his elbows on the bar. Jack's gaze ticked down and he saw that the ghost's arms actually passed an inch or so through the wood. Sometimes he wished that Artie did not try to behave as if he were still alive; it made it creepier, and sadder as well.

"Most everyone who has their wits about them over

here moves on before too long. So far, most of the spirits I've met who have been here a long time are either completely self-involved or not quite all there. Either way, they don't pay much attention to what's going on around them. So what I know, I know from things that have been passed down—"

A long beep broke the silence in the pub. Jack and Artie both turned to stare toward the back of the restaurant, at the door that led into the kitchen. The beeping stopped and then a door slammed.

"What the hell?" Jack muttered as he rose from the stool. It was going on two in the morning.

The kitchen door swung wide and Bill Cantwell stepped into the restaurant followed by two uniformed policemen and a woman in street clothes who wore a badge on a chain around her neck.

"Bill?" Jack asked, alarmed.

"Are you Jack Dwyer?" the woman asked.

He nodded.

"Amy Pepper," she said. "I'm a homicide detective. I'd like to ask you a few questions about Mr. Cantwell's whereabouts the past few days."

Homicide. The word lingered in his mind and he stared at Bill. *Homicide.*

CHAPTER 6

The air conditioner hummed in Courtney's window. The late-night city lights cast the room in a soft yellow glow. On nights Bill went home, she had taken to sleeping with the radio on low. Her door was open to let the cool air waft out into the rest of the apartment. Even when Bill slept over, she kept the door partially open. It wouldn't be fair, otherwise.

Eyes closed, she let the details of the day swirl in her head and blur into one another, and it was not long before she began to drift off, an old song by the Eagles on the radio. In this twilight state between waking and dreaming, she heard the door to the apartment click open. Her eyelids fluttered but did not open. It was just Jack, she knew, finally turning in for the night.

Gonna have a hell of a time waking him up in the morning, she thought. Then she nuzzled more deeply into her pillow. It smelled like Bill, and a smile flickered across her face as she at last fell asleep.

"Court?"

She snapped awake, eyes wide open. For a second she was not sure if she had really heard Jack's voice, or if she had dreamed it. Then she saw his silhouette in her doorway out of the corner of her eye, and she sat up. The cotton pajama top she wore was twisted around wrong, and she fixed it unconsciously as she gazed at Jack, mind still sifting the real from the sleep world. Her brother looked more than uneasy.

"What?" she asked.

"Better put some clothes on and come downstairs," Jack said. "We've got trouble."

"Jesus," Courtney whispered as she stared at this woman, Detective Pepper. Her gaze went instantly to Bill and she shivered. From the detective's description of the dead man, it was obvious he had been killed by a Prowler. But Bill could not have done such a thing. *Well*, she corrected, *he could, but he wouldn't*.

Her mind whirled as she tried to make sense of it all. Even presuming a Prowler had killed the man in Bill's trunk, the question remained, why? Why put him there.

"Who was he? The dead man, I mean," Courtney asked the detective.

"No idea, yet."

"Bill didn't do this."

"We're not saying that he did," Detective Pepper replied. "From the look of things, the trunk was forced open with a crowbar or something. That much I'll give you. But the body was in the trunk of his car and we encountered Mr. Cantwell at the scene. He claims he was chasing the person who put the body in his trunk, but we have to consider the possibility that he was after the person who forced the trunk open and *discovered* it there."

Courtney frowned and sat up straighter, smoothing the wrinkles in the pants she had pulled on quickly. "Yes, you have to consider it. Just as long as you realize that isn't what happened. Now let me ask *you* something. How did you know to check out his car, to look in that lot in the first place? You didn't just happen by."

Detective Pepper sat back in her chair and regarded Courtney coolly. "No, that's true. We didn't. We had an anonymous tip actually."

Satisfied, Courtney nodded. "So there you are. An anonymous tip from the person who put the corpse there, the person who's trying to cast suspicion on Bill."

"That's yet another possibility we have to consider," the detective replied.

But somehow Courtney thought that Detective Pepper wasn't going to spend too much time considering that alternative. And talking about Prowlers as yet another alternative would only make the woman less likely to listen to reason. Courtney was about to protest again when she remembered that there was at least one detective on Boston's homicide squad who might.

"Do you know a homicide detective named Castillo?"

*   *   *

Castillo groaned as he came awake with a start. His eyes opened and he sighed as the cell phone on his night-stand trilled a second time. He snatched it up even as he glared at the luminous numbers on the clock.

2:27 A.M.

He had been asleep for a little more than two hours.

"Yeah?" he rasped into the phone.

"Jace, it's Pepper."

"My shift was over hours ago, Pepper," he grumbled.

"If you say so. Do you know a woman named Courtney Dwyer? Owns Bridget's Irish Rose on Nelson?"

"Yeah?"

"We've got a DOA down here. The Dwyer woman asked me to call you. But it's my case, mister."

Castillo could hear the pique in her voice, but he paid no attention to it. The second she had mentioned Bridget's, he grabbed for his jeans and was pulling them on, phone clutched between his shoulder and jaw.

"Sorry, Pepper," he told her. "Not anymore."

"What?"

"If you have an issue with it, talk to the lieutenant," he said as he pulled socks from his drawer, glancing around in search of his shoes. "I'll be there in fifteen."

"You know we're going to be useless in the morning," Jack said.

From the table in the middle of the pub where he sat with Courtney while the police continued to question Bill, Jack could just barely see the clock behind the bar. It was a few minutes past three. Molly still slept upstairs, and so they had been careful not to wake her.

"We might have to send Molly to the fish market in the morning," Courtney said tiredly.

Yet in her eyes Jack saw the worry that weighed upon her now. He knew she must be asking herself the same questions he was. Or at least the one overriding question that boomed in the back of his head. Not who, or what, but why?

"I'll go," Bill said. "I can go to the market, then sleep in the afternoon and still take the dinner shift."

Courtney nodded. "We'll work it out."

A long silence ensued. After another minute Jack rose to get himself another soda from behind the bar. He had not gotten very far when there came a rap on the frosted glass of the door. A dark silhouette stood outside. He glanced quickly at Detective Pepper, who nodded in assent, and then he strode over to disarm the security system and unlock the door.

Jace Castillo stood on the sidewalk. The street outside was completely silent, the storefronts all dark, most of the windows unlit as well. Only the wan illumination from a few street lamps and the dim glow of distant city lights alleviated the darkness, and they made the night look surreal.

"Jack," the detective said cautiously.

Jack stepped back to let the man enter. Castillo was fortyish, about six feet tall, and slim. From previous conversations, he knew that the man was a combination of Irish and Puerto Rican, and the mix had been good to him. Both Molly and Courtney had commented before about how handsome the detective was. Jack wasn't so sure about that, but he had to allow that the guy had that dark, George Clooney thing going on.

Castillo glanced curiously around the pub as he walked to the table where Detective Pepper sat with Bill. When he seemed to find nothing remarkable about the place, he gazed at the other detective.

"I'll take it from here, Amy."

Pepper frowned deeply, angrily. "I want to know what this is about, Jace. I may be new to the division, but not the department. I don't like the smell of this."

Castillo fixed Pepper with an admonishing glare. Jack figured he didn't think it was a conversation they should be having with civilians in the room, never mind the uniformed officers who stood there. It was a lesson he and Courtney had learned a long time ago. Never argue in front of your subordinates.

"What you're told or not told is up to Lieutenant Boggs, not me," Castillo told her. "Now if you'll excuse me, I'd like you all to clear the room."

Silent but fuming, Pepper stood and led the other officers back through the kitchen and presumably back out into the alley crime scene. When they had all gone, Castillo studied Bill, then glanced at Jack and Courtney.

"Talk to me," he said.

Courtney did not smile. "Maybe you'd better have a seat."

Castillo crouched down and studied the marks where the trunk had been forced open. Probably a crowbar, he figured. He touched nothing as he took another look at the remains in the trunk. It looked too damn familiar. Over the years he had seen a lot of bodies like this, most of them just a few months before, when Owen Tanzer's pack had slaughtered more than a dozen people in the city, including a local organized crime capo. The fallout from that was still taking place. It was one thing to tell an average civilian that a murder was unsolved, or that their spouse simply disappeared and has never been found. Quite another to keep mob leaders from killing each other in vengeance for something none of them had anything to do with.

Fortunately, that was really the FBI's job.

He stood up again, studying the inside of the trunk. The body had clearly been dumped there, but anyone could have done that, even a human. Someone might have found the body and put it there. Cantwell, Jack, and Courtney had all been involved in taking Tanzer down. More than likely this was a warning to put them on alert that they were targeted for payback, but that was just a guess.

"All right," he said, turning to the crime scene analysts who had been working on the site already. "Sorry for the interruption. You'll all have instructions from Al Pratt on how to handle the remains and the evidence in this case. Do nothing until you hear from him."

Like Lieutenant Boggs, Pratt, who headed up the forensics team, had dealt with Prowler murders before, and could keep a secret. Castillo strode away from the scene and back to the rear entrance to the pub, where Cantwell stood with the Dwyer siblings, observed at a distance by a pair of uniforms.

"All right, Mr. Cantwell. Why don't we go down to the division and talk about all of this?"

The kid, Jack, stared at him. "Is that really necessary?"

Castillo studied him. Once upon a time he had felt bad for the kid. His best friend had been one of the first people murdered by Tanzer's pack when they started hunting in Boston. But it turned out Jack Dwyer had some secrets of his own, the biggest one being that he could talk to the dead. He and his friend Molly Hatcher had killed Tanzer themselves, which was a major mark in their favor in Castillo's book. But Jack talking to ghosts was still about the creepiest thing Castillo had ever run across. Though he had once told the kid to call him Jace, he was glad Jack had gone back to *detective.*

Castillo glanced at Courtney and Cantwell, then back at Jack. When he spoke, he made certain to whisper so that his voice would not carry to his fellow officers. "If this guy turns out to be a transient or something, or if it turns out there weren't any witnesses, it's not impossible to make all the evidence collected disappear. Trust me, it wouldn't be the first time."

"Jesus," Courtney muttered. When Castillo stared at her, she brushed at the air. "No, no. I mean, of course that's best. It just amazes me, the size of the conspiracy that requires. That it's been kept so quiet all this time."

"It isn't difficult to hide the truth from people if they don't want to believe it in the first place," the detective replied, glancing along the alley at Pepper, who caught him looking and glared. "But this is a human corpse, not some monster we can just incinerate. If there were witnesses, we're going to have to account for what happened here somehow. That means we have to conduct it like a criminal investigation. Forensics, everything."

He turned to Bill. "It also means that once the other detectives arrive, I'm going to want you to come back to the division with me to give a more formal statement about all this."

The burly bartender stiffened, a dangerous look in his eyes. Both Jack and Courtney moved closer to him as though they felt the need to protect him somehow.

"I didn't do anything," Cantwell said sharply.

"Probably not," Castillo allowed. "But it's my job to investigate, and that's what I'm going to do. Are you going to give me a problem with that?"

Cantwell bristled, but he shook his head. "No. I'm ready when you are."

The security system in Bridget's Irish Rose Pub was like millions of other similar setups in homes and small businesses all across America. Ninety-nine percent of its effectiveness came from its mere existence. The average small-time burglar, second-story man, or crackhead willing to B&E for a fix would see the symbols for the security company on the doors and windows and not give the place a second look. In reality, a handful of stickers would probably deter most would-be thieves without actually even activating the system.

On the other hand, anyone who really wanted to get inside a home or building was going to find a way, depending on the level of their determination. In some cases, they might risk setting off the alarm in hopes they could be in and gone before the cops arrived. Or, if they had the skill and the patience, they might be able to find a way to circumvent the system altogether. There were expensive high-tech devices that could do exactly that.

Dallas didn't like to spend money on that kind of crap. The tech stuff was too unreliable, too sensitive to being jostled or jarred.

He stood in the alley that ran parallel to Nelson Street, downwind, and watched as a police detective took Bill Cantwell away. It was precisely his plan—more of a hope, really. This way, he knew that Cantwell would be otherwise occupied. One-stop shopping for his real targets, no waiting.

There were other vehicles there, of course—police, a tow truck, a crime scene team, and someone from the Medical Examiner's office. But Dallas was patient. When the last police car was out of sight, Dallas let the minutes tick by. Ten, fifteen, twenty. Enough for the rest of the people in the apartment above the pub to slip back into bed, maybe even fall asleep. If it were earlier, he would have worried more about them staying up to talk about what had happened to Cantwell. But at this hour, he banked on their going back to bed.

A warm breeze blew back his long, straight hair, but he liked that. It made him feel as though, even in the midst of all the steel and concrete around him, the wild was ever present. No matter how much humanity had scarred the face of the earth, nature, the wilderness, was still there beneath and above it all.

A single light burned in a window on the apartment level of the building. The restaurant took up two stories, he knew. The third story was where they all lived. When the light blinked out, he padded silently across the alley. When he had put the corpse in Cantwell's trunk, he had spotted a broken table up against the Dumpster. The table was still there, two shattered legs and a long crack down the middle. Fortune had smiled on him; the garbage collectors had not been around to pick it up yet.

Still wearing the masque of humanity, Dallas sniffed at the air and peered around the alley. When he was certain he was not observed, he lifted the table and propped its two unbroken legs against the base of the wall, so that it sat at an angle next to the building. Just beneath the fire escape. It took strength to do such a thing silently, but a Prowler had the physical power for that and more.

Carefully, he scaled the smooth face of the table and balanced his feet precariously on the edge that jutted upward. Dallas splayed his hands against the brick wall and stood up straight. The ladder that ought to have protruded from the bottom of the fire escape was missing, as though it had been removed to help deter the possibility of just such an intrusion. But standing upon the table, it was a simple thing for Dallas to thrust himself upward and wrap his right hand around the iron grating of the fire escape.

His left hand came up, fingers slipping into the grating as well. He had seen the humans within, the Dwyer siblings and the Hatcher girl, moving about for a time, while he waited, but then lights had been turned off and it seemed all of them had at last returned to their beds. Still, he could not be sure they were sleeping. Intent upon stealth, he moved slower than he could have, pulled himself soundlessly up into the fire escape and then climbed the ladder to the top. The window there was barred.

Even a determined thief would likely have been turned away by those bars.

But Dallas was not a thief.

Outside the window he caught the scents of those within and a bloodlust rose in him. His heart began to thunder in his chest and his human skin began to feel tight, constrictive around him. His body yearned for the change, the freedom of revealing his true self. With a quick shudder, he let his tongue slip out, slide over his teeth, and he tasted the night, and the flavor of his prey in the air.

The beast within surged forth, but Dallas forced it back down. It was no simple feat, but he had practiced controlling himself and focusing his bloodlust for decades. He was not some foolish animal, controlled only by instinct and savagery. Not like the others of his kind. Dallas was an assassin, a calculating killer, a cunning taker of lives. And it was that calm killer, not the savage beast, who refused to be deterred. He had taken on this job, and even without the help in finding his daughter that Jasmine had promised, even without the money involved, he would have followed through.

With a low rumble in his chest that only he could hear, Dallas stepped onto the window ledge, then up to the railing at the top of the fire escape, then onto the tiny lip on top of the window. His arms shot up and he gripped the edge of the roof with his fingers, then hauled himself up with only the hush of his clothes against the brick to give him away.

On top of the roof he walked only on the edge to avoid any sound below. The window at the top of the fire escape had been barred, but the others were not. Once, twice, three times he stopped to dangle himself headfirst over the edge of the roof. He saw Jack Dwyer shifting fitfully in bed, uncovered, sweating with the heat of the night, when even the breeze through his window must be unpleasant. His sister had an air conditioner in her window, and Dallas could see that the door was open, but the cool air did not seem to help much in the rest of the apartment. He could not tell if Courtney Dwyer was awake, but he suspected she would be the most likely to have trouble falling back to sleep. Cantwell was her lover, after all, or so Dallas had been told.

The third window that he hung down and peered through led into the kitchen. It was empty and quiet save for the tick of the moon-and-stars clock that the Prowler's eyes could make out on the wall, even in the dark. The window was wide open to let in the breeze, but there was a screen. How simple it would have been to tear the screen out with his hand. But that would be too loud. Though he had no doubt he could kill them all even if they knew he was coming, Jasmine had warned him that these humans were formidable and seemingly fearless. They had killed Tanzer, after all.

So, caution.

Dallas retreated back to the roof and removed a small pair of wire cutters from his pocket. He had expected screens. Hanging once again from the edge of the roof, he cut away the bottom corners of the screen slowly, methodically. Finished, he slipped the wire cutters back onto the roof then reached into the two holes he had made in the screen and undid the latches that held the frame in place. Carefully, he popped the screen inward and set it gently aside.

Swiftly, flesh tingling with anticipation, he turned around and lowered his feet down onto the windowsill, then slipped through.

He was inside.

For a seemingly endless span of moon-and-stars ticks, Dallas simply stood in the kitchen, inhaling the scents of life, of this odd family, their cooking and their dirty laundry and the sweat of their emotions. Silence reigned. Nothing moved. He could hear the hum of the air conditioner in the next room.

Quickly now he went into the hall. Outside the door to Courtney's room he paused, then glanced around the edge, ready to pounce if she noticed him. Ready to change, to tear out of his human skin and then to savage her. A tiny grin slipped across his features.

That was one of the few things he liked about the human form. It felt good to smile, especially when it was a smile of pleasure rather than amusement.

Courtney lay on her side, turned away from the door. The sheet barely covered her, and he admired her still form a moment, thought what a shame it would be to have to kill her. But he had a reputation to uphold and had long ago dismissed any real regret for his victims. Or, at least, any regret that might hold him back.

PREDATOR AND PREY

Soft and precious in a cotton pajama top, Courtney's chest rose and fell with a gentle rhythm. She might have been awake, staring into the darkness, or trying to will herself to forget the events of the night long enough to drift off. But he thought she was already there, already sleeping.

Dallas would come back to her.

He slipped along the hall, wary of the open door at the far end where Jack had his room. Halfway along the corridor, on the side opposite Courtney's room, he caught the scent of the other female, Molly Hatcher. Dallas moved through the darkened apartment and slipped into the girl's room. Though the air conditioner in Courtney's room was turned up high, still it was too warm. Molly was sprawled in a tangle of sheets, her red hair in a wild spray around her head. Her eyes were closed and her lips parted in a strangely seductive display of innocence.

Asleep.

The T-shirt she had worn to bed was rucked up to expose her gently sloping belly, a stretch of pale, smooth, perfect flesh that made Dallas growl low in his chest, despite the risk. He felt fur begin to sprout through his false human visage and his teeth grew longer, sharper. The lure of that perfect, creamy white skin would have presented him a great challenge if he had still needed to control himself.

But the time for control had passed.

Her life would pass into him as he tore her flesh apart, as her blood spattered his fur.

Dallas slipped farther into Molly's room and the

111

change came over him. He could feel the skin tear as his fur pushed up from beneath, as his limbs restructured themselves in a shifting of bone unlike any other possible in creation. The false human skin flaked off and sifted down to the floor in a fine dust. Part of the transformation, particularly the elongation of his jaws and the thrusting up of fangs, was painful, but it was a glorious pain, as though with every fiber of his being he were reaching back to the primal heart of his ancestors.

His nostrils flared, his pointed ears twitched. He breathed in this human girl, this prey. Slightly crouched, he moved to the edge of the bed, tilted his head at an angle, and watched for a moment the way she slept, the simplicity of it. There was human prey that tasted awful, like some wretched refuse.

But just looking at this girl, he knew she would be succulent.

Dallas crouched low over her, the growl rising in his chest, becoming just a little louder. He brushed the hair from her face and waited for her to open her eyes, to look up at him.

To scream.

CHAPTER 7

Beyond the Ghostlands, this world of lost souls and shadows in which Artie Carroll now existed, there was something more. He knew that it waited for him there, some final destination, some afterlife. Heaven? Paradise? Some dull, smoky coffee bar where all anybody ever wanted to talk about was beat poetry, Picasso, and Kurt Cobain?

Artie did not know, though he suspected it was not the latter. Whatever yearning tugged at him, urged him on, there was a sweet benevolence to it unlike anything he had ever known. It sucked being dead. No question about that. But he felt that if he would just allow himself to be swept up into the maelstrom of warm lights that he glimpsed so often just beyond the edges of his awareness, he might be able to forget all about the regrets and longings that still tied him to the fleshworld.

It tore him apart. In his heart, Artie held his pain and

grief close. He did not want to move on, to let go of those emotions, for they were the only things that made him feel as though a spark of life remained in him.

Soon, he thought. *Soon I won't have a choice.*

He knew it was true. The pull of the maelstrom, of eternity, grew greater each day. Only by fractions, but inevitably it would be too much for him. Artie had been preparing for that from the moment he had understood that he was dead, that he was a ghost now, just a wandering spirit. When Jack and Molly had killed Owen Tanzer and most of Tanzer's pack, the unfinished business that kept him tied to the earthly plane was complete.

The Ghostlands themselves were a dreary place, woven of clouds and dreams, shadows and phantoms. Yet from there Artie could keep an eye on those he loved, his friends and his parents, on Jack and on Molly. There was one other benefit. During his life he had been almost obsessive about conspiracies, from the Kennedy assassination to the secret war in Laos during Vietnam to the sins of omission committed by big tobacco. In the Ghostlands, one could learn almost anything from the lost souls. It gave Artie a certain amount of pleasure to learn which of his pet conspiracy theories were true and which false. But he had also learned first hand about other conspiracies, including the tacit cooperation of numerous law enforcement and government agencies around the world to pretend, on an extraordinary scale, that Prowlers were merely a myth.

It was a conspiracy that had naturally evolved over the course of thousands of years, those in authority deciding again and again what they thought their people ought to know, and what their own superiors would believe. Not the United Nations, of course, but individuals in key positions who hid what they knew in order to avoid panic or an uprising that would call their own power into question.

After all, there were so few Prowlers, or so they thought. Every time there was a sighting, or a conflict, people convinced themselves that was the end, that the Prowlers were now extinct, or nearly so. Artie knew that was far from the case. Jack and Molly and Courtney, and in his own way, Bill Cantwell, had begun an effort to seek out Prowlers individually or in packs and destroy them if they seemed to pose a threat to humans.

Artie had begun it all. He felt that he may have pulled the thread that would unravel this ancient conspiracy. It felt good. But it was becoming more and more difficult for him to pretend he had purpose here any longer. Now he was just holding on, having overstayed his welcome. It would be better for all of them, he was certain, if he would just let it go, just move on. Just die, once and for all. In a part of his consciousness he tried to ignore, Artie knew that when the Ravenous had been dealt with, it would be time for him to go.

Nothing left for him to do, to contribute.

No more Jack. No more Molly.

Molly.

All through this strange night, Artie had stayed with her, knowing that time was short and unwilling to give up a moment of these last days he had to be near her. Now, nothing more than a specter, a flutter of the wind, a shadow glimpsed from the corner of her eye, he hovered by her bed and watched as she slept. Her restless tossing and turning had caused her shirt to slide up just beneath her breasts and though he knew she must be warm, Artie bristled at that exposure. She seemed so vulnerable. He wished he could reach out and fix her shirt, pull it down to cover her again.

But he could not touch her. Not ever again.

He could only watch.

And in that crystalline moment of understanding, he was shamed. *Only watch. But it isn't just watching. I'm haunting her.*

Then, as the ache in his soul deepened, he heard a sound from the hall. After what had just happened with Bill, he would not be surprised if Courtney or even Jack were having trouble sleeping. Curious, he drifted toward Molly's door.

A face peered around the corner.

Not Courtney. Not Jack.

The man had dirty blond hair, darker than Artie's had been in life, but too long as Artie's was. A stubble that wasn't quite a beard grew on his chin and his grey eyes sparkled with an intensity even the ghost could feel. There was a power, a raw, primal energy to his very presence, and Artie knew what it was at once.

Not just a burglar. A Prowler. The intruder slipped into Molly's room and Artie could hear a low rumble coming from the monster's gullet. Fur began to spurt up through the skin as it moved closer to her, breathed in her scent.

"No!" he yelled, as loud as he could. "Get away from her!"

He even tried to grab the Prowler, but of course he could not. In his soul, in his mind, Artie still recalled what they had done to him the night he was killed, the way they had torn at him. Images of that same savagery inflicted upon Molly flickered through his mind, of Molly suffering the loneliness and loss he had felt in all his time in the Ghostlands.

"No, damn it!" he screamed again.

The Prowler did not so much as twitch. It neither heard nor sensed him. But as Artie screamed again, the monster began to transform fully, the façade of humanity torn away to reveal the beast within.

Molly slept on, blissfully unaware.

"Jack!"

In the depths of hard-earned slumber, Jack heard the voice calling out his name. Even in his subconscious mind, he tried to ignore it, to push it away. His eyes burned beneath the lids, his throat was dry, his joints ached. Sleep had been difficult to come by this night and so he clung to it with desperation.

"Jack! Wake up, wake up, wake up!"

No, he thought, but it was more plea than denial. His eyes opened, heavy and itchy as though someone had poured sand into them. He listened, eyes slitted, to see if it had been a dream or something real. Then Artie manifested in front of him, the lower portion of the ghost barely coalesced into any form at all. The phantom's bottomless black eyes were wide and his expression frantic.

"Prowler. In Molly's room."

The weight of those words suffocated Jack. He lay completely still, considering. *The bed'll creak if I move; will he hear it? But I might just move in my sleep, turning over. So slow, then. Very slow.*

Like a serpent he slid from the bed to the floor, screaming silent prayers. With each tiny noise of bed and floor he was tempted to pause to listen, but knew that would be folly. The Prowler might come after him before Jack was ready, or it might just kill Molly instantly at the first noise.

No time for self-doubt.

Jack reached under the bed and his fingers closed around the barrel of the pump shotgun he hid under there. It wasn't all that long ago that he abhorred guns, a feeling he had developed partially because of Artie's crusade against them. Never had he imagined he would have a weapon in his house, but it had come to seem necessary after their skirmishes with the Prowlers.

Now he rejoiced at the feel of the steel against his flesh. Guns were instruments of death, and he would never turn one against a human being. But there were things in the dark corners of the world that had to be met with savagery equal to their own.

Jack stood, loaded shotgun in his hands. The ghost watched him, its gossamer form wavering, barely holding the human silhouette that made it recognizable as Artie. Fear had done that, Jack realised. Artie had lost his focus.

With a single brush at the air, Jack waved the ghost away, nodding in the direction of Molly's room.

"You want me to check it out, see where he is in the room?" Artie asked, getting it instantly.

They had been best friends most of their lives. And after.

Jack nodded. The reluctance in Artie's expression was painful to see. The ghost said nothing more, but Jack understood nevertheless. The last thing Artie wanted to do was go back in that room and find that he was too late. But it had to be done. He was nothing but a shade, a phantasm, and as such, invisible to the Prowler.

Artie floated out of the room. Barefoot, Jack hurried along behind him, careful to avoid the floorboards he knew squeaked. In the hall, Artie passed right through the wall into Molly's room and was gone. A horrible feeling slipped into Jack's mind, curled tendrils of almost crippling dread into his brain. Despite the heat of the night and the sweat on his forehead and his bare chest, he felt a chill snake through him.

Too many things had gone wrong in one day, one long, seemingly infinite day. He had always believed that a new dawn brought a new chance to figure things out, but after all that had happened, the way that he kept awakening to new horrors this night, it felt like the dawn would never come.

He held his breath, hoping Artie would tell him something he could use, but Jack dared not wait more than a few seconds. No sound came from within Molly's room and that ominous silence weighed heavy around him, as though trying to crush him.

From within, suddenly, he heard the rustle of sheets. Molly began to mutter something in a sleepy drawl and then her voice rose abruptly in alarm. It was cut off with a strangled cry and a low growl that seemed almost like a purr, a sound of animal pleasure.

Before Jack could run into the room, Artie shouted his name.

"Say something!" Artie told him from within. *"But don't let on that you're armed."*

Thoughts careened through his mind, collided, and he pushed them away. There was no time for thought, only instinct. He had to do as Artie said.

"Molly?" Jack asked, praying that the anxious quaver in his voice would be heard as the weariness of someone woken in the middle of the night. "You having a bad dream or something?"

Jack froze, there in the hall. He could have moved closer to the door, but the Prowler knew he was out here now. As the thought skittered across his mind he understood what Artie hoped for. That it would forget Molly and come for him instead.

His fingers were wrapped painfully tight around the shotgun's barrel. He would have to pump it before he could fire, but if the Prowler knew he had a weapon . . .

Within her bedroom, Molly screamed his name, trying to warn him. Almost in that same instant there came a crash and her voice was cut off again.

"It's coming, Jack! Now!" Artie cried.

But he did not need the ghost to tell him. The Prowler had been furtive and clever, a quiet killer. Now it snarled loudly and its tread upon the ground was clamorous. It leaped out into the hallway in front of him, a slavering thing with golden fur and blood on the claws of one hand—*Molly's blood*. Its eyes seemed to dance with violence and amusement, but then it saw the weapon and its lips curled back with surprise and fury.

Jack racked a shell into the shotgun's chamber.

The Prowler lunged for him, one huge hand drawn back, claws slashing down.

The shotgun thundered in Jack's hands. The blast caught the Prowler in the left shoulder, tore a chunk of flesh and fur out of the beast, spattered the wall with blood. With a bark of pain, the monster spun, twisted around by the impact.

But it didn't go down.

The thing was agile as hell and it used the momentum of the shotgun blast to take off in the other direction. Jack pumped the slide again, took aim and fired, and a piece of the frame blew off the kitchen door as the Prowler fled, bleeding.

"I'll be back, Jack," the monster snarled as he disappeared into the darkness of the kitchen.

Swearing loudly, Jack ran after him, racking another shell into the chamber. As he passed his sister's bedroom he heard Courtney call out to him, saw her limping toward the door in his peripheral vision, but Jack did not slow down.

Just inside the kitchen he stopped and leveled the shotgun, aiming at the dark, bestial form silhouetted in the window. His finger tightened on the trigger and the shotgun bucked in his hands. He had aimed high, and the open window shattered with the cascade of broken glass.

The Prowler was gone.

"Damn it!" Jack pumped the shotgun again and went to the window. He stood back carefully, aimed at what remained of the window, and tried to see outside. After a moment's anxious hesitation, he stuck his head out the window. It was much too far down to jump without something to break the fall, even for a Prowler. From above him there came a low grunt. Jack glanced up, searching for some sign of the intruder. He heard the sound of receding footsteps as the Prowler ran off across the rooftops on Nelson Street. For a moment, Jack considered trying to climb out the window and onto the roof to give chase, but he knew the thought was foolish. Never mind the drop to the street below if he lost his grip, the monster was much faster than he was.

By the time he would have gotten onto the roof, the Prowler would likely already have scrambled down some fire escape on a building up the block. Jaw set in anger and frustration, he ducked back into the kitchen. The shotgun was warm in his hands as he rushed back to Molly's room. He had pushed aside his fear for her in order to drive away the intruder, but now it came rushing upon him again, a knot of anxiety tightly twisted in his gut.

Molly sat on the floor, her back to a small bookcase that had been jarred somehow, knocking books and knickknacks to the floor. Several small pieces had shattered, ceramic animals and a crystal vase. He could barely make out the shards in the dim room, the only illumination coming from the streetlights outside. With her bad leg, Courtney could not crouch and so she was seated on the floor beside Molly, holding the girl in her arms.

On the other side of the bed Artie's ghost shimmered in front of the window, light passing through his diaphanous form as though he were nothing more than an afterimage burned into Jack's eyes. The memory of something he had seen, rather than the actual thing. It occurred to Jack how true that was, and he shuddered.

The ghost would not even look at Molly. Instead, Artie stared out the window and hugged himself as though he were cold. Jack wondered if that was possible, if it was cold for them over there in the Ghostlands. If they could feel it.

"Molly," he said softly.

Eyes red more from lack of sleep than tears, she lifted her head from Courtney's shoulder and looked up at him. Her red hair fell in tendrils across her face and Molly brushed them away. Though he had seen her do things that were extraordinarily courageous, in that moment, there in his sister's arms, in her nightshirt, Molly looked like a little girl to him, soft and vulnerable.

There were long scratches on her throat where the beast had grabbed her. Thin trails of blood trickled from them and stained her shirt. On her forehead there was a welt where she had struck her head. Jack could see it in his mind, the way the Prowler must have thrown her when he had called out; he understood that she had crashed into the bookshelf and hoped that she was not hurt any worse than he could see.

"I . . . I hit him once but it didn't stop him." It was one of the hardest things he'd ever had to say. "He's gone, though."

"But he'll be back," Molly said, her voice hushed. "I heard him say that. He'll be back."

Jack bristled. "Maybe not. I wounded him. He's bleeding. He was probably just talking big to make up for the fact that he turned tail and ran."

Courtney gazed up at him gravely. "He called you by name, Jack. Somebody went out of their way to set it up so Bill wasn't here when this happened, and that thing called you by name. He *will* be back."

Anger burned in him and Jack went to crouch by them.

"Let him come. We'll be waiting."

Jace Castillo rubbed tiredly at his eyes and let out a long breath. The Boston P.D. homicide division was air-conditioned, of course, but whoever wielded the authority to control the thermostat was stingy at best. While not nearly so warm as it was outside, most would have been hard-pressed to call the temperature cool. As a result, the air in the building was close and stale. Castillo had not showered in going on twenty hours and his skin felt grimy, oily. All in all, he would rather have been outside sweating. At least then he could have breathed fresh air.

What made it worse was that Bill Cantwell, despite his size and the fact that the man had been working at the pub most of the day, seemed fresh as the proverbial daisy.

His eyes were bright and alive, his features open and aware. The bartender's hair was a mess, but beyond that, he looked ready for just about anything.

It pissed Castillo off.

"So you're sure you never saw the guy in the trunk before tonight?" he asked, scratching idly at the back of his head.

Cantwell sighed, though not impatiently. "I appreciate that you have to at least pretend to do this by the book, Detective. Make it look like a real investigation. But you and I both know that is not what's going to happen here."

The big man had a gravelly voice that, like his overall appearance, made it difficult to judge his actual age. Castillo would have put him at forty, but he might have been off a few years in either direction. It would be simple enough to find out, but when Castillo had run Cantwell's name he had found that the man had no criminal record and so had not bothered to look at much else. The bartender had played professional football for the New England Patriots some years before. It would not be difficult to get a whole dossier on him if necessary.

The thing was, Cantwell was not the problem. It would be easier if he had been.

"Please answer the question, Mr. Cantwell," Castillo instructed.

Cantwell's nostrils flared angrily but his face hardly betrayed his pique otherwise. "I already answered the question. Several times. The dead guy isn't familiar to me. Even if his face wasn't torn up, I'm pretty sure I wouldn't recognize him."

"And you have no idea how the corpse got into your trunk?"

The big man lost his cool. His open palm slapped the table like a thunderclap and it shook with the impact.

"What are you screwing around for?" Cantwell demanded, eyes narrowing dangerously. "I came down because I know you've got to cover your asses on anything like this. I get that. But we're both tired, Castillo. You want to keep asking the same pointless questions, come see me at Bridget's tomorrow and you can ask all you want as long as your ass is on a bar stool and you've got a beer in your hand."

With that he stood up. Sitting across from him, gazing upward, Castillo had a moment to appreciate how big Bill Cantwell actually was. Not freakishly so, to be sure, but imposing without doubt. The lieutenant who ran Boston Homicide, Hall Boggs, was taller, maybe even wider, but across the shoulders and in the arms, Cantwell was bigger.

The detective sat back in his chair and rubbed again at his eyes.

"Why you, Bill?" he asked.

Cantwell frowned and glared skeptically down at him. "Now we're back to first names, *Jace?*"

"Why do you think we're in the break room and not one of the interview rooms?" Castillo asked.

"You wanted to be alone with me?"

Castillo chuckled softly and nodded. "Pretty much, yeah. There's no observation area for this room. Anything we talk about, I don't want anybody listening in even if they're on the job. The wrong person gets wind of what this is all really about . . ." His words trailed off and he sighed, then gestured to Cantwell. "Look, why don't you sit down another minute."

Grudgingly, the big man sat.

"You know all this. Even if we've never really talked it out. You and the Dwyers and the Hatcher girl, you know what we know. Truth is, I'm pretty sure you know more than we do. So you know why we keep it as quiet as we can. Before I was with homicide I used to work narcotics. Honestly, there are a lot of truths the public is better off not knowing because as long as we do our jobs the odds that they'll be affected by those things are almost nil.

"And we do, Bill. We do our jobs."

Cantwell nodded grimly. "I'm not saying you don't. We've been over this. I know why you brought me here. You know how this guy really died. But you keep asking me these questions when you know I had nothing to do—"

"Don't presume to tell me what I know," Castillo interrupted.

The bartender studied him carefully. The detective folded his hands on the table and leaned over to make sure he had the man's full attention.

"I don't *know* you didn't kill this guy. I'm pretty sure that's not how it went down, but I don't *know* it. I don't know *you*. What I do know is that you and your friends were instrumental in cleaning out one of the worst . . . pest problems this city has ever had. I know you've had at least one other run-in with that sort of pest. But even if you didn't kill the guy, someone put him there to get your attention. Maybe you have an idea who that might be. Not *what*, 'cause you're right that we're both pretty sold on the answer to that question, but *who* specifically. Makes sense to me to wonder if you knew the dead guy."

Cantwell let out a long slow breath and Castillo was forced to revise his impression. The man did look tired.

"Not so far as I could tell," the bartender said. "But when you identify the body, let me know and I'll be able to say for sure."

The hum of the snack machines on the far side of the room suddenly seemed too loud, and the flicker of a dying fluorescent light above was beginning to give Castillo a headache. Cantwell was making it worse.

"I get the idea there are things you're not telling me, Bill."

"You get the strangest ideas, Jace."

The two men stared at each other for a time, but then the moment was broken by a knock at the door. Castillo did not bother to reply, but the door swung open anyway.

Lieutenant Boggs filled the doorway. "You almost finished here, Detective?"

"We're done," Castillo confirmed.

Boggs glanced curiously at Cantwell, then nodded. "Good. Why don't you run Mr. Cantwell back to Bridget's then. You're going to need to take a statement, have a look around."

Castillo had half-turned to look at the lieutenant when the man had come in, but now he swiveled all the way around in his chair. "The crime scene unit was almost done when I left. We've taken all the statements I think we're going to need, Lieu."

Boggs shook his head. "Not about the DOA. About twenty minutes ago, someone B&E'd the place, assaulted at least one person on the premises. We had two separate calls from the neighbourhood about shots fired, but the guy who phoned it in, Dwyer, didn't say anything about that."

"He wouldn't," Castillo replied dryly.

But even before the words were out, Cantwell sprang from the chair and strode toward the door. Lieutenant Boggs stepped out of his way and Castillo had to rush to catch up with the bartender out in the hall. He had gotten the idea Cantwell and the Dwyer woman were involved, and now he was pretty certain of that.

"Hey, hey, slow down," the detective urged him. "It's over. Doesn't sound like anyone was seriously injured."

"Yeah? Well when I figure out who's behind this, that's going to change," Cantwell replied, his voice a low growl that startled Castillo with its ferocity.

"You think the two things are related?" the detective asked.

As they rushed down the steps toward the door, Cantwell cast him a sidelong glance.

"Don't you?"

CHAPTER 8

Morning came too soon. Even after one of the longest nights of his life, Jack cursed the daylight. Bill had returned to the pub by three o'clock in the morning with Detective Castillo, who put a patrol car in the alley for the rest of the night. The detective had asked a few questions, poked around the kitchen and the alley, and then left. Once Jack had told him it was a Prowler, Castillo knew all he needed to know. There would be no crime scene unit in the apartment. Castillo would keep in touch, and so should they.

Jack had taken Molly to the hospital, where they had cleaned the scratches on her throat—none of which, thankfully, required stitches—and checked her to make sure she didn't have a concussion. Then the doctors had sent them home. They had to call the police, of course, so Jack gave them Castillo's number. The last thing he needed was some nurse filing a report that implied he had beaten Molly up.

It was five in the morning when they got back, and the sky was already lightening. Molly fell asleep in the Jeep on the way home and he had to guide her up the stairs and into her room. He worried that she would be afraid to sleep in there alone, but she was snoring softly within seconds of her head hitting the pillow.

Courtney had also been sleeping when he got back, but Bill had been awake and sitting in the kitchen. He cleaned up what little glass had actually fallen inside rather than out, and replaced the screen despite the damage. Jack had been dubious about his own chances of getting any sleep, but with Bill there watching over them and his shades drawn, he drifted off after only a few minutes.

To his dismay, however, he had found it impossible to sleep past nine o'clock. Not wanting to disturb anyone else he had moved quietly through the apartment. Molly was still sleeping, sprawled across the bed in what would be her room only for a few more weeks. In Courtney's room, Bill lay on his back with one arm thrown over his head, a low, rattling snore issuing from his open mouth. But there was no sign of Courtney herself. Jack stiffened a moment before he realized that Bill would not have gone to sleep unless Courtney had gotten up. It still bothered Jack to see Bill in his sister's bed, but this morning that small discomfort was the last thing on his mind.

On the kitchen table he found a note from Courtney.

Went to market. Called alarm company. Back soon.

Jack never ceased to marvel at his sister's capacity to rebound from things that would at the very least knock the wind out of the average person. On what was probably no more than three or four hours sleep, she had gotten up and gone to the seafood market to get the pub ready for business. Jack himself hadn't had any more sleep than that, but his was a case of having been unable to sleep. Courtney had chosen to get up. It didn't help that he felt guilty because he had told her that *he* would go to the market this morning, but there was nothing to be done about it now.

His gaze went to the hastily scrawled note again. *Called alarm company.* More than likely she meant to have the windows wired to the alarm system. It made sense to Jack, but for it to be really effective, they might have to finally get central air-conditioning in the apartment so they could actually close the windows on hot summer nights. Not that he was going to complain.

It was a beautiful summer morning, already above eighty degrees he was sure. Out the shattered kitchen window was nothing but blue sky and sunshine. The wind must have changed, he realized, because the breeze that came through the apartment now actually brought some comfort. An ocean breeze, then, off the harbour.

Though he wished he had been able to sleep, he knew it was best for him to be up and around now. There were far too many menacing things happening for him to sleep any longer. He felt lost enough trying to figure out what the Ravenous was and how to destroy it, how to stop it from consuming the lost souls in the Ghostlands. How to keep Artie safe. But now he had to deal with this as well.

Though no one could prove it, even Detective Castillo agreed that it seemed likely that the golden-furred Prowler who had broken in and tried to kill Molly—probably meaning to kill them all—had also planted the corpse in Bill's trunk. And Castillo did not know what the rest of them knew, what Bill told them when the detective was gone. The scent the intruder had left behind was the same. They knew for certain it was the same beast. In some ways that was better; it might mean there was just the one. In others, though, it was even more unnerving.

It meant the monster had a plan.

Careful not to make too much noise, Jack took a shower and tried to figure out how to deal with both things at once. Given that he wasn't sure where to start in either situation, all he got for his efforts was a lot of frustration. Things were lurking in the shadows in the flesh-world and in the afterlife, waiting to hurt Jack and the people he loved. The Ravenous had his scent. This other guy, the flesh-and-blood monster, it knew where he lived. And on top of all that, though he had taken her to the hospital the night before, Molly was still obviously pissed at him.

Artie, he thought as he dried off after the shower. *Where'd you go, buddy?*

Back in his room he ran a brush through his hair and then put on shorts and a worn Harvard University T-shirt, the kind they sold at every tourist spot in town. Warm as it was, he saw no point in dressing for work until it was actually time to go downstairs.

Jack's mind went back to the conversation he had had with Father Mike the day before. It astonished him to think of all that had taken place in less than twenty-four hours earlier. Going to the priest with questions about the Ravenous and the afterlife and ghosts in general had seemed like an obvious choice, but the visit had proven fruitless.

"The church hasn't a formal position on the matter, and frankly, neither do I."

The priest's words reverberated in Jack's mind now. Ghosts existed. Jack saw them, spoke to them, but this man of God wasn't quite sure they were real. It did not undermine his faith in any way—after all, who knew better than he did that there was an afterlife? But it had been a huge disappointment. Now he had no idea where to start.

"All right, Artie," Jack said to the empty room, his voice low so as not to wake the others. "After last night I know you haven't gone far. If you're still around, we need to talk, don't you think?"

"Hey."

Without any surprise at all, Jack turned to see the ghost coalescing on the other side of the room. The sunshine was so bright in the windows that the spectral form was barely visible. Sheer and nearly colorless, Artie did not obscure the walls and windows and bookshelf behind him. It was almost as though he were made of cool, clear water that somehow pooled in the middle of the air.

He seems farther away, Jack thought. It was an odd idea to have spring into his mind, and he had no idea where it came from. Now was hardly the time to examine it, however.

"Hey," Jack replied.

"Is she all right?" Artie asked.

They didn't have to discuss who *she* was.

"Didn't you look in on her?"

Artie's form shimmered. *"After last night, I thought I should give her some space."*

A silence fell between them. Jack kept turning both of his present dilemmas over in his head. Artie drifted a bit closer, taking on a bit more color as he moved away from the windows.

"So what now?" the ghost asked.

Another minute ticked by until Jack sighed and met Artie's black gaze.

"This corpse in Bill's trunk last night? He died ugly. His spirit's gotta be wandering around somewhere. I need you to find him, track him down. That's the only way we're going to get a lead on who's trying to kill us before he tries again. In the meantime, I'll keep looking into the Ravenous, try to find someone who has a clue what I'm talking about who isn't already dead."

Artie had his hands shoved into the pockets of his torn sweatshirt, and he nodded as Jack spoke.

Suddenly the ghost's eyes widened, and then Artie glanced guiltily at the ground, a stricken expression on his face.

Without turning, Jack knew Molly had entered the room.

"Good morning boys," she said, her voice a sleepy rasp. "Don't you think it's time we all had a talk?"

Molly felt as though something had given way inside her, like she had been suffocating and now she could finally breathe again. The emotions that had twisted up inside her, all that grief and anger, began to melt away like snow on the first warm spring day. She had no explanation for this sudden purge, but it seemed to her that her ability to reason had been drowned in emotion, and the events of the night before had given her a fresh perspective.

On her way to the shower, clad only in the things she had slept in and a blue cotton robe Artie had bought her the previous Christmas, Molly heard Jack talking quietly in his room. There had been no doubt in her mind with whom he was speaking with.

Now she stood in the open doorway and Jack stared at her awkwardly. Molly glanced about the room and a tenderness blossomed in her heart. She had always believed that one could tell a great deal about a person simply by visiting the place where they spent most of their private time. Her own mother's bedroom, for instance, was a domestic crime scene scattered with unwashed clothes, too much makeup, the detritus of bad relationships, and a line of bottles on one windowsill she insisted on referring to as "the liquor cabinet." Molly had not so much escaped her mother's self-destruction as she had survived it.

Jack's surroundings spoke well of him. The sunlight that washed through the windows gleamed off the hardwood floor. The room was almost too neat, a place for everything and everything in its place, as though it were a hotel room and the maid had just been through. Yet the bookshelf laden with biographies and paperback westerns, the neatly stacked twin towers of CDs against the wall, and the framed photograph of his late mother on the bureau were in stark contrast to that impression.

"So you've got nothing to say?" she asked.

"Molly, I . . ." Jack ran a hand through his short, spiky hair and his eyes darted toward the opposite corner of the room near the windows. When he looked at her again, he raised both eyebrows and shrugged, a penitent expression on his face. "I guess I just don't know what I can say that isn't going to piss you off."

For a moment Molly made no response. Her attention was focused on that corner of the room. She tried to imagine she could see Artie there and for a moment it was as though he stood with them, fidgeting, shaking back his shaggy blond hair, just as awkward as Jack was.

The ghost was there, she was certain of that.

But Molly could not see him.

"You're probably right," she confessed, her gaze drifting back to Jack and then focusing on him fully. "You've apologised enough. That doesn't make it okay, and it doesn't take any of the hurt and the weirdness away."

Jack started to speak but Molly held up a hand to hush him.

"You've explained it enough, Jack. I get it. Artie's . . . not coming back," she said, her eyes darting toward that sunlit corner again. "He didn't want to keep me from moving on. And you promised you wouldn't say anything. We'll get back to that part. First I have a couple of confessions to make. Sit down."

Arms still wrapped around herself, Molly walked toward the spot in the corner where Jack had looked. She stepped into the pooling sunlight and felt its heat, felt it begin to warm her instantly. Her back to Jack, she closed her eyes, relished the sun on her face, and imagined Artie was there with her, his arms slipping around her from behind as he kissed the back of her head. But this silent moment of intimacy between them would never have lasted more than a few seconds while he was alive. His mind was so full of thoughts and curiosities and his heart so full of passion and doubt that in life he had been unable to be still for very long.

When Molly faced Jack again, he was seated on the edge of the bed.

"You were right. I knew. And when you lied to me, I knew it was a lie, but I convinced myself it was true because that's what I needed to believe. For the same reasons Artie gave you. So some of this is my fault."

Jack nodded slightly. "Well—"

"Don't even start. I said some, not all. No fooling around, Jack, I don't have a handle yet on how to sift through the blame on this, but I know I'm still angry at you. At *both* of you."

And there it was again. *Both of them.* In the moments of awkwardness since she had entered the room Molly had been painfully aware of the ghost's presence but had mainly addressed her comments to Jack. But now . . .

"Where is he?" she asked, her voice barely a whisper.

Jack hesitated only a moment before pointing to a place between where she stood in the warmth of the sun-splashed floor and the bed where he sat. Molly realized she must have walked right past him, even through him, and she felt an electric tingle of fear run through her. It was irrational, she knew. Artie would never hurt her. In the past few months there had been several times when she had been with Jack and *known* there were ghosts there, the lingering spirits of the dead. So why this trepidation now?

Then she knew. It was not Artie she feared, it was his death. Her own death. Having his ghost there, so close, was an intimate whisper in her ear reminding her that one day she would also pass into whatever limbo he now wandered.

Stop it! Molly told herself. *It's Artie.*

"Artie," she said aloud, addressing him for the first time. Her eyes searched for some point in the room to focus on as a substitute for him, but found nothing and so she turned again to Jack. "Can he hear me?"

"Yeah. He's sorry too, Mol. He—"

Jack stopped midsentence and stared at the spot in the middle of the room where he had pointed a moment before. Molly swallowed, her throat suddenly too dry. The way Jack gazed into nothingness, she knew he was listening to Artie, hearing the voice of the dead.

Then he looked at her. "If you want to talk to him, I can tell you what he says. Like a translator or—"

"A medium," Molly finished for him.

Jack nodded, but Molly wasn't looking at him anymore. Barely aware of her own movements, she sat crosslegged on the floor and stared at that spot just a few feet away. In her mind she tried to summon an image of Artie again, the way she had when she first walked in, but it wouldn't come.

When she spoke again, it was to Artie.

"Hi," Molly began.

From across the room, Jack responded. "Hola, chica."

A smile rippled across her face and Molly laughed softly. It was surreal, certainly, and more than a little unnerving. But it was real. *Hola, chica.* That was Artie, all right, just one among a thousand little expressions that were all him, like the way he often called Jack "bro."

"I . . . I miss you."

"Don't get me started," Jack replied.

If she closed her eyes, she could almost hear Artie's voice. Her chest tightened as joy and grief warred within her.

"I know you've been watching me, you little perv," she teased.

"Only in the shower. And getting ready for bed. Good thing I was watching you last night."

Molly glanced away, looked out the window. "I guess."

There was a long pause before Jack spoke again, giving her Artie's words, his sorrow.

"I know it can't be like this. When this thing with the Ravenous is over, and after I've done what I can to help get rid of the Prowler from last night . . ."

The words trailed off and Molly glanced around to see Jack staring at the center of the room. Once again, in that moment, she thought she might have been able to see a silhouette there of her laughing boy, her crazy love.

"What is it, Jack?" Molly asked. "What's he saying?"

An expression that was almost one of anger swept over Jack's features, and then he turned to Molly. "He's going to go on. When all this is done, he won't be around anymore. He says to tell you it's best for all of us. You and me and him. That his business is done.' "

Tears threatened at the corners of Molly's eyes, but at the same time, she was nodding. "Maybe so. But will you . . . will you be able to come back?"

"He doesn't know. 'I'll try, if you need me, or if I learn more about the Prowlers. But it isn't right, you having to feel this.' "

Molly dropped her gaze. "You know, after all this, I guess I don't mind so much. I told Jack before that I didn't need anyone to take care of me. It turns out last night proved me wrong. God knows with the family I've got, I've never been very good at that kind of thing. Maybe I do need someone, but no more than Jack does."

"Everyone needs someone to watch over them. To watch their back."

After a long moment, her throat still dry, Molly turned to address Jack. "So what now? I heard you talking to Artie before. He's going to look for the ghost of the dead man in Bill's trunk. But what about the Ravenous? You have no idea how to find more information on it?"

Jack offered a small shrug. "The priest I talked to was no help. I thought I'd look into some other religions. We talked about mediums, but they all seem like such bullshit artists."

"You're a medium," she said sharply.

"I guess. But I don't know a damn thing. It's the ones who claim to know everything that probably aren't worth asking."

Molly turned that one over in her mind. "My mother

went to one up in Newburyport a couple of years ago. She might not be for real, but Mom sure thought so."

Obviously skeptical, and understandably so given that her mother was the source, Jack gazed at her for a long moment before nodding in agreement. "I guess it's worth a shot."

It was only silence in the room then, the two of them—probably the three of them—shifting uncomfortably, knowing that they had reached the end of things. A true end, now, or at least its preamble.

I love you, she wanted to say. But what she said instead was more true. "I loved you. I don't think I can say good-bye."

Jack said nothing, only stared at the ground.

"What?" Molly urged. "What did he say?"

He raised his eyes and she wondered in that moment if looking from the right angle she might not have seen Artie reflected there.

"Good-bye was a long time ago. I just didn't hear it then."

Molly's right hand came up to cover her mouth as though she might scream. But it was not a scream she was trying to hold in, it was a plea to this ghost not to go, not to leave her. She knew those words would not be fair to either of them, for he was already gone.

Then Jack was speaking once more, this time directly to Artie, and a moment later she realized that Artie was gone and it was just her and Jack now. She stood up, pulled her robe tight around herself again, and walked to him. Jack rose from the bed to greet her, but they both hesitated awkwardly.

"Thank you for that," she said.

"I'm sorry about everything," he said. "You know I am. I just . . . I promised him."

Molly narrowed her eyes and was surprised at the bitterness she felt still within her.

"He's dead, Jack. You have a responsibility to me, not to him," she said. "You're about the best friend I have. I love you. But I'm going to be angry for a while still, and you're just going to have to deal with that. Now I'm going to take a shower and you're going to Newburyport. Let me know if you learn anything."

With that, she turned and walked from the room, leaving a mightily chagrined Jack to stand there and watch her go.

The smell of garlic was strong inside Concetta's Trattoria, a tiny restaurant whose atmosphere and decor was so quaintly Italian that it might have been a film set rather than an actual place of business. *Too self-aware*, Dallas thought. *That's what it is. They went to the best spots in the North End and recreated it here. It's not a real restaurant. It's Epcot.*

On the crackling sound system, Frank Sinatra sang "The Best Is Yet to Come." The dining room was dark, shuttered off from the outside world so that even at high noon they could light the candles in the precious red glass votives to get the desired effect. The air conditioner hummed softly. The walls were adorned with maps and drawings of Rome and Venice and shelves outside the swinging kitchen doors were stocked with salamis and enormous slabs of cheese, fat jars filled with peppers. Yet those nods to the working-class Italian restaurant were belied by the crisp white tablecloths and the starched, effete waiters.

This was Wellesley, after all. The city stank of money, and the faux-perfect Italian restaurant only lent itself to that stench. Dallas was certain that the food would be exquisite. In a city like this, with a clientele that could afford the prices on the menu, it had to be. But all of it just pissed him off.

"Did you decide what you wanted?"

He looked across the table at Valerie and she smiled.

"Never have been able to," she replied playfully, and yet there was a gravity to her gaze that touched him. "That's the trouble with all of us thinking creatures, isn't it? Caesar or House? Veal or chicken? Privacy or company?"

Dallas smiled thinly. "Funny."

Valerie was dressed in a wardrobe from Nine West and Lord & Taylor, blending into the culture of these wealthy communities as though she were born to it, as though she were human. It was not merely a skill she had learned over decades, even centuries, just as Dallas had. It was also a talent. She had the flair for it. And yet there were moments, like now, when instead of fitting in, she seemed so very lost.

"I wasn't trying to be funny," she said softly. Then she stared at the menu and spoke to him again without looking up. "What about you, Dallas? Have you decided what you want, what you're hunting for?"

He gazed at her. "Isn't there value in the hunt itself?"

For a long while she said nothing, merely perused the

menu. As he watched her, words from out of time floated into his mind, the final thing she said to him before their last split.

"You give all your intimacy to the prey," she said. Even then he had known she was right, but could never manage to work out what was so wrong with that. Those thoughts led him to his worry for his daughter, and the emotion surprised him, as it always did, for it was a very recent development. When her mother died and she set off into the human world, trying to find human music within herself, playing her guitar in roadhouses and dive bars she was too young to drink in, he had barely thought of her at all.

Now, though, to know she was lost . . . Perhaps there were other things worth hunting than prey.

Dallas watched Valerie closely. Sometimes he wondered why he never stayed with her for very long. Other times he wondered why she ever took him back.

"You look beautiful," he told her.

A reluctant smile appeared upon her face. "Not so bad yourself."

Yet already his mind had gone back to the prey. The quickly healing wound in his shoulder seeped blood into the white shirt under his black jacket. A ferocious darkness coiled inside him, not merely angry but driven to rage by the bloodlust that had gone unquenched the night before, the mission that had gone unfulfilled.

She saw it in him, as she always had.

"Hey," Valerie said softly. "You'll find a way."

A waiter arrived at the table and filled their water

glasses from a pitcher filled with clinking ice cubes. He sped off a moment later as though he had other glasses to fill, but there was no one else in the place. The maître d' and the bartender and a trio of waiters were the only other people there. It was just coming up on noon on a weekday, too early for most people to have lunch apparently, and Dallas figured that a place like this did most of their business at dinner anyway.

He stared at the menu and grumbled inwardly at the errors in the translations from Italian to English.

"What did Jasmine say?"

Even as Valerie asked the question, Dallas tensed. He could feel the weight of the cellular phone hanging in the inner pocket of his suit. His nostrils flared and his upper lip curled as he glared up at his lover.

"I haven't called her yet."

Valerie's eyes widened. "Oh. Oh, I'm sorry. I just . . . wanted to cheer you up."

He grunted, and it was almost a laugh. "You're doing a hell of a job."

Her hand slipped across the table and closed upon his. Dallas let the menu slip to the table and paused a moment before reaching up to hold her hand in both of his.

"I know," he said reluctantly. He gazed at her, this beautiful creature that he was never quite fair to. "Just ignore me, all right. I'm more than a little ticked off about my shoulder, but mostly I'm just angry with myself. Only twice before have I missed the mark the first time out, but this is different. The job is for one of us. This is exactly why I don't work for our kind. How will it look when word gets around?"

"And that's why you haven't told her," Valerie said, nodding in understanding. She offered him a too-bright, supportive smile. "Well, why should you? You can take care of this and she'll never even know."

Dallas took a long breath and let it out. He stared at the red glow of the candle flickering in its glass. It was true, things weren't as bad as all that, but that did not prevent him from feeling as though he had failed. It would be so much easier if he were willing to kill Bill Cantwell, but he did not want to have to explain that to Valerie or, more importantly, to Jasmine. Reluctantly, he realized that it might have to come to that. Cantwell might have to die.

In the end, he had to decide what was more important, his reputation or his honor.

Thinking about it hurt his head and made the sting of the shoulder wound all the more acute. Dallas winced and stretched out his left arm, feeling the stiffness begin to relax. The wound was healing, but it would take a few days before he was completely recovered.

"Do you need more time, or would you like to order now?"

The waiter had suddenly appeared and he hovered over them now, a short, middle-aged Italian man with a mustache he had probably been instructed to grow. In his crisp white shirt and black tie, he regarded them with an air of disdain, as though they had inconvenienced him with their patronage.

Dallas felt the buzz of a low growl in his throat but it was not loud enough for the waiter to hear.

He forced a false grin onto his face. "You know what? We need another minute."

The waiter sniffed. "I'll come back in a few moments with some bread."

When they were alone again, Valerie looked at him with what might have been excitement or anxiety. "Oh, baby, what can we do to make you feel better?"

Dallas grinned again, but this time it was for real. His life, his profession, was all about order, but in that moment he wanted more than anything to do something for Valerie. And the greatest gift he could give her was chaos.

"Why don't you lock the door?"

CHAPTER 9

Jack had been to Newburyport only once before, so it took him several minutes to locate the right street even though Molly gave him directions. She and Artie had often visited the quaint old seaside town, whose well-groomed streets were lined with eighteenth and nineteenth century homes. It was the kind of place that would eventually—probably soon enough—be totally overrun by young executives whose presence would drive the real estate values through the roof. Already it was far from cheap. But it was still the sort of place that felt like a real town, where people knew their neighbours, called the postman and the librarian by name.

As Jack drove through Newburyport, he felt a tug of yearning in him. He could not imagine a time when he would not be helping to run Bridget's, but a town like this—the old homes, the little restaurants, the parks—it all appealed to him.

Molly had not been able to remember the name of the street but just from her description Jack had vaguely remembered it, so that when he passed it suddenly on his left he recognised it immediately and turned around. The road was lined with cars parked on either side and had more traffic crawling along it than any other spot in town. It sloped down on a gentle curve he knew would eventually lead to a restaurant that sat on a wharf and looked out upon the ocean. There were bars and boutiques and bookstores crammed along both sides of the road, tiny little shops that seemed to be squeezed in too tight on each block. Jack spotted an ice-cream store he remembered as he drove down the street, though many of the storefronts were invisible behind the crush of humanity that strolled up and down the sidewalk.

Jack was grateful that the traffic moved so slowly on that road. He had to bend over the steering wheel slightly to glance at the buildings that passed by on the passenger side. There was supposed to be a small sign that hung out from the side of the building, but if Molly had not told him to be on the lookout for it, he would have driven right by Madame Stefania's Psychic Studio.

The sidewalk was crowded with ghosts.

Jack hit the brake so quickly that the driver of the car behind him lay on the horn. The windows of the Jeep were rolled all the way down and he heard the man cursing him loudly, but barely registered the words.

There were dozens of them, milling about on the cracked pale concrete sidewalk. Some sat on the three brick steps in front of the door that led to Madame Stefania's second-floor offices. These phantoms were an odd array of individuals, men and women of varying ages and races, and children as well, many of them clad in styles that were years, even decades out of fashion.

Window shoppers and tourists passed right through them. Young couples with small children and tribes of teenagers merged on the sidewalk with people in business suits and a stunning trio of fashionably attired twenty-something women who would have drawn a long stare from Jack on any other day. Today he barely glanced at them.

He found a parking space a block up and walked back toward the cluster of ghosts in a sort of daze, bumping people without realizing it, mumbling barely formed apologies. As he moved closer, he half-expected the ghosts to turn and look at him, to *see* him, but they did not.

Many of them, perhaps even most of them, had far-away looks in their eyes and a sort of lost, empty cast to their features that Jack had seen on spirits before. But not like this, never in these numbers. He stared at them, fascinated and saddened at the same time. The ones who appeared to be less than sane were difficult enough to see, but the others were somehow worse. Even in life, he had rarely seen such anguish on human faces. Each appeared lonelier and more pitiful than the last, and yet they were all together.

Together.

And then it struck him, something that had been unnerving him without him even recognizing it at first.

They were all together, and yet none of them spoke to

the others, even looked at each other, as if each of those sad, lost souls were unaware of the others. The children were the most difficult to see, gazing up at the windows of the second floor with despair on their faces, and yet none of the other ghosts tried to comfort them.

Jack stood among them, there in front of Madame Stefania's, and he knew he had to try to reach out to them. He cast a self-conscious glance around, and then he closed his eyes and tried to see them. His stomach did a queasy little flip, he opened his eyes, and the world shifted around him, became the photo negative of reality. The buildings and the people, the couples and teenagers, the cars going by on the street were pale shades, just whispers of what he knew was real and tangible.

But as it always was when he truly *looked* into the Ghostlands, the spirits themselves were solid, tangible.

"Hey," he said.

As one the ghosts turned to stare at him in astonishment, even those he had thought barely sane. For just a moment, the sadness and loneliness left them all. Some even turned to glance at the others. A woman reached down to grip the hand of a little girl with curly blond hair. A horrible understanding came over Jack; these spirits were not unable to see one another. Rather, they could not provide one another with the things they all craved.

Light. Warmth. Hope. Rest.

He felt it from all of them, that craving. Though he would not have said he sensed their emotions in any supernatural fashion, he could not avoid a certain empathy with them. *Call it intuition,* he thought.

The woman who held the little blond girl's hand had dark, exotic features and almond-shaped eyes. Her light summer dress rustled as she moved, as if blown by some ethereal wind. She took a step closer to Jack.

"Who are you?" she asked.

"My name is Jack," he replied, not really knowing how to explain any better than that. "I'm a friend."

"Jack!" the little girl piped up, prompting the others to all stare at her as though they had no idea she could speak at all.

"What are you all doing here?" he asked.

A murmur began to build among them, their voices like whispers, the flutter of a flock of sparrows taking wing from the branches of an oak tree. Though the real world continued on around him and Jack knew he must be drawing unwanted attention for what must seem to flesh and blood passersby like the behavior of a madman, he could not tear his attention away from these forlorn spirits.

"It's her," the spectral little girl said, craning her neck to gaze up at Jack. *"She called us here."*

He knew without being told exactly who the girl referred to. When he glanced up at the building beside him, the world reverted to normal around him with a pop like the flashbulb on an old-fashioned camera. Sound came rushing in, car engines and voices and the radio from a van passing by. An elderly man whose hair seemed woven from silver thread stared at Jack.

"You all right son?" the old man asked.

Jack shivered, his heart touched with the chill of the

despair of the phantoms there on the sidewalk. The old man could not see them, of course. The way he looked at Jack was the way people must have looked at Columbus when he said the world was round. But Jack could still see them.

The ghosts watched him, each of their faces etched with a silent plea.

"She called. You heard her?" Jack asked.

The old man frowned, shook his head, and walked on, having used up whatever bit of Samaritan he had in him.

The ghost of the woman in the summer dress came to Jack now, reached up and tried to touch him. Her hand passed through, but Jack felt her essence on him, felt a warmth instead of the chill he expected, and he thought he smelled cinnamon.

Cinnamon girl, he thought. And in his mind, that's who she became, this beautiful dead woman.

"She called to us," the cinnamon girl told him. *"And we heard. But when we tried to answer she couldn't hear us. She pretended like she could, and she told my husband that I was happy now and he paid her."* A flicker of rage passed over the specter's features and then was gone. *"He paid her, you see? She's a charlatan. But we keep hoping that she'll hear us one day, if she'll only listen."*

A *charlatan.* Jack flinched at the word, though it was what he had expected. Seeing the ghosts had given him hope that Madame Stefania might be the genuine article, but the truth did not surprise him. There was nothing the woman upstairs could do for him now. He knew he should just turn around and go home.

But he could not.

"Come with me," Jack said, and he walked up the three steps to the door and pushed it open. On the street, several tourists gave him a wide berth, alarmed by his words and by his tone.

The stairwell smelled of mildew and cats. Jack climbed to the second floor with a parade of ghosts behind him. At the top of the stairs was a landing, and a white door with a sign on it identical to the one that hung from the front of the building. It was close and too hot and humid there in the stairwell, and Jack felt oddly claustrophobic.

Just before he reached the top, the door opened. The woman who emerged was perhaps fifty-five, her hair dyed bright red and wrapped in a gaudy scarf. She wore dozens of gold bracelets on either wrist and a brightly colored floral print dress that clashed with the scarf. When she spotted Jack where he had paused on the stairs, there was no alarm whatsoever in her face.

"I'm sorry. I don't have any openings today. My next appointment is in half an hour and I'm just running out for coffee," Madame Stefania said.

For he was certain now that was who it was.

Jack glanced at the cinnamon girl, whose ghostly form shimmered in the stairwell behind him. Through her he could see all the other ghosts, their gossamer figures lined up on down the stairs, and through them, the door out to the street.

"What's your name?" he asked the cinnamon girl.

"Letitia Soares," the dead woman replied.

When he looked back up at the fraud, the supposed

medium had finally registered something more than curiosity. Her hand reached back toward the door to her office.

"Letitia Soares," Jack said.

Madame Stefania only frowned.

Jack looked back at the cinnamon girl again. "She doesn't remember you. When did you die?"

"December twenty-first, in nineteen eighty-seven. My husband Esteban came to see her."

Though he was horrified by how long the ghost had lingered here, waiting to be heard, Jack pushed those thoughts away and turned to the medium again.

"Esteban Soares came to see you in nineteen eighty-seven after Letitia died. You called to Letitia, lady, and then you pretended to talk to her and you took Esteban's money. You stole his money and you lied to him."

Madame Stefania stiffened. It was clear that she was used to being challenged and, now back on familiar territory, she returned to her familiar role.

"I don't have any specific memory of the man you mean, but if he was one of my clients, then I did precisely as I promised. And I gave him the peace of mind he came here searching for," she said indignantly. "Now if you'll please move aside, I have to run an errand before my next appointment arrives."

"Your next victim, you mean," Jack said.

That pissed the woman with the jangling bracelets off. "Do you want me to call the police, kid? 'Cause I will."

Jack sighed and shook his head. "Please do. Maybe we

can have a talk with them. You called Letitia Soares, lady. What you never knew is that she came. You said you could help her speak to Esteban and she *believed* you. She's been here ever since. She's here right now, on the stairs with us, and there are others here, too. A lot of others. Men, women, little kids."

Madame Stefania stared at him, her penciled-in eyebrows arching suspiciously, her burgundy-smeared lips pinched together. "You're out of your mind."

"Why does that seem so impossible to you? Isn't it what you claim to do? The difference is, I can really see them. I can talk to them. You've trapped them here, don't you get that? Until you tell them you can't really hear them, until they know there's no hope, they're going to stay here because they're afraid to go on. You've given them something to hold on to, and that lie is keeping them from going on to whatever their final destination is meant to be."

Madame Stefania looked as though she were about to shout at him, and Jack steeled himself for it. But even as the woman shook one hand at him, bracelets clanging, and started to speak, she faltered. With a deep frown, she looked at him again.

"Prove it," the medium said.

Jack understood her, then. Though what she did was criminal, all of it a hoax, Madame Stefania wanted to believe it was possible. Something inside of her was crippled by the fakery of it, because she wanted to believe. He could see it in her eyes.

All at once, the ghosts began to whisper behind him,

talking all at once, telling their own tales of loved ones cheated by the false medium. Jack shushed them loudly and Madame Stefania actually took a step back, doubt and fear on her face.

The little girl with the curly blond hair stood beside Letitia's ghost, and Jack knelt and looked at her. He didn't like being so close to them, not with the way their eyes seemed to fall away into some eternal darkness. But ghost or not, she was just a little girl.

"What's your name?"

"Amy."

"Amy what?"

"Amy Duvic. My mommy came to talk to the bracelet lady after me and Daddy crashed the car. Mommy didn't have 'nuff money, but she had a nice bracelet and the lady said she could pay with that. I tried to tell Mommy no, don't give the lady the bracelet, but she couldn't hear me. 'N I tried to yell at the lady, but she didn't hear either."

It was all Jack could do not to weep. The ghost of the little girl lifted her chin high, proud of herself.

"Good girl," Jack told her. "That'll help."

As he stood up again, he glanced at the cinnamon girl's ghost, and Letitia smiled at him. Jack could see water stains on the wall right through her face, and though he smiled back, it was only halfhearted.

Madame Stefania glared at him imperiously. "Well?" she asked.

And so he told her Amy Duvic's story. Even as the words left his mouth, he could see from the woman's reaction that it was true.

"You could be some extortionist or something," Madame Stefania snapped. "The Duvic woman could have told you all that herself."

Jack felt tired. It was not even noon and this bitter, horrid woman's disbelief had exhausted him.

"Amy, can you show me which bracelet it was?" he asked.

The little girl smiled and ran right through him. Jack flinched and his stomach felt queasy again. While he watched her go up the stairs, her small feet trailing a sort of ectoplasmic mist, Madame Stefania stepped back to the door and glared down as though she could see the phantom girl.

"This isn't funny," the woman snapped.

But she did not go inside, and she did not want to call the police. As much as she did not want to be revealed as a fraud, Jack thought, she wanted too much to believe to run away now.

"*This one!*" Amy announced.

Jack started up the stairs. Madame Stefania looked as though she might order him to stop, to come no closer, but she said nothing. When he reached her, the woman reeked of incense and cigarette smoke, and he had to breathe through his mouth.

"Are you sure?" he asked the ghost.

Amy pointed at a bracelet that was not a chain but a solid piece made of two bands of gold in different shades, twisted together. The woman wore at least two others that were similar, but the little girl nodded firmly.

Jack reached out and tapped the bracelet. "That one."

Madame Stefania flinched when he touched her. And then she began to cry. "Oh my God—" she began.

Whatever else she might have said then was blotted out by a sudden clamor on the stairs as the ghosts began to shriek in a deafening chorus. Jack spun frantically to see what the cause of it was. At the bottom of the stairs, the ghost of a man in an old brown fedora was torn apart, his essence lashed into tendrils of mist by some invisible force before the spirit disappeared entirely.

Even before he concentrated, focused his will on seeing into the Ghostlands, Jack knew. But then the world inverted again, and the ghosts were tangible and solid, and their screams seemed even louder in Jack's ears. Letitia looked at him with those almond eyes, and he wanted to hold her, to save her. She was already dead, but that was not the worst that could happen to her.

For the Ravenous had arrived.

The moment Jack *shifted* his vision, the beast sniffed the air and it looked up at him, glaring, slavering. It was hideous, but beyond that, when he saw it he felt a terror that seemed to come up from his subconscious, as though it were some ancestral memory passed down through the millennia in the most primal part of his mind.

The Ravenous stood eight feet high, even hunched, its arms long enough to touch the ground, its silver claws like knitting needles. It had a thick, skunk-stinking black coat with those soul-remnants, soul-maggots, squirming in it. From its fur jutted rows of spiked bone horns that started on its forehead and ran up over its skull and down its back, where they joined just above a leathery red tail like a bullwhip. It wasn't an animal, at least not a single animal, and yet it seemed like a sort of union of every beast that had been feared by primitive man.

Its eyes burned with hunger as it stared at him. It snuffled as though laughing and Jack tried to work out the coincidence of its being here at the same time he was.

The Ravenous slashed out at another ghost, its eyes on Jack, never leaving him, as though he were its real target. As though he were its prey.

Oh, God, he thought. *I am.* He knew that it could not follow his scent unless he was seeing the Ghostlands, but he had done exactly that only a few minutes earlier, out on the street. *It must have scented me the second I did that. And it followed the scent here.*

I'm the prey.

The Ravenous roared its hunger, and the ghosts kept screaming.

Jack's every instinct told him to look away, to back up the stairs, to get the hell out of there. All he had to do to save himself from the Ravenous was to force himself, as he had done before, to *stop* peering into the Ghostlands. The monstrosity would not be able to see him then, would not be able to track his scent as long as he was not using the second sight he had somehow developed.

But how could he turn away? These people, the lost souls who clasped to the false hope offered by Madame Stefania, crowded the stairs between him and the Ravenous, and they would not flee. At the bottom of the steps, the hideous thing opened its jaws and they distended, stretched wide. With needle-claws it slashed out at the ghost of a bony, bespectacled man with only wisps of hair. The Ravenous, eyes burning bright, tore the skinny man open, then grabbed him up in its claws and began to rip at him with its jaws, consuming the dead. Its tail, ridged with bony spikes, jutted up behind it as though it had senses all its own.

Horrified, Jack could only stare. They had color and life to him when he peered into the Ghostlands, depth and weight, as though they were the living and he himself the spirit.

"Jack!" whispered the ghost of the cinnamon girl. "What do we do?"

A shudder went through him, his eyes locked on the Ravenous as it tore apart and ate another spirit. Twenty steps away, perhaps less. There were ten or twelve souls between him and the phantom beast. They backed up the stairs toward Jack, eyes wide with terror, clutching at one another and screaming, but they did not run. It made no sense. They could simply disappear, fade through the walls or stairs or ceiling, but the sight of the thing had paralyzed them all.

"Run!" he screamed at them. "Why don't you run?"

He turned to look at the cinnamon girl, Letitia, where she stood just beside him with little Amy Duvic. Beyond them, on the other side of the landing, up against the door to her office, he saw Madame Stefania. The medium looked like a ghost to him now that he was using his second sight, but even so the terror on her own face was clear.

"What is it?" the flesh-and-blood woman cried out. "What do you see?"

Jack ignored her. He stared at Letitia and Amy instead. "Why don't you run?"

"We can't! Where would we go?" the cinnamon girl replied.

Amy did not even look at him. The ghost of the curly-haired girl only stared at the monster as it slaughtered and ate the others on its march up the steps toward Jack.

"Is it the devil?" the little girl asked softly. "Is it?"

A horrible rage blossomed inside Jack, and he rounded on Madame Stefania. He could barely make her out, but he heard her bracelets jangle as she held up her hands as if to ward him off. She was a shade in a world of gray shadows.

"Damn you," he snapped. "Listen to me. There's a thing here, a demon if you want to call it that. It's *eating* them, and they won't run away because of you. *Tell* them! Tell them to go!"

The shade of Madame Stefania shook her head in denial. If she were not backed up against the door and he so close, he knew she would have tried to escape by running inside and might even have really called the police. Instead she raised one arm even further as if to brandish the bracelets at Jack. Madame Stefania grabbed at the jewelry there frantically.

"Look, I get it now. I know what you're doing. Trying to scare me. Fine! The lady wants the bracelet back, she can have it."

The medium tore the twisted band of gold Mrs. Duvic had given her from her wrist and held it out toward Jack. He only stared at her, this gray shade of humanity there in the formless landscape of what he knew was the real, the solid world. He stared at her and he knew she could not hear the screams of souls who would never reach their final destination.

"Keep it," Jack snarled at her. "You earned it, lady."

Then he crouched by Amy, reached out to try to touch her face but his own hands were little more than shades as well, *his* fingers ghostly now, and they passed through the girl's cheeks.

"You've got to go," he said. Then he stood and stared at Letitia, the cinnamon girl. "You've got to run away."

With only one more moment's hesitation, Jack started down the stairs. A ghost of the living, a phantom of flesh and blood, he passed through the souls whose own hopes and inability to let go had trapped them here, and as he touched each one, his essence pushing through them, the screaming stopped. They moved up the stairs toward where Madame Stefania stood and watched in confusion as Jack ran down the steps toward the Ravenous.

It sensed him coming. Its head snapped up, jaws leaking the mystical residue of another spirit it was consuming, and it growled with menace and anticipation. A ripple passed through the thing and it shuddered, its flesh beneath the filthy matted fur shaking. Some of the soul-maggots that squirmed through its dark fur fell to the floor and then simply disappeared. The Ravenous was crouched over just slightly, the rows of spiked horns that ran over its forehead and down its back seemed somehow sharper now. Its scorpion tail swung like a puppy's.

Jack clenched his jaws together to trap the scream that

tried to erupt from his throat. *What the hell are you doing?* he thought. *Back up, Jack! They're already dead, you moron. What does it matter? Let it have them.* But he could not do that. The Ravenous was a spiritual entity and Jack was still alive. He could see it, it could scent him when he shifted his vision into the Ghostlands, but how could this thing hurt him if it was just a ghost?

And even if it could, how could he just let it have Letitia and Amy, when they could not even run away?

Every muscle in his body was heavy with reluctance, but he forged ahead, down the stairs. Only a few steps above the Ravenous, he stopped. The thing snorted and then roared and then it swung that spiked tail around at him. It would have crippled Jack, but he dodged backward, out of range of the tail. The second it had swept past his chest, Jack kicked at the thing's face as hard as he could, though in the back of his mind he feared his foot would strike nothing and he would simply tumble down the stairs.

The kick connected. His foot struck the Ravenous in the side of head, its snout snapped to one side, and the spirit-beast roared again in surprise and fury. Terror raced through Jack in that instant—if he could touch it, then it could touch him—but it was too late to retreat.

And if he could not retreat, there was only one option. The Ravenous raised both huge taloned hands and reached for him. Jack cracked it in the face with a hard elbow, taking advantage of his greater elevation. Then he threw himself at the thing, thinking to drive it down the stairs. But its claws flashed at him. One mighty hand clutched him by the left arm and tugged him right off the stairs. Jack swore and all the fear he had been pushing away came rushing in. His heart hammered in his chest and he felt a surge of panic that seemed to race through his whole body as though it were trying to find a way out.

At the top of the stairs, Madame Stefania must have seen him lifted off the ground by what to her was some invisible force, for she began to scream in shock and horror, trying to ask him what was going on, what was happening.

Jack barely heard her.

The Ravenous shook him, roared in his face, and he could smell the stench of the thing's rancid breath as though the ghosts it had eaten had been made of flesh and blood, and the stink that came from its mouth was that of the dead. Jack cracked it across the face again with a hard backhand, kicked at its chest, but the Ravenous held him up as though he were a rag doll and examined him for just a moment.

Don't look! Jack's mind screamed. *Get out of the Ghostlands. Stop looking!*

The spirit-beast gripped him in one taloned hand and with the other it slashed razor-claws down at him, raking deep furrows across Jack's chest, tearing him open, cutting flesh and muscle and cracking bone. Jack screamed with pain unlike anything he had ever felt, and he closed his eyes.

Then he was in freefall.

He struck the steps and banged his head and when he looked up, the wooden stairs and the stained floral wallpaper in the stairwell were back in focus. The Ravenous was invisible to him now, but he could still see it. The creature was there, just above him, probably enraged that he had escaped it again.

But he had not escaped it, had he? The pain in his chest was excruciating and he gritted his teeth, fear of the Ravenous replaced by fear that these wounds would kill him before paramedics could arrive. The way his head lay on the stairs, he could see up toward the second-floor landing. Madame Stefania stood there, staring down at him, both hands covering her mouth, her skinny body quivering enough so that her bracelets clanged together.

Between them, Jack could still see the others, the ghosts. They were transparent again, shimmering specters who stared in abject horror down the stairs at him.

Not at me. At the Ravenous.

And if I die now, then it will be able to get what it really wants. My soul.

"Tell them," Jack gasped. "Tell them they'll never be able to . . . talk to the people they left behind. Tell them to *go.*"

Madame Stefania threw back her head and cried out as though the ghosts were flying around her head rather than clustered by her on the stairs in terror. But then, she did not know any better.

"It's true!" she said. "Go! Find your own peace. There's nothing I can do for you!"

Little Amy Duvic began to weep, the truth of that even worse to her than her fear of the Ravenous. Letitia

Soares picked the dead girl's ghost up in her own gossamer arms and looked down at Jack.

"How can that be? What do we do now?"

"Go!" Jack pleaded. "There's another place for you, but if you stay you'll be destroyed."

There was a single moment of hesitation, and then the ghosts began to flee. Some of them passed through walls, others seemed to float up and right through the ceiling, and one spectral old woman simply dissipated like a breeze had blown her away. Letitia, carrying Amy in her arms, ran right at Madame Stefania. The ghosts passed through the medium, and Madame Stefania gasped and shuddered with a sudden chill.

"Was that . . . ?" she asked.

"Yes," Jack said softly, relieved to see that there were no more ghosts there in the stairwell.

Now he only had to worry about himself, about staying alive. He lay on the steps, the hard wood against his back, his neck craned up to stare at the medium. His chest felt numb and though that was better, he knew it really was not. That numbness was very bad. Thus far he had avoided trying to look at the ragged wounds on his chest.

"Are you all right?" Madame Stefania asked softly, beginning to walk down the steps toward him.

"Jesus," Jack whispered. "Do I look all right?" He wondered why the woman had not gone in to call 911.

"Um . . . yes?"

Yes?

Slowly, Jack raised his head and looked down at his chest. He was sprawled on the stairs and his back hurt from where he had landed, but there was no blood, no tear in his shirt, no wounds at all on him.

Physically.

But as he struggled to stand, pain lanced through him and he had to lean against the wall for support. There were no wounds in his flesh, the Ravenous had not been able to harm him in that way. But though even now it began to fade, the pain was there, the echo of torn skin and cracked ribs.

The wounds were only on his spirit, yet still he could *feel* them.

CHAPTER 10

In its way, working the narcotics division had been even uglier than working homicide. Being a detective in narcotics meant spending every single day down among the most reprehensible creatures on earth, men and women who had no respect not only for the lives of others, but for their own. Soul-dead men, dealers, poisoning people in their own neighborhoods, turning the children of their community into junkies. Women who sold themselves not for money but on the barter system; anything for the next fix. He came across mothers who had given away their children in trade when they ran out of things anyone wanted.

In comparison, Jace Castillo felt that homicide was the easier job. The victims were already dead. There was nothing he could do to save them. The job was to make sure the people responsible ended up in prison, to keep murderers from taking any more lives.

Today was the first time Castillo regretted moving to homicide. For in all the years he worked narcotics, Jace had never had to tell a mother that her child was dead. That had always been somebody else's job. Today it fell to him. It did not make him feel any better that the victim, Paul Manning, had been twenty-three years old when he died. Would it make a difference to his mother? Would it make a difference that he was an adult when somebody tore him apart and stuffed him in a car trunk?

Ellen Manning lived alone in a small split-level in Chelsea, a grimy, run-down little city so full of corruption that it ran out of money and had to be adopted by the city of Boston for a while. Even so, the blue-collar neighborhood where the Manning house was located lacked the usual signs of neglect Castillo so often saw in such places. No cars up on blocks in the driveways, no groups of young men sitting on stoops and smoking cigarettes.

If this was a working-class neighborhood, then it truly was *working* class. In the middle of this weekday the only people at home were the few women whose husbands made enough money as electricians or painters or plasterers so that they could stay at home with the kids. Mrs. Manning had been one of those—all the bills paid by her ex-husband—and she apparently still got by on her alimony, for she had only a part-time job at a local greenhouse.

The flower beds in front of Ellen Manning's house were well taken care of, the perennials in glorious bloom on that hot summer afternoon. The colors were rich and vibrant, and Castillo shuddered to see them. In his mind he shouldn't have had to come there on a day like today. That did not make any sense, of course, but it did not have to. News like he had to deliver ought to arrive under the cover of rain and dark thunder clouds. Not with the sky so blue with just wisps of clouds. Not with the sounds of a sprinkler running on the lawn next door, or the children laughing and shouting as they rode their bikes just up the road. Not with the flowers thriving, so brilliant and vivid, bees buzzing from bloom to bloom.

No, he should not have had to come here today and tell this woman her son was dead. But the Prowlers did not care about such things. They were only predators, monsters.

One of these monsters, at least one, had it out for Jack and Courtney Dwyer and their friends. Castillo wanted to help them, and not only because it was his job. The idea that these creatures lurked in the night, these Prowlers existed there, hiding away among humanity waiting for someone to walk into the wrong shadow . . . it horrified and repelled him.

Paul Manning had been murdered at least two days before he was put in that trunk. If Castillo could trace his activities in the time leading up to his death, find out where and when he had been killed and if anyone had seen his killer, or what the killer looked like with its human face on, then he might be able to stop it. He might be able to prevent any further harm from befalling the Dwyers and Bill Cantwell and the Hatcher girl. And he might be able to kill another one of these things. That was an honourable ambition all on its own.

But he could not help thinking how much simpler it would have been if Manning had turned out to be another John Doe, a nobody, a nothing, someone they could have swept under the rug and never thought about again.

Castillo parked in front of the house rather than in the driveway, not wanting to be that close, that intimate, as though he were a friend. He walked up the short driveway and then the paved walk rather than cutting across the lawn. As he reached up to ring the bell, a petite brunette in her mid-forties came around the side of the house. She wore work gloves and had a trowel in one hand, smears of dirt across her cotton blouse. In his head, he had envisioned this woman whose heart he was about to break as a gray-haired, fragile thing, but now those preconceptions were dispelled in an instant.

"Can I help you?" the woman asked, her features aquiline and attractive.

"Are you Ellen Manning?"

She cocked a hip and put a hand on it, stared at him expectantly. "I'd say that depends on who's asking."

Castillo removed the small leather wallet in which he carried his badge and held it up, open, for her to see. "Detective Jason Castillo, Boston P.D., Mrs. Manning."

"Hasn't been *Mrs.* Manning in a long time," the woman replied, but there was a catch in her voice now, the tiniest bit of alarm. "But I'm her, yeah. What can I do for you?"

As he came down off the steps, Castillo slipped the wallet back into his pocket. He took a few steps onto the lawn, maybe ten feet from the woman, and stopped to regard her.

"It's about Paul, Ms. Manning." He saw the spark go out of her eyes even as he said the words, but he rushed on to get it all out, so she would know it all. "I'm sorry to have to tell you this, but his body was discovered in the early hours of the morning. We believe he was murdered."

The trowel dropped from Ellen Manning's hand and stuck blade-first into the lawn. Her right hand, covered in dirt, came up fast to cover her face, and then she sat down hard on the grass. Castillo froze a moment, just staring at her. He knew he had more questions to ask, things he ought to be saying, but could not think of a one at the moment.

At last words came to him. "I'm very sorry for your loss," he said, and hated how trite and hollow the sentiment sounded.

After a few moments, she wiped at her tears and stared up at him.

"You believe?"

Castillo blinked. "I'm sorry?"

"You said you *believe* he was murdered. You don't know?"

He felt the urge to look away from the intensity of her eyes but held her gaze out of respect. "We know. The M.E. has not established an exact time of death, but his best guess so far is that it happened sometime in the afternoon the day before yesterday. Do you have any idea of his whereabouts at that time?"

Though she seemed to have somewhat regained her composure, Ellen Manning did not rise. She sat on the grass and stared up at Castillo, and she shook her head slowly, eyes red and tan face now paler.

"He's not . . . not the kind of son who calls his mother every day. That never bothered me, though. I know he loves me, he's just got his own . . ." Her voice broke then, dropped to a whisper, and her eyes were wide as though she expected to be interrupted with some sort of explanation for this tragedy. "His own life."

Castillo did not want to be here anymore. "Did he have any close friends you think I should talk to, people who might have had a better idea of his comings and goings?"

She rattled off three names, guys Paul hung around with, and Castillo jotted them down on a pad he carried in his pocket. After a moment's hesitation, he asked her to go down to the morgue and identify the body. Once there the process of claiming her son's remains would be explained to her. She took all of this in with heartbreaking poise.

Castillo thanked the woman, offered his condolences again, and walked back to the car. The worst of it all was not what he had had to tell her, it was what he could not tell her; that she would never know what had really happened to her son, never have the satisfaction of knowing his killer had been caught and dealt with.

But the monster would be dealt with, Castillo vowed. It might not bring peace to Ellen Manning, but it would save some other mother the same kind of torment. Today, that was the best he could hope for.

Castillo wondered if the narcotics division would take him back.

Jack was sick of driving, sick of banging his head against a wall and coming up with a whole lot of nothing. He was not a scholar, not a theologian, not a holy man. Madame Stefania had suggested to him, just before he left her office, that he could make a great deal of money as a medium if he so desired. Wealth beyond his imagining, or so she had implied. The more he thought about it, the more he knew she was right. If people were willing to pay good money to suspend their disbelief for charlatans, how much more would they pay for the real thing.

But Jack wasn't really a medium. Not in the sense Madame Stefania was. He could talk to the spirits of the dead, that much was true. But he had never asked to be able to do that, and had no interest in making money from it. All he wanted was to stop the Prowlers and to run the pub and to take care of the people he loved.

That included Artie, and taking care of him meant trying to figure out how to stop the Ravenous. But all these dead ends had started to depress him. If not for the phantom pain in his chest where little bits of his spirit had been torn away, he probably would have just gone home. As it was he was due to start his shift at five o'clock and it was going on three.

But he felt that pain, the dull ache of scars forming on his soul, and he knew the Ravenous had to be stopped. So in spite of his frustration, and against his better judgment, he had decided that he would make one last stop today. Tomorrow he would start calling local colleges, tracking down professors who taught theology and spirituality. But Jack was quickly losing faith that that would lead to anything substantial.

Still, he had more hope for college professors than he did for this stop, especially since his source for this one was Madame Stefania. Even as he drove the Jeep down the beautiful, old New England, tree-shaded street in Winchester, he wanted to turn around, felt stupid for even taking the woman's advice long enough to drive out here.

He found number Seventy-three with no trouble at all, pulled the Jeep into the driveway, and climbed out. For a moment, he stared at the front of the elegant brick colonial, this home that probably cost ten times the profit Bridget's Irish Rose Pub made in a year, and hesitated.

What the hell, he thought. *I'm already here.*

With a sigh, Jack walked up the concrete path to the front door and rang the bell. He batted at his leg with his left fist, rattling the keys in his pocket. The door was opened by a girl no more than twenty, probably younger, and she was beautiful. Her hair hung in a tangle of dark ringlets over her shoulders and part of the way down her back, and it gleamed with a luster all its own. Her eyes were a deep azure blue like the sky at dusk and there was a curious set to her mouth that he suspected was there all the time.

The girl looked at him oddly, expectantly, but Jack was so stunned by her, so thrown off after the thoughts that had been spinning through his mind as he approached the door, that he said nothing. At last, she smiled.

"Do I know you?"

"I don't think so."

At that point, most people would have wanted to know what he was doing on their doorstep, who he was, the questions anyone would have asked. She only sighed.

"Happens to me all the time. It's frustrating, of course, because I'm certain it's mostly with people I *have* met before, some other place, some other when." Her smile became almost demure and she glanced away. "Story of my lives."

Understanding dawned on Jack then. "Wait. *You're* Eden Hirsch?"

Her eyebrows shot up. "My, you have me at a significant disadvantage, my friend."

Doesn't talk like she's eighteen, he thought. Then he recalled what Madame Stefania had told him about her. *No, I guess she wouldn't.* For according to the medium up in Newburyport, Eden Hirsch was among a handful of people who had not only been reincarnated again and again through thousands of years, but who remembered each and every one of their lives.

"You're staring," she said, and then she blushed like a high school girl, which he realized might be exactly what she was.

"I'm sorry. I'm Jack Dwyer," he replied, and he stuck his hand out for her to shake, feeling absurd. "The woman who told me I should come see you didn't mention how old you were."

A flicker of irony across her face. "Age is relative, don't you think, Jack? Would you like to come in?"

Jack hesitated. He frowned as he looked at her. "I . . . are you sure? I mean, how do you know I'm not some serial killer or something? Madame Stefania said you had . . . well, that you had memories of things but that you weren't a psychic or a medium or anything."

A grave expression appeared on Eden's face. She reached up to brush a few errant ringlets behind her right ear and studied him. *"Are* you a serial killer?"

"No."

"Didn't think so. I'm a pretty good judge of character, but I wasn't always. It comes with experience, and experience is basically just surviving your mistakes. Or, in my case, remembering them the next time around."

With that she turned and walked back into the house and Jack was left to either stand at the door or follow her in. He chose the latter. The foyer of the house was all white tile and wood, and a grand staircase wound up to the second floor. Eden led the way into a parlor off to the right and Jack followed. She wore a lilac-colored blouse that was quite sheer with a white tank beneath it and a pair of cuffed denim shorts with no shoes. He could hardly keep his eyes off her.

She sat on a delicately built loveseat and stared at him intently. Jack took a seat in a wingback chair across from her and glanced around the room with its antiques and faded paintings, and he wondered if she still lived with her parents or if this were somehow *her* house. With any other girl her age, that would never have occurred to him, but he found himself believing in what he heard about her without even realising it had happened.

Those dusky eyes watched him, and he wondered what they had seen. Jack had loved history since he was a little boy, but to this girl, if what he'd been told were true, there was no history. Only memories. The idea fascinated him.

"Talk to me, Jack," Eden prodded, leaning toward him with her elbows on her knees. "You have a story to tell, maybe more than one. I can see that. Share."

So he did. For nearly half an hour, he laid it all out for her, the Prowlers, and Artie, and the Ravenous, and the souls he had met and the dead ends he encountered. Madame Stefania suggested he go see Eden because she knew that over Eden's many incarnations she had learned a great deal about the spirit world and the occult. Jack just wanted to find someone, anyone, who had heard of the Ravenous. But as he spoke, he could tell from the expression on Eden's face that she was not that person. Just as he could see how her eyes lit up every time he talked about the ghosts he had encountered.

"The Ghostlands," she said softly when he had run out of words. She spoke as though she were tasting the syllables. "I have never heard it called that before, though I've been there countless times."

A clock chimed once somewhere deeper in the house. The windows were open, but it had grown still and close and too warm in the parlor, no breeze rustling the lace curtains. Jack gripped the arms of the chair and sat perfectly still.

"What do you mean you've been there?"

A high little laugh like a child's rose from her lips. Eden smiled. "I'm sorry. It isn't funny. It's just so strange to me to have someone who is so . . . normal, though I beg your forgiveness for using the word. It's odd to have someone so normal seem to believe me without reservation. To be honest, it's almost unsettling. I have always been home schooled, you see. So I must confess I am quite unused to talking with people who are in my own age group."

"I wouldn't think there are very many people *in* your age group," Jack replied.

"Touché."

Jack had never known anyone who actually used the word *touché* in casual conversation. To his surprise he found that he liked it.

"You seem to have accepted my story at face value," he told her. "I'd say we're even."

Eden seemed to roll that around in her head a few moments. Then she nodded as if coming to some agreement with herself. "You're quite something, Jack Dwyer. A true medium is almost as rare as a recurring soul such as I have. So let me be direct."

She shook her hair back, and those curls fell across her shoulders like silk. Her gaze was intense, locked on Jack, and he did not think he could have looked away even if he wanted to. He doubted he had ever met anyone with the simple presence of Eden.

"I cannot tell you how old my soul is. The more time passes, the more lives I have lived, the less clarity I have in my memories of those early times. I remember the Roman Empire, Jack. And the French Revolution. The American Civil War. Hiroshima. I can only dimly recall the many times I have died, though I suspect that has more to do with choice than clarity. But between my lives I have memories of another place, a world like a sea of clouds, of souls who wander and some who cannot."

"The Ghostlands," Jack said, his throat dry.

Her eyes shone. "If you say so. I'm no medium, Jack. While I'm here, in this life, I cannot touch that place except in my dreams. When I dream, I can see and speak to old friends, the parents and siblings and lovers I have had over so many lives. The reason so many people believe I am what I say I am is that in those dreams I have learned things I could not possibly have known otherwise. But I know I don't have to prove myself to you, so let's put that aside.

"In those dreams, and every time I have walked that netherworld for as long as I can remember, I have had a guide there. His name is Seth, and I suppose I look upon him as a sort of guardian angel. I have never heard of this Ravenous creature, but if it exists upon the Ghostlands, I am certain that Seth has."

Though Eden had intrigued him, Jack had reached the conclusion already that she would be of no help in his search for clues about the Ravenous. When she told him about Seth, he sat up straighter in the chair and stared at her. This was a possibility, an opportunity he had never expected, but it presented certain problems of its own that he had to work out.

"If I try to look for him, to see into the Ghostlands, the

182

Ravenous will scent me and come here. I can back out, but it might put . . . Seth? It might put him in danger." He turned the problem over in his mind and then he thought about Madame Stefania, and the strength of the connection Eden felt with this spirit. "His presence right now isn't strong enough that I see him. But maybe if you called for him?"

A sadness swept across Eden's features. "As I said, I'm not a medium. I understand if you cannot—"

"You don't have to be able to hear him for him to hear you," Jack said hurriedly. "Try."

Eden regarded him for a long moment and then settled back onto the loveseat, her lilac shirt clashing with the red and yellow floral design on the furniture. With a self-effacing grimace that revealed that despite all she had learned over the millennia, in this form she was still a teenaged girl, she closed her eyes and began to call for Seth. Her voice was soft, slightly embarrassed perhaps, but she called for him nevertheless, told him how she missed him, and that Jack was a friend who might enable them to speak. Entire minutes went by, though Jack could not be certain how many, and then just as Eden opened her eyes and gave Jack a look of frustration, a new presence entered the room.

Just over Eden's shoulder, it appeared as though it had always been there and Jack had just opened his eyes to it. Seth was a silhouette of light, a man, perhaps, or just the shape of one. He wore robes and had no discernible features save for his eyes, which were a brilliant green quite unlike the dark eyes of other spirits he had seen. This being was more a construction of glittering light than a ghost.

Guardian angel, he thought. That's what Eden had called him. Jack had no idea if that was really what he was, or if he was simply a ghost who had remained on the Ghostlands for all these thousands of years. Whatever Seth was, though, Jack felt a wave of benevolence from the spirit that seemed to suffuse him with good feeling. In the quaint, richly decorated parlor in Eden Hirsch's home, it ought to have been absurd. Instead, it was sublime.

"Seth," Jack whispered.

Eden's face lit up. "He's here?"

Jack nodded, staring at the figure of Seth. "I'm—"

"I know," Seth said, and his voice was like the tumble of a waterfall across stone. *"I've been listening."*

Surprised, Jack frowned. "You've been here? Why couldn't I see you?"

Though he could not make out the spirit-guide's mouth, he was sure that Seth smiled.

"I did not want you to."

"He's been here all along," Jack told Eden quickly. Then he gazed at Seth again. "Can you help me? Do you know anything about the Ravenous?"

For a moment it was as though he could make out a definitive shape after all, a handsome face with aquiline, almost feminine features, and a kind of sash that was draped across the robes with some sort of insignia on it. Then the moment passed and the light flickered again and Seth was just a silhouette, a mirage of a man.

"Tell Eden I love her, will you?"

Jack swallowed, his heart racing with the intensity of Seth's presence. He looked at Eden. "He loves you."

"I love you, Seth," she said, speaking to the room, to the air, to her guardian angel.

But Jack was no longer listening. He was captivated by the clear green eyes in that splash of light. Seth stared at him for a time, then the silhouette grew closer, and Jack tensed.

"There is not one creature called 'the Ravenous,'" Seth began. *"They are creatures who appear in the realm of lost souls from time to time. In truth, they are lost souls themselves, but they are not human. I listened as you told Eden of the Prowlers. While I do not know them by that name, I know of them, this race of beasts who mask themselves in the guise of men. A Ravenous is the spirit of one such creature who has died but whose essence has become lost, wandering far from the netherworld that awaits it."*

"Wait, back up." Jack frowned and shook his head slowly. "The Ravenous can't be a Prowler. That doesn't make any sense. I was told that Prowlers have no souls, that there's no afterlife for them. And the Ravenous doesn't look anything like a Prowler . . . or at least not very much."

"You have been misinformed," Seth replied, and his form somehow became both brighter and more transparent. *"As for the beast's countenance, the appearance of the Ravenous is that of the heart of the beast, the true primitive. These creatures did not always appear the way they do now, could not always alter their forms."*

"So. What? You mean this ghost is what Prowlers looked like before they evolved?"

"Precisely that," Seth agreed. *"They changed to survive."*

Prowlers had spirits, an afterlife. The Ravenous was nothing more than the ghost of a monster. Mind whirling with the implications of all this, Jack immediately thought of Bill. The big man thought there was no heaven waiting for him, no eternity. *Won't he be surprised?*

"I have a friend who'll be happy to hear that."

"Perhaps," Seth whispered, and now his form became even more diffuse, as though he were fading from them. "Remember, however, that the afterlife for these beasts is molded to them. It is a different plane of existence altogether, a savage, hellish place of almost constant battle. That is the wildness in them."

It felt as though Jack were crackling with the energy he felt now. Finally he had discovered the truth about the Ravenous. The problem was, how did he use that truth? He paced a moment, feeling Eden's eyes upon him, knowing that it must be driving her crazy listening to him talk with Seth when she could not.

"I guess you don't have any idea how to stop one of these things?" he asked finally. "How to destroy it."

"I do not. But the Ravenous only does what instinct tells it to do. It is not meant to be here among us. If you can guide it to its own netherworld, it would no longer be a threat. I would be happy to help if I can."

Jack blinked, surprised. Seth knew the risks involved in that, what the Ravenous could do to him, but he was still willing to take that chance. It made him wonder just how long a soul would have to linger upon the Ghostlands to look the way he did, so pure and bright. Eden stared at Jack, and for a moment he only studied her face, so open and kind.

"Tell you what," he said to her. "It's probably a quarter to four. I've got to leave in about half an hour, but I'd guess you two have a lot to talk about. If you want, I'll help."

Even as he spoke, Eden's face lit up into a brilliant smile, and tears began to form at the corners of her eyes.

Jack stayed.

The shades were still drawn, and there was nothing Bill wanted more than to fall back into bed. But he had been away from the pub long enough already. That morning after he had finally woken up he promised to return for his shift and headed home to clean himself and his apartment up and to get a few more hours' sleep.

Despite the events of the previous twenty-four hours, his own bed, in his own place, still called to him. But all he had to do was think about Courtney, and remember that whoever planted that corpse in his trunk and broke into the pub last night was still out there, and it was easy to walk away from the bed.

When he walked out of his bedroom, the shades were still drawn and the room was dark. Bill patted his pockets for his keys, glanced around to make sure there wasn't anything he was forgetting, yawned once, and then pulled open the apartment door.

He caught the scent too late. That familiar scent.

PROWLERS

And he looked up into a face out of his past, a face he remembered though he had nearly forgotten the scent.

"Dallas," Bill said.

Then Dallas shot him with a taser gun and Bill stiffened with the pain as electricity surged through him. He slipped to the floor and unconsciousness claimed him.

CHAPTER 11

There are the clothes had several she had brought with her into the Dwyers' a small ready to go. On the bed she had the clothes in neatly folded piles, ready to be packed. To one side she had set a bunch of things she planned to

Molly's room was organized chaos. Everything she had brought with her when she moved into the Dwyers' apartment—most of her clothes, a lamp, and a small nightstand—was ready to go. On the bed she had stacked the clothes in neatly folded piles, ready to be packed. To one side she had set a bunch of things she planned to wear in the nine days before she was to leave for Yale, and a Bridget's sweatshirt just in case it got cool. All she needed now were the old radio CD player from her mother's and enough boxes and suitcases to transport her clothes in.

With a sigh she stood and stared at the clothes, at the two open suitcases on the floor, and she knew there was one other thing she had to do. An uneasy feeling in her stomach, she walked out of the room where they had made her feel so at home and headed for the door. In the hall she paused outside Courtney's room and glanced in.

There were the bulletin boards, tacked with stories of horrible mutilation murders and monster sightings that might or might not have indicated the presence of Prowlers. She felt the dark lure of that room, of those stories, as though she were shirking some responsibility. A sadness had been growing in her as she packed and now it came to a head.

Home. Moments before, she had thought of this as home. And it was home, now, more than her mother's house had ever been.

And the time had come to leave.

For a few more seconds she just stood there in the hall and stared into Courtney's room. The papers on the wall fluttered in the hot August breeze. Then Molly pushed her hair away from her face, turned, and went out of the apartment. She walked down the stairs into the restaurant perhaps a little too fast, though she was certainly in no hurry to reach her destination. Though never the most self-aware girl by her own standards, it struck Molly as ironic that she was rushing away from the one place she really wanted to be.

It was nearly five o'clock but there were already a couple of tables filled by people having an early dinner or a very late lunch, mostly suits in the midst of business. The bar was practically deserted, but that would change almost as quickly as the situation in the dining room. Fortunately the lunch crowd had thinned out early and Courtney had let Molly off around three to start organizing her things for the big move.

Now, as Molly walked among the tables, she glanced

around for Jack. He was supposed to come on at five but he had not come up to the apartment yet, so she assumed he just started working. But there was no sign of him.

Courtney was talking to Matt Brocklebank, the young guy who usually covered the bar when Bill wasn't on. She leaned against the bar, lion's-head cane clutched tightly in her hand. Though she looked completely put together in black pants and a cream top with spaghetti straps, and her sandy blond hair was pulled back with nary a strand out of place, there was an intensity to the set of her jaw that worried Molly.

"Hey," she said as she approached. "Everything all right?"

With a frown that knitted her brows and made the light spray of freckles across her nose look almost sinister, Courtney turned to her. "Jack and Bill are both late."

"Oh," Molly said, her voice small. "Guess that answers my question, then."

Courtney focused on her for the first time, then shook her head. "Sorry. I'm ticked at the boys, not at you. What was your question?"

Molly shrugged. "I was hoping I could borrow your car to take a run over to my mother's. But if you want me to stay to cover until Jack gets back—"

"No, the hell with it. Matt's going to cover the bar for a while, and I can spot Jack half an hour or so. Not without tormenting him, of course, but that's what sisters are for. I think my keys are in the kitchen upstairs."

With a mischievous smile, Molly held up Courtney's key ring.

The older woman threw up her hands with a laugh. "Good. Go. Have fun."

It was Molly's turn to frown. "I did say I was going to my mother's, right?"

"All right, then, hurry back."

"Don't worry. I will."

When Jack pulled into his spot in the alley lot, he was surprised to see that his sister's car was gone. A spark of alarm went off inside him and burrowed into his brain. Though lack of sleep had combined with his busy day and the emotionally draining time he had spent with Eden and Seth, he felt his exhaustion burn off as he rushed down the alley toward the rear kitchen entrance into the restaurant. The door was propped open with a cinder block, letting out some of the heat from the stoves and ovens. Jack walked right in, startling one of the line cooks as he prepped salads. Tim Dunphy glanced over in alarm but then waved when he saw it was Jack.

"Where'd Courtney go?" Jack called over the loud radio and barked orders in the steaming kitchen.

Tim grimaced a second as he tried to decipher the words through the clamor. Then he got it, and hooked a thumb toward the dining room. "Out front."

"Her car's gone."

With a mystified expression, Dunphy shrugged his shoulders. Jack waved and hurried through the swinging doors and into the dining room. He was half an hour late, and that didn't include the time it was going to take him to run upstairs and change his clothes. When he saw his sister on the phone at the front of the restaurant, standing by the hostess's station and taking reservations on the telephone there, relief surged through him. Then Courtney glanced back into the dining room. When she spotted him, she shot him a withering glance that made him feel every single minute of his tardiness.

As he approached he gave her a sheepish grin, waiting for her to hang up the phone. She scribbled a reservation into the book that lay open at the hostess's station, then used her cane to turn around and stare at him, awaiting an explanation.

"It's complicated," he warned, though not without an apology in his tone.

"We don't have time for complicated," Courtney said, her voice strained. "Bill hasn't shown up yet. Matt's been on since eleven o'clock. As soon as you're ready, why don't you spell him and I'll keep hostessing with Wendy."

As if summoned, Wendy Bartlett returned to the hostess station after having seated a party of four. Jack exchanged pleasantries with her, a sort of awkward break in his conversation with Courtney. Then a thirtyish couple laden with shopping bags came in and Wendy grabbed menus and escorted them to a table. The moment she was gone, Jack studied his sister again. Several strands of hair had come loose and hung at odd angles around her face. He doubted he had ever seen her so harried.

"Have you heard from Bill?" he asked. "I mean, did he call?"

Courtney gave a sharp shake of her head that betrayed the tension she felt, but she said nothing.

"You tried him?"

She nodded. "Three times. I left messages. He's probably on the way here. Could be traffic, or a fender bender or something. He drives that boat around, he's gonna hit something eventually, right?"

"I'm sure he's fine," Jack said. "Don't start worrying yet."

But they both knew that the worrying had already begun. The Prowlers were back, or at least one of them, a killer with a vendetta. A corpse in Bill's trunk, an attempt on their lives. Jack shot the bastard in the shoulder, but he was a Prowler. A wound like that was not going to slow him down for long.

As Wendy returned, Jack stepped close to his sister and gave her a quick hug. "He'll be here."

Courtney tried to tuck the loose locks of her hair back and seemed to prop herself a bit higher with her cane. "Go get ready for work."

"Gone. You don't even see me." He started toward the stairs at the back of the restaurant that would lead up to the apartment, then turned to regard her again. "What happened to your car?"

"I let Molly take it to Dorchester to see her mother."

"Oh."

Jack tried to process that as he trotted up the stairs to the apartment. Molly avoided going to her mother's unless she absolutely had to, so he wondered what had prompted her to make a drive over there. The door stuck slightly, swollen with humidity, but he got it open and pushed inside. The air-conditioning unit was off when no one was home, and it was sweltering inside. He wished he had time for a shower.

Instead, he went quickly into his room and changed into dark pants and a hunter green, collared Bridget's shirt. In the bathroom he splashed some water on his face and into his hair, then ran his fingers through it, trying to neaten it up a little. As he walked to the door, ready for work, he caught a glimpse inside Molly's room and saw her clothes laid out on the bed, open suitcases on the floor. Jack paused and leaned against the doorframe.

"Ah, Mol," he whispered to himself. "Damn it."

"Sucks, huh?"

Jack's heart skipped a beat, but even before he went farther into the room, he knew it was Artie. He glanced around and spotted the ghost in a corner on his left. Though his spectral form was diaphanous, as always, the wall visible through him, Artie seemed to Jack unusually vivid. The color of his hair and his sweatshirt, the dirty laces trailing untied from his sneakers, all seemed a bit more tangible.

"Hey," Jack said. "Did you get anything?"

"I found a few new arrivals over here, three definite murder victims, but all of them are basketcases still. I'm trying to shake them loose, see if I can figure out which one is our guy."

"All right. Keep at it," Jack replied. Then, quickly, he told Artie about Eden and what he had learned about the Ravenous, and that somehow the Ravenous had caught his scent and could track him if he truly looked into the Ghostlands.

"Whoa."

"No kidding. Look, stick around. I can't call for you, so you're just going to have to hang out for now. The faster we get this over with the better. I'm going to call Eden, see if she can come down. Let's see if this Seth guy can help us out."

"Not like I have a hot date waiting," Artie said. *"I'll linger. It's what I do best."*

Molly's mother lived in a decrepit little two-bedroom house in a Dorchester neighborhood where most people Molly knew would never go after dark. There were a hundred things her mother could have done to improve the appearance of the house and the postage-stamp yard around it. A simple paint job and some grass seed would have done wonders. But even in her lucid moments, when the alcohol tide had receded in her brain, Tina Hatcher's attitude had always been laissez-faire. What was the point, after all, of improving her own property if the rest of the neighborhood looked like shit?

Molly had told her several times that if it did not matter to her, then there really *was* no point.

With traffic it took her nearly three quarters of an hour to drive to her mother's house. She was almost surprised to find that her key still fit in the front door. The inside was as bad as the outside, maybe worse. The paint was peeling and the dust thriving, and the smell of mold and human sweat and stale beer filled the place. Despite the heat there were not enough windows open.

"Mom?" she called.

"Who's that?" her mother barked from her bedroom at the end of the hall.

"Who else calls you 'Mom?' " she snapped back. Molly had given up being surprised by her own bitterness a long time ago.

At the door to her mother's bedroom, she paused and gazed inside, her stomach queasy. Guilt raged in her over her revulsion at this place, at this woman who had borne her and somehow managed to raise her even through the alcohol and pills and men. But guilt or no guilt, Molly could almost not bear to be here. Now that she had a place where people wanted her, a place where she felt she belonged, it hurt to come back to this place.

How sick is that? she thought. *I'd rather be somewhere my life is in danger than here with my own mother.*

But she stared into her mother's room, and her guilt dissipated. The bed was a mess, soiled sheets spilling onto the stained carpet. The room reeked of marijuana smoke. Half empty bottles of vodka and tequila lined the windowsill, and there were empty beer cans stacked in towers on the bureau. A man's work boots lay cast aside next to the bed, but to Molly's great relief, her mother was alone.

Tina Hatcher stood in front of a full-length mirror dressed in a shirt that was too tight and a skirt that was too short. She was only thirty-seven years old, and despite how she had ravaged her body, she still had a decent figure. Tina might have pulled off the outfit if it weren't for the way her makeup was caked on, and the beer bottle in her left hand.

"What do you think?" she asked without turning, her voice too loud, too forced.

Molly wondered how many of the beer cans on the bureau had been emptied today.

"I just . . . I leave for college the end of next week, and I wanted to pick up a few things."

At last her mother turned, but there was a dark anger on her face, almost a sneer, that made Molly look away. No one in the world could make her feel badly about herself as quickly or as easily as her mother.

"So you're just gonna leave? Taking off, big college girl?" Tina said, voice heavy with loathing. "What about me? What am I supposed to do?"

Molly only sighed. She had given up trying to tell her mother what she ought to do years earlier.

"So you figured you'd come by and see what you could sneak out of here?" her mother went on.

Nausea rushed through her, and Molly felt as though she might have to run to the bathroom to throw up. She forced the feeling down and shook her head.

"I just came to say good-bye."

Her mother took another swig of beer and set the bottle down. Then she picked up a brush and ran it through her red mane, puffed up with too much hairspray.

"So you didn't say. How do I look? Got a date tonight with this new guy, Rob."

As Tina went on about the new man in her life, Molly turned and went back down the hall and out the door, furious with herself for even coming out here in the first place. There was nothing inside the walls of that place that she needed, or wanted. Nothing.

Even as she went to the car, started it up, and drove back toward Boston, she kept insisting that to herself.

★ ★ ★

predator and prey

The first thing Bill was aware of as he returned to consciousness was the sharp almost-pain of fingernails being dragged slowly, languorously across his face. Not hard enough or fast enough to break his skin, but enough to leave light scratches, enough to hurt. Confused, he opened his eyes and tried to swat the hand away, but he found he could not move. Before him stood a lithe, petite woman with spiky hair that was dyed a deep ebony black to offset her pale features. She wore a tight, belly-baring white T-shirt with the words SNOW WHITE printed on it in red, and a wraparound cloth skirt that fell barely mid-thigh. She watched him, amused.

Metal rings encircled his wrists and Bill struggled against them, fully expecting them to snap off. They did not. If these were handcuffs on him, they were far more substantial than average police issue.

"Mmm, look at you squirm. You are a big boy, aren't you?" cooed his captor.

Still putting together the pieces in his head, reconstructing the last thing he remembered, Bill caught that familiar scent in the air again, and he remembered it all. Despite the manacles on his hands—and the chains he now realized bound his legs—Bill pressed his back to the wall and ratcheted himself around.

Across the room, in a brown leather chair with a reading lamp craned above it, sat the wiry, swift killer whose western outlaw features and overlong blond hair he had recognised instantly. They were the features Bill's own sister, Claudia, had fallen in love with several decades before. Images flashed through Bill's mind then. Claudia, tall and elegant as a human, but as a Prowler, her body sleek with a coat of burnt copper fur. He had always been so proud of her, but never more than when she became a teacher in a public high school. Though as brother and sister they often disagreed, Bill and Claudia had one thing they could be in absolute agreement about—their desire to live peacefully among the humans.

Their history together was a scattering of moments, playing in the desert as children, hunting in the mountains of Europe as youngsters, exploring American cities with only each other for company. But those were only the images of them together. Both of them had had their own lives, their own loves. And Claudia had never loved anyone the way she loved the laughing, charismatic, bright-eyed killer she met one hot summer when America was tearing itself apart over a war on distant shores.

Fifteen years or more they had done a dance of heartache and longing, Dallas always coming back, but never to stay. Until at last Claudia had become pregnant. With her child on the way, she told Dallas he had two choices, to stay or to go. She would not allow him to treat their daughter the way he always treated her.

But Dallas could not promise her, it was not in him. He had never been part of any pack, no matter how small. Claudia told him to leave, but he wanted to stay to see his daughter born. The mother-to-be had driven him away with claw and fang and the two, as far as Bill knew, never talked again. Yet now here he was. The scent in the alley the night before, all around his car, the figure he had chased through Quincy Market, the intruder who might have killed Molly and Courtney and Jack.

"Dallas," Bill growled. "How's the shoulder?"

The female clucked her tongue. "That's not very nice."

"It's pretty sore, actually," Dallas confessed, rotating his left arm with a grimace of discomfort. "But I'll get over it. Dwyer's a tough kid."

Something in his tone made Bill hesitate, a twist of dread in his gut. From the moment he realized who his attacker was, he had presumed that this was all about him. But now . . .

"You stay away from them," Bill warned. He bared his teeth and snarled long and menacing. "You stay away."

Dallas gave him a regretful look and began to pace the room. The place was decorated with tasteful antiques, an Oriental carpet on the floor, several plants placed where they would get the most sun. The house was as much a mask as the human faces all three of them wore, Bill thought, but beneath the surface of it rippled the wild, the predatory nature of the beast. Dallas shook his long hair back and scratched at the week-old stubble on his chin. Then he reached out and traced his fingers across the female's back as he passed her, still pacing. She shuddered and smiled shyly, as though he had tickled her.

"I can't do that, Bill. I have a contract." Dallas paused and shot him that regretful look again. "Truth is, the contract includes you. But I figure the client has to give me some leeway given our history. Plus my daughter would never forgive me. So for Olivia's sake, I'm going to keep you here until it's over."

"No," Bill growled, and the sound grew louder in his chest. He bucked against the shackles that bound him, and he began to change. The fur spiked up through the skin all over his body and he strained to free himself. His jaw clicked and bones slid painfully over one another as his facial structure changed, elongated. Claws lengthened and muscles became more prominent beneath his fur.

Dallas produced the taser from inside his pocket and held it ready just in case he freed himself. But as hard as Bill struggled to break the manacles on his wrists, he could not. After a moment, Dallas relaxed again. The female had retreated a few feet and stared with wide eyes, almost salivating. Now she ran her hands through her short-cropped hair and chuckled nervously.

"Had us going there a second, didn't he, Valerie?" Dallas said to her. Then he regarded Bill closely. "You know what amazes me, Bill? Your focus, your level of concentration. I mean, I have worked very hard to be able to hold off the change even if I'm in pain, being tortured, whatever. It's part of what I do. But you? I zapped you good with that taser more than once, and again to keep you unconscious, and you never lost your concentration, never let your focus be shattered so much that you let the animal out. I've got to admire that. The way I've got it figured, you spent all those years playing football, getting hit, you had to be focused enough not to reveal yourself every time you got knocked down.

"Do you think that's it? The football?"

Bill's gaze ticked from Dallas to Valerie, who stared at him in fascination, and then back to his sister's former mate again.

"You said you had a contract," Bill growled. "Who's your client? Who sent you to kill us?"

Dallas sighed as though it were the most ridiculous question in the world. "Come on, Bill! You know I can't answer that. Where would my reputation be if I didn't keep the identity of my employers confidential?"

But Dallas did not have to answer. Bill knew of only one creature who hated them all enough to hire an assassin, and yet would also be reluctant to try to do the job herself.

"Jasmine."

As though scandalised, Dallas put a hand over his mouth. "Oops. Well, you said it, I didn't." Then he walked over to kiss Valerie deeply, hungrily. Her hands roved over his body until they broke apart. "Keep an eye on him for me, darlin'. I'm going out."

"Dallas, don't do it!" Bill shouted as the other Prowler, his captor, began to walk from the room. "I swear if you touch them, any of them, it will be to the death for us. Either way, you'll break your daughter's heart."

All the mockery and amusement disappeared from Dallas's face then, and he stared back at Bill with sad eyes.

"I don't even know if Olivia is still alive, Bill. Word is she's been missing for months. I need allies if I'm going to find her, and so I need Jasmine on my side. I've got a dilemma here, and I'm trying to solve it as best I can. If you make me kill you, and Olivia hates me for that . . . well, at least I tried."

With that, Dallas turned and strode from the room.

"Wait!" Bill shouted after him. "What do you mean you don't know if she's alive? What the hell do you mean?"

The house threw back echoes, but that was the only response. Valerie stared at him, and a few moments later he heard the front door slam and an engine fire up out front.

Courtney, he thought, and he began to struggle again, twisting his wrists so hard against his bonds that they cut his flesh and he began to bleed. Valerie watched for a few minutes, but soon grew bored and left the room.

Oh, Courtney, no . . .

CHAPTER 12

Molly made the drive back from her mother's house in a kind of daze, where the music on the radio merged with the sound of the engine to numb her mind and heart. Emotions tore at her, crashing against one another, regrets and anger at her mother, grief over Artie's death, longing for someone to help her make sense of her feelings, not only for Jack but for the pub itself. A place she belonged; a place she even now planned to leave.

All her life, Molly had felt like a girl out of place, detached from life. Artie had changed that, given her moments, sometimes entire days when things felt right and good. But then he had been killed. Now, with Jack and Courtney at Bridget's Irish Rose, she had found somewhere she was not only wanted, but needed.

How could she leave now?

The clash of her emotions overwhelmed her so much

that she was still in a daze when she parked Courtney's car in the alley lot and walked around the front of the pub. It was nearly seven and the kitchen chaos would be in full swing. Through the windows she could see people seated around tables inside Bridget's, laughing and talking, eating their meals. Others lingered just inside, sat at benches to one side of the hostess's station waiting for tables, or crammed into the bar until their names were called. When Molly clutched the brass handle on the door, it thrummed with the noise and energy from within. She pulled it open and stepped inside; it enveloped her, and she felt it again, that certainty that she was not only welcome here, but that this was where she belonged.

Whatever her true feelings for Jack, she would have to work them out for herself. Meanwhile, she could no longer deny a simple truth of her heart: she did not want to leave.

A hand fell on her shoulder and Molly turned to see the harried expression on Wendy Bartlett's face. The hostess looked as if she had already had a long night, and it was early yet.

"Molly. Courtney wanted to talk to you as soon as you got back."

"Where is she?" Molly asked.

The hostess frowned and her eyes searched the restaurant for a moment before she shrugged. "She was just here. Ask Jack, maybe?"

Then Wendy went back to her station, marking the erasable map of the restaurant's table layout and grabbing up a few menus before turning to call out a name to the people waiting for tables. Molly avoided making eye contact with those impatient folks, not wanting to see how they glared at her when they thought she was there to have dinner and had been bumped ahead of them on the waiting list.

She glanced over at the bar and noticed that Matt Brocklebank was still on duty and Bill Cantwell was nowhere to be seen. A buzz of alarm passed through her entire body as her brain began ticking through the frightening math she had been learning of late. One missing bartender and no sign of Jack. Throw in that Courtney was looking for her, and all Molly could think was that something else had happened.

Great, a cynical little voice in her mind said. *This is the place you're so sad to leave?*

When she did not see Jack in the restaurant either, Molly headed for the steps that led up to the apartment. She had already started up when he pushed through the kitchen door with a tray of salads in his hand. Jack did not notice her, but Molly pursued him to a table where two thirtyish couples were deep in conversation about babies' bathroom habits. Jack dished out the salads and asked if he could get them anything else. When they demurred he slipped the tray under his arm and turned around, nearly bumping into Molly.

"Hey," she said.

Jack was startled but only for a second. Then he laughed softly. "Good thing I wasn't carrying anything breakable. Have you talked to Courtney?"

"Not yet."

A shadow seemed to cross his features and Jack beckoned her to follow him back toward the kitchen. In a corner where one of the computer registers the wait staff used blinked silently at them, the two stood face to face for the first time since Jack had played interpreter for her and Artie. Molly felt a kind of electric static in the air between them, as though she had reached out to touch Jack and they both felt an instant shock.

"What's happening?" she asked anxiously.

"A lot," Jack replied, his expression grim. "I finally got a lead on the Ravenous, what it is and maybe . . . I hope . . . what to do about it. I met someone I think can help, and she's on the way down right now. There's more to it than that, though. Bill didn't show up for work. He's two hours late, more if you consider he's almost always early."

Molly stared at him as the implications of that statement sunk in. "Oh, shit," she whispered.

"Yeah." Jack nodded. "Courtney's out of her mind. Matt's been filling in, but it's busy as hell. And when Eden gets here, I'm going to have to bail for a little while to deal with this Ravenous thing, if I can."

Molly had a feeling there was a great deal he was not telling her about the Ravenous, that Jack was more than a little afraid. Still, the situation with Bill seemed both more immediate and more frustrating. At least he seemed to have a plan where the Ravenous was concerned. With Bill, there was not much they could do.

"Has she called—"

predator and prey

"Castillo," Jack interrupted. "She went up to call."

His gaze ticked past her, and Molly turned to see Courtney hurrying down the stairs, her momentum making her look far more dependent upon the cane than she truly was. The three of them met at the bottom of the stairs. Courtney's focus was on Molly.

"Jack told you?"

Molly nodded. "I'll do whatever I can. Just let me change my top."

Courtney sighed gratefully.

"What did Castillo say?" Jack asked.

"Took me forever to get him on the line," his sister replied, shifting her weight off the cane and against the post at the bottom of the steps. "He's investigating the body but he said he'd go by Bill's right now. He'll call the restaurant number if he has any news."

Molly touched her arm. "He'll turn up. He'll be okay. I'm sure he's just trying to track down our visitor from last night."

Courtney nodded but said nothing, fear in her eyes. They both knew that Bill would have called unless there was trouble, but neither of them was going to say it. Then Molly frowned and looked at Jack.

"Do . . . do you think Artie can help?"

Jack glanced away, then scratched at the side of his head as he looked back at her. "I'll ask," he said. Then his gaze shifted toward the front of the pub and something flickered across his face. "Here's Eden now. If this works, we can get rid of the Ravenous. And hopefully, figure out what's up with Bill."

PROWLERS

He started toward the front of the restaurant, and Molly followed his path with her gaze until she spotted a beautiful girl standing by the hostess's station and staring around expectantly. *Eden*, Molly thought. *What the hell kind of a name is that?* The girl was maybe eighteen, though she could have been younger. Her porcelain features seemed to have a glow all their own, and the way her face was framed by babydoll curls, she looked almost angelic.

Then Jack was striding toward the girl, taking her hand and smiling as he greeted her. Eden's eyes shone as she spoke to him, and he led her on a weaving path back across the floor to the stairs. He paused for only a moment to make introductions.

"Let me know if Castillo calls," Jack said, before going up to the apartment with Eden.

Molly stared after them, and struggled to pretend she did not feel the things that were in her heart at that moment. But she was not fool enough to lie to herself for long. The feeling in her was jealousy, and not a simple twinge of it either, but full-blown possessiveness, enough to make her blush with the realization of it.

"She's pretty," Courtney said, her voice soft and knowing.

When Molly glanced at her, this bright, stylish young woman who had become almost a big sister to her, she saw in Courtney's gaze that the other woman had registered her response to Eden immediately.

Embarrassed, Molly glanced down. "I'm so confused," she confessed, and until that moment she had not even

210

realised just how tangled her emotions were. She had been hiding from those feelings, and now they had been tugged into a knot inside her.

"Sometimes things are less confusing than we make them," Courtney said. "It just takes someone to snap their fingers and wake us up to make us see that. Take it from someone who knows."

With that, she turned and hurried toward the front of the pub, once again ready to deal with the difficulties involved in running the place. Molly bit gently on her lower lip, amazed at Courtney's strength, and deeply afraid that she was about to lose this home she had spent her whole life waiting to find.

Castillo left his car double-parked in front of the brownstone in Brookline, the bubble light flashing blue on the dashboard. Bill Cantwell lived in a second-floor walk-up in what was an upper-middle-class city neighborhood. Real estate values in this part of town had skyrocketed years earlier and though it was no longer the trendiest place to live in the Boston area, it was still on the list.

Even the foyer of the building was cleaner than most. It made Castillo wonder why Cantwell bothered working at Bridget's. There was no way he made enough as a bartender to afford an apartment in a building like this, so it only stood to reason he had saved some of the money he made playing in the NFL. A lot about the guy didn't make sense, but at the moment, the biggest question was, Where the hell was he?

Castillo had buzzed the apartment three times, but

there was no response. The building manager wasn't home either, so he had to resort to hitting the buzzer for all twelve of the building's apartments. One responded, home during the day.

"This is Detective Jason Castillo with the police. I understand if you don't want to let a stranger into the building, but if you won't buzz me in, I'd like you to come downstairs to see my identification, and then open the door for me."

There was a protracted silence. Castillo sighed and was about to hit the buttons again.

"You here to see me?" a voice asked on the intercom.

"Not unless you've seen Bill Cantwell in 2C today."

"I live on the fourth floor. Haven't seen him. Come on in."

The door buzzed, and Castillo pushed it open before it could stop. It amazed him that in any modern city a stranger could be buzzed into a building like this simply by claiming to be a cop. He could have been lying, after all. But today was not the day to try to alter the fundamentals of human nature.

He went up to the second floor two steps at a time. Though there were a million reasons Cantwell might not have shown up at work today, Courtney Dwyer's feelings on the subject had been pretty clear. The guy would not have pulled a no-show without checking in. To Castillo that meant one of two things: either Cantwell really had killed Paul Manning and stuffed him in the trunk of his car, or something had happened to the bartender. The latter, unfortunately, seemed more likely.

Much as he had not wanted to be pulled away from the investigation into Manning's murder—he wanted to get it wrapped up and swept under the rug as quickly as he could officially manage to do so—Cantwell's disappearing just had to be related. The DOA's mother had given him the names of a few of her son's known associates, and Castillo had tracked two of them down already. Nobody seemed to have a clue about where he was the day he was murdered, but they did share a piece of information that Ellen Manning apparently did not know.

Her son Paul had a girlfriend, an older woman in Newton. The relationship was supposed to have been a big secret, but Paul hadn't been very good at keeping secrets. He considered the girlfriend a major find, and had crowed about her loud and clear to his drinking buddies.

That was the next stop, this Padgett woman's house out in Newton.

First, though, he had to see if he could figure out what happened to Bill Cantwell. Castillo stood in the hall in front of apartment 2C and glanced around. Nothing out of the ordinary as far as he could see. Plants on small tables at either end of the corridor—despite the fourth-floor resident's willingness to let strangers into the building.

He knocked hard on the door, called out to identify himself, even though he was certain in an almost preternatural way that there was no one inside. Cop instincts. Like knowing sometimes just by looking at a kid on the street whether he was carrying a weapon or not. Instinct.

The big man was not home, but Castillo knocked

again just to be sure. Then he paused and wrinkled his nose. Something in the air, an acrid odor like burnt hair, maybe an electrical short. He was going to have to try to track down the building manager or the super. Just before he turned to go back down to the first floor, Castillo tried the knob.

It turned. The door was unlocked, and he pushed it open and stepped inside.

The apartment was immaculate, no sign at all of a struggle or any kind of foul play. But the place was empty as he had thought, and that burnt smell was much stronger inside, trapped in the air-conditioned room. Castillo walked through the apartment once and then went out again, deeply troubled. He closed the door and went down to his car, and wondered whether or not he should risk putting an officer on to watch the building for Cantwell's return.

Lieutenant Boggs would not like that. The boss wanted to keep anything relating to Prowlers limited to vital personnel only. Already they were stretched. A restaurant massacre in Wellesley looked an awful lot like a Prowler attack, and the mayors of Boston and Wellesley were putting their heads together with Lieutenant Boggs to spin it for the papers and put it into Boston P.D. control without *really* ticking off the Wellesley homicide boys.

So for now, Castillo would go it alone. If it turned out he needed more men, Boggs would have to give him a few from the Wellesley detail. Particularly if there seemed any indication that the restaurant killings were in any way related to the murder of Paul Manning. Castillo knew most of the cops in Boston who had dealt with Prowlers before and who could be trusted. But the lieutenant had been clear that no one should be involved with the truth in this case, or any case involving those monsters, unless they absolutely had to be.

Castillo would come back and check on Cantwell's apartment again.

Meanwhile, he would take a ride out to Newton to try to meet the late Paul Manning's girlfriend.

When he got back, he would phone Courtney Dwyer with the bad news. If they were all really lucky, Cantwell would have turned up by then in one piece with a big apology and a good excuse for his girlfriend. If not . . . Castillo was pretty certain that this whole thing was not going to end well.

Any animal could kill. Any animal lurking long in the darkness could find likely prey, stragglers among the herd of humanity. But Dallas had always relished the difference between murderer and assassin. To mark a target, particularly a difficult one, to track that target, isolate it and bring it down, that took more than savagery. It took skill.

There was an exhilaration in the triumph of assassination, of murder for hire. There had been times in the past, working for government agencies or for various independent contractors, when Dallas had found utter glee in the successful completion of an assignment. The truth of it was, assassination could be fun. But there was no fun left in this job.

From the moment he had seen Bill Cantwell come out

of Bridget's Irish Rose Pub, Dallas knew that this assignment was going to get ugly, messy. Jasmine was never going to be completely content with the fact that he would only take three of the four targets she had hired him to eliminate. But she understood the importance of the pack, the nature of it. And though they had not seen each other for many years, though they had never really been part of the same pack, the fact that Dallas's own daughter was Cantwell's niece would be enough of an explanation for Jasmine.

She might not like it, but she would accept it.

Now with Bill out of the way, it would have been simple enough to track the others. Dallas could have taken them in quiet moments, one by one. He could relish the hunt, the chase, the prowl. Or he might have been able to if he did not have his daughter Olivia and her mother Claudia on his mind. It was not supposed to be like this. In all the years he had been working as an assassin Dallas had never had an assignment bring him so close to home. It wasn't merely a question of whether he was willing to kill Bill Cantwell, but whether or not his daughter would ever forgive him. He did not want to kill Cantwell; he liked the guy, no matter how he had behaved in response to Cantwell's fury and pleas, his words had not fallen on deaf ears.

There was no pleasure in this now for Dallas. He just wanted it over with as soon and as fast as possible, even if that meant it was going to get messy. There would be no game to it now, no challenge, no lingering in the shadows waiting for the perfect moment. He would have to make the moment.

predator and prey

Any animal could kill.

Night was falling over the city of Boston, shadows creeping along the streets. It was a war that was waged every single day all over the world. Despite the strength of the sun, the power of daylight, the onset of darkness was inexorable.

On the horizon, the sky was still deep blue, darkening, but along the streets lined with towers of steel and stone, ominous shadows grew longer and deeper. Unlike werewolves of myth, legends of which had sprung up among mankind's tribes to explain the existence of the Prowlers, Dallas's kind had no need for the night or the moon. Yet there was freedom in darkness, in the anonymity it provided. Primal, brutal things ran wild under cover of night. Thus had it always been, thus would it always be.

It cradled him, the night protected him. The world changed its face from light to dark, and to Dallas it always felt as though the sunlight was the false face, like the human skin he wore to cover the animal within.

Shortly after eight o'clock, he stepped through the front door of Bridget's. The clash of scents and sounds was almost overwhelming. Voices and music, food and human musk. It would be difficult for him to separate out the scents of his targets in this crowd, but all he really had to do was sit and wait. He did not need to scent them when he could see them.

When he first walked in he had thought for a moment that the redheaded girl at the front of the restaurant taking names and reservations was Molly Hatcher. But the impression lasted only a moment.

"Can I help you?" she asked.

Her voice was too singsong, too high, too pleasant. Forced, but that was considered professional in the service industry. Dallas could sense it, he could read humans from their scent, from every twitch. It was part of what he was, and partly what he did.

"Dinner," he said.

"Oh," she replied, apparently taken aback. "You're dining alone?" She seemed genuinely surprised at the prospect.

Dallas gave her his broadest smile, and he could practically feel her reacting to him. There were certain women he had an immediate effect upon, and this girl was apparently one of them. A bit of cruel irony swept through him. *Animal magnetism,* he thought. And she did look tasty.

"It's just me," he confessed.

"If you want to eat at the bar, I can seat you now. Otherwise it'll just be a few minutes."

Dallas decided to wait for a table and took up a position next to the door from which he could see most of the restaurant and part of the bar.

Only a few minutes after he had arrived he saw Molly Hatcher emerge from the kitchen with a tray in her hand. She went about serving her customers, patrons of the restaurant, chatting with people. The girl hustled to take orders, bring meals, settle bills. A short time later, Courtney Dwyer emerged from the back room, hobbling on her cane. She came to the front of the restaurant and chatted briefly with the hostess. The woman passed within inches of Dallas's hands. The urge to kill her then and get it over with was strong.

But now was not the time. Not yet. There were enough people in the restaurant that they might get in his way, might interfere with his chances of killing all three, and that would be a disaster. More than that, however, he wanted to wait for Jack. The Dwyer boy had shot him, and Dallas was not going to forget about that easily. Whatever reluctance he felt about killing these people because of Bill Cantwell seemed to evaporate with every throb and dull ache he still felt in his shoulder. But there was another reason to wait for Jack Dwyer. He might be barely more than a boy, but he had killed Owen Tanzer and other Prowlers as well. Jack was dangerous, and if there was one thing Dallas knew, it was that when you had more than one target, you took down the most dangerous one first.

So he would sit and he would eat and he would keep his eyes on the doors and the stairs that led up to the apartment. When the moment came he would take Jack Dwyer first.

And then there would be screaming.

The seconds ticked by on the moon-and-stars clock in the kitchen. Jack sat at the table across from Eden and fidgeted awkwardly. She sat almost primly, slightly on the edge of her chair with her hands folded on the table in front of her as though she'd come for afternoon tea rather than to confront and hopefully destroy a savage spiritual entity.

"Can I get you anything?" he asked her. "A cup of coffee, a soda . . . tea?"

"No thank you," she said pleasantly, patiently. Eden seemed content to just sit there waiting, satisfied with the silence and with his company.

Jack knew he ought to have a thousand more questions for her, things about history, her lives, and the things she had experienced. The girl was fascinating, and the way she held herself—somehow both confident and innocent—just drew him in. He hoped that in the not so distant future he would have a better opportunity to talk to her about those things, to learn more about her. Not because of the attraction he felt toward her—for it was Molly he loved—but simply because he had never met anyone quite like Eden before.

Now was not the time. There were things that had to be done. But they could not really start without Seth and he did not want to start without Artie. Jack was very concerned that the ghost of his friend was not there. He had expected to see Artie waiting for him when he returned upstairs with Eden. Where the hell had he gotten off to? After all, what else did he have to do?

Jack knew anything he would say to Eden now would just seem like small talk, and yet what else was there for them to do now as they waited. It was odd there in the darkening kitchen, in the dying light of day, the night coming on outside the window and him yet to turn the lights on, for them to just sit alone together, intimate. And he did feel a kind of intimacy with this girl he had only met earlier that same day. Jack felt some sort of connection between them, almost as if . . .

He chuckled softly to himself at the feeling he'd been

having, that somehow they'd met before. In light of who Eden was and the lives she claimed to have led, there was a certain irony to that. It was funny, though, Jack could believe that she had led all these lives, but not for a moment would he even entertain the idea that the same might be true of him. He brushed the thought away. They had never met before. It was not déjà vu. It was just the power of her presence, the innate charisma that she had.

"Y'know," he said as the thought occurred to him, "I never asked what you do with your life. You said you're finishing with high school but you never mentioned what your plans were."

She smiled softly. "I had thought about going to college to become a history professor, but I thought that might be cheating a little bit. I think, in all honesty, that I'd like to be an architect. It's something I've been thinking about for quite some time. Something I tried to do once before, but unfortunately the opportunities did not present themselves.

"With all the chances I've had to see the world, I've watched buildings go up, and then be torn down. I've watched whole cities crumble. And yet so much of architecture endures for hundreds, thousands of years. I think it would be an extraordinary feat to be able to design something beautiful, to be able to build something that would endure, that would last. Something I could return to again and again over the course of my life, and whatever comes after."

Jack stared at her, unable to find words to respond

with. Eden shifted, blushing slightly under his gaze. After a moment he realized he was making her uncomfortable.

"Sorry," he said. "I've just never had a conversation like that before. I mean, I know people who want to leave something behind, something to be remembered by. But you have to admit your perspective on it is pretty unique. For myself, I never thought about it much. This place has been my whole life up until what happened to Artie, up until the Prowlers. In a way what Courtney and I have done with this place has always been about remembering my mother. Sure we have to live and we have to make a go of it, but it's all for her, really. For my mother."

"Have you ever wondered if she knows?" Eden asked. "If she sees and understands?"

Jack glanced away, shuddering slightly.

"Oh, I'm sorry. Was that too personal?"

"No, it's okay," Jack said, looking up again. "It's just hard for me to talk about. Most people aren't that direct. I do think about it, though. I hope she knows. I hope she understands how much we miss her."

"I'm sure she does," Eden said confidently. "I'm sure she knows and sees, and one of these days, you'll find out for sure. Someday you'll see her again. The people we love in our lives, the people that matter to us, they crisscross our existence forever. Someday you'll find out."

Jack paused and took a breath. He did not know if she was right, if what she said was true, but it felt true and he hoped that it was.

"Someday," he agreed. "Just not today."

predator and prey

A voice came from across the room. *"Hope I'm not interrupting anything."*

Jack looked over to see Artie's gossamer spirit coalescing in the corner near the boarded-up windows, not quite whole, not quite clear. Below the knees, the ghost was merely mist.

"Hey, where've you been?" Jack asked with a grin. Then he shot an apologetic glance at Eden. He'd forgotten that she couldn't see him. "Sorry, Artie's here."

She turned to look into the corner, but of course she saw nothing. Artie threw back his hair and scratched a bit at the side of his neck as though he still had nerve endings, still had skin to scratch.

"Thought I'd see if I could find anyone else to help. If the Ravenous can touch us, we can touch it. If it can attack us, we can attack it. Not that we can do much, but as you know a lot of folks around here have a grudge to settle with the Prowlers. You helped with Tanzer and his pack, but the kind of grudge this is? It's for eternity. A lot of them wouldn't come, and some of the recent ones are still too whacked to talk sense about anything. So I still can't figure out who that was in Bill's trunk. But those that would come . . . they're here."

Even though Jack wasn't looking into the Ghostlands, he could sort of see them then, outlines in the shadows of the room. Even from their silhouettes, he thought he recognized one or two of them: a nurse named Corinne Berdinka and Father Pinsky, an elderly priest, both of whom had been victims of the Prowlers and had helped Jack before. Jack was tempted to turn the light on because it was growing very dark in the kitchen, but he didn't because he thought it would make it more difficult to see them. And Eden did not seem uncomfortable in the dark anyway.

A tremor of anxiety passed through him. "Artie, are you sure this is a good idea? I mean, they're just putting themselves in harm's way. And so are you."

Artie shook his head. *"Listen, bro, you can't do this on your own. You already told me what happened the last time you ran across this thing. Who knows what'll happen if it really gets its claws into you. If you don't switch your sight back in time, it could consume you. What would it leave then? Some empty shell?"*

"He's right, Jack Dwyer."

Behind Eden, light flashed in the darkened room, a pillar of illumination flickering like fire, brilliance in the form of a man.

"Whoa," Artie muttered. *"What the hell are you supposed to be?"*

"That's Seth," Jack told him. "The one I told you about. Eden's spirit guide."

"Seth's here?" Eden asked brightly, and then the brightness disappeared from her features. A dark shadow fell across her face. "It's time to start, then, isn't it?"

Artie drifted toward the table. *"Damn, Jack, she's a babe."*

Jack shot him a withering glance. He wanted to tell him to be quiet, even though Eden could not hear him. The sudden change in her tone and expression concerned him.

"You *are* okay with this, right, Eden?"

She hesitated a moment, then nodded. "There's not much else we can do, is there? This thing, this Ravenous, it can't be allowed to run free, destroying people's souls. Whether they're supposed to go on to their final destination or come back to learn more, to *live* more. The way I have. They have to have that chance, that opportunity. The Ravenous can take that away, and we have to stop it."

There was a rustling in the shadows of the room like the whisper of the wind through the trees. The ghosts of the dead, the victims of the Prowlers, shadows upon shadows in that room, the moon-and-stars clock ticking on the wall, counting off seconds until Jack would become one of them, until Eden would be one of them again. Until they both would be prey for the Ravenous.

Jack felt the burden then, greater than he ever had before. All he ever desired was the peace and security of his family and his home, this place, the people he loved. But the existence of the Prowlers threatened all that, whether they were attacking his sister and his friends directly. They were a threat that would probably always be there to some degree. He could not feel that burden and do nothing. As long as he drew breath, he would fight the Prowlers. Any time he learned of their existence he would have to do something about it. But now he also had to fight the Ravenous, had to do everything he could to destroy it, whatever the risk. Much as he wanted to tell Artie to leave now, to go, he knew that the more spirits were there the better chance they had of holding the thing long enough to show it what it needed to see, to reveal to the spirit of this beast the netherworld that it was meant to embrace, its own dark, savage realm, its bestial heaven. In its way, the Ravenous was a lost soul, just like the others. Only its destination was different.

"Seth, did you find out what you needed to know?" Jack asked.

The spirit guide's shining form flickered again, brightened. *"I have spoken to others here in this realm, those even older than I, beings without form or image. They are the purest souls and totems clinging to this earth, phantoms of ancient times, heroes and kings who still watch over their people. Still they linger, haunting these lands, too in love with the world and what it meant to them to go on.*

"They have been here so long that they could not coalesce even for a moment to speak to you, could not communicate with you in any way that you would understand. But these ancient men and women have shown me the borderlands of this afterlife, the destiny awaiting the spirit of the Ravenous. It exists beneath the world you see, beneath the Ghostlands.

"Just as you have been shown things, been allowed to see things other humans cannot, this realm that exists side by side with your own, so have they allowed me to see. So have they pulled back the veil to show me where my world meets that of these beings you call Prowlers. If you can bring the Ravenous here, I believe that I can show it the eternity it is seeking, longing for. I only hope that once it arrives, I can do this quickly enough that it does not destroy you first; destroy us all."

Jack took a long breath, sitting there at the table. Eden watched him expectantly, waiting for him to repeat to her all of the things that Artie and Seth had said. He did not want to. She knew that there was danger to him and to

Seth, but Jack did not want to have to explain to her just how perilous what they were about to attempt would be.

He felt Seth's gaze upon him, this ancient being waiting on him. Then Jack looked at Artie, and he saw the way the ghost of his friend fidgeted, stuffed his hands in the pockets of his old sweatshirt. For the first time it occurred to him to wonder what had happened to that sweatshirt, the real one. Was it still stuffed in a drawer in Artie's old bedroom in his parents' house, or had they thrown it out, given it to Goodwill with most of his other clothes?

Jack had begun to realise that in those moments when he peered into that other world, that spirit realm, he became a part of the Ghostlands. His spirit shifted into that place along with his perception, sliding into the afterlife in a way that was not supposed to happen for people who were still alive. Yet somehow, if he focused, he could *see*. All Jack needed to do was shift his perception slightly, and for a moment he could touch that world. Much to his regret, however, he had learned recently, and quite painfully, that it could touch him back.

He felt the presence of the spirits around him, Eden watching him carefully. Jack looked at the wise, benevolent countenance of Seth, her spirit guide, and then took one more long breath.

"All right," he said. "Let's do it."

CHAPTER 13

Beyond the window, the sky was a deep indigo blue quickly darkening toward black. The stars had begun to appear, more with each passing moment, as though somewhere a universal hand turned them on, one at a time. The celestial display was breathtakingly beautiful, but where the night almost always brought Bill Cantwell a sense of contentment and tranquility, this evening it brought him only terror.

Courtney, he thought for perhaps the thousandth time since Dallas had left the room, the very air about him laden with menace. Of course Bill worried for Jack and Molly as well, and anyone who happened to get in Dallas's way, but it was Courtney who was foremost in his mind. The scattering of freckles across the bridge of her nose and her cheeks, like the early stars in the gathering dark of the evening sky. The silky feel of her pale skin under his touch. The way she curled up in the crook of his arm when they were in bed, her head on his chest, her breathing slow and steady.

Blood streaked Bill's hands and coated his wrists, sticky and pungent. Valerie had left him alone a while ago, he could not be certain how long. Though she had teased and taunted him for some time, even caressing him and whispering to him the words of a temptress, when Bill did not respond the Prowler had grown bored. Even now he could hear the blare of a television down on the first floor, shouts and explosions. Valerie was watching a movie.

Thirty, maybe forty minutes had passed, though that was just a guess, and Bill had spent the entirety of that time struggling against the shackles on his wrists. A fire of rage burned inside him, the savage heart of the beast thrashing to be free, but he had forced the wildness in him to recede once more behind the human mask. His false human flesh was slicker than fur, his arms slightly thinner, and that was useful, so now he blocked out the pain in his wrists in order to maintain that form.

Still seated on the floor, he pulled at his bonds, muscles rippling in his arms, shoulders, and chest. The manacles tore at his wrists and more blood spilled down across his palms and along his fingers. The skin had been rubbed raw at first when he tried to use sheer force to snap his bonds. When he realized he could not break them, he began trying to pull his wrists free, contorting his hands, forcing the bones painfully together, working the flesh against steel.

And he had begun to bleed.

If there had been more play in his bonds, enough so

that he could have slipped his hands beneath him, gotten his arms out in front of him again, things might have been different. A coyote caught in a trap would gnaw its own paw off to be free, and to save Courtney's life, Bill would be willing to do the same. He had run the scenario over in his head a dozen times, get the cuffs beneath him, slide them out under his legs, then let the beast out, reveal his true self. His jaws would have been more than up to the task of snapping his own hand off. But even if he could have done that, there was no guarantee he would not bleed to death before he could help Courtney.

Still, he would have tried.

But as tight as his hands were bound by the steel shackles on his wrists—no mere handcuffs these—that option was not open to him. There was only one way for him to get out of this. He had to tear free.

And it was taking too long.

There was no clock in the room, but he almost wished there was. Still, he did not need to see the hands ticking across the face of a clock in order to feel the time passing, to know that Dallas moved closer to the people he loved with every passing second.

Courtney, he thought again.

For just a moment, Bill rested. Then, once again, he began to pull, to twist his fingers and hands up, trying to force the bones to bend without breaking. Slowly, with excruciating pain, he felt the skin of his wrists begin to tear further as he strained against his bonds. The flesh ripped. He bared his teeth and snarled low and deep, enraged at his pain, as if the pain itself were his enemy.

The blood flowed.

The metal became slick.

His right hand slid down half an inch, the bones forced together so tight he thought they would crack. The blood had lubricated his skin enough to allow for just that much movement, the steel circlet sliding over the torn flesh. He feared that one more tug might snap those bones, but did not care. With that slight movement he had forced the width of his hand down into the manacle.

He *would* be free.

Bill gritted his teeth again, and they lengthened slightly as another snarl rolled from deep in his chest. There would be more pain, he knew, but beyond that pain freedom awaited. Dallas had to be stopped.

He braced himself, tension in every muscle, about to put all his strength into one final effort. A sudden growl filled the room, and he looked up to see Valerie standing in the hall just outside the room, her bright eyes glittering with reflected starlight.

Downstairs, the TV still blared.

"What the hell are you doing?" she snarled.

Bill ignored her. He took a deep breath. Even as he did so, Valerie began to change. Her shag cut hair and her pixieish body, clad tightly in that midriff-baring T-shirt and short skirt, changed almost instantaneously. Despite the pain of shapeshifting, her form altered with stunning speed. It was all one fluid transition, fur tearing through flesh that flaked away to nothing, face distending into fanged snout. Her clothes were so tight that they ripped as her skeletal structure altered, and they hung on her in tatters as she crouched, tensed, and sniffed the air.

Valerie bounded across the floor at him, slavering, fangs bared.

Heart pounding in his chest, legs still wrapped in chains, Bill roared in pain and fury and hauled at his bonds, twisting and pulling simultaneously. Smeared with blood, contorted, his right hand slid free. Even as it did he began to change, the Prowler beneath his human masque emerging in a frenzied instant.

She was upon him then. Valerie's claws slashed down, raked his snout and chest as she drove her jaws toward his throat. Bill felt the wounds, the skin sliced open, but the pain seemed a distant echo now, his blood pumping with the adrenaline of freedom and the knowledge that Courtney's life was in peril. Even as Valerie's razor fangs began to close on his throat, Bill lashed out and grabbed a fistful of her fur. He brought his left hand up, bloody shackles still locked tightly around that wrist, and backhanded her. With a crack of bone on bone, he knocked her backward and Valerie sprawled onto the floor.

The chains were still tight around his legs and Bill bent to tug at them, tried to pull them down and off. His knees were so tight together and the chains wrapped so snugly that he could not get them over his thick calves. The chains were heavy and strong, but the lock, he now saw, was a cheap, shoddy thing. With a grunt of determination, he grabbed the chains on either side of the lock and pulled, muscles in his shoulders and back straining and popping.

The hasp of the lock began to bend.

With a shriek, Valerie leaped on him. Her claws slashed down across his back, digging deep furrows in the flesh, and Bill roared in agony. Her jaws closed on his shoulder and blood spurted out onto her snout and into her mouth. Bill felt it dripping down his back, soaking through his oversize shirt. For a moment his blood-slicked, fur-covered hands slipped on the chains. He thought he felt her fangs scrape his clavicle.

He tore at the chains again and the hasp of the lock bent and cracked, popped loose. The chains fell away. With all the strength he could muster he rammed an elbow back into Valerie's chest, and her jaws loosened for just a moment. Long enough for Bill to lunge forward, away from her, to roll and come up to face her again.

Her snout was soaked red from his blood. It flowed freely from his wounds, and he was bent over, hurt and vulnerable now. But he was free.

"I don't have time for this," he snarled at her. "Let me pass and you'll live long enough to get out of here."

The female's feral eyes narrowed. "I don't think so. Dallas told me to keep you here. He didn't want to kill you, but that doesn't mean I can't. You're half-dead already."

Blood dripped onto the hardwood floor. Valerie lunged toward him and he met her halfway, clawing a long gash in her abdomen as with his other hand he began to choke her. Together they crashed into a book-case against the wall and then went down, snapping at each other.

Bill was blind to all but the scent of her blood now; the instincts of the Prowler had overwhelmed him. Yet somewhere in the back of his mind, he still knew what he was fighting for.

Courtney.

Castillo was just about to knock when he heard the crash of breaking furniture from the second floor. Through the open window above him came snarls and grunts of pain, of animals fighting.

Animals. But he knew what it was. What they were.

He glanced once over his shoulder at his car. Inside was a radio he could have used to call for backup, but how many cops would hear the call? How many would respond? He had his cell phone in his pocket, but there was no way to know if he'd get Lieutenant Boggs right away and he didn't have time to wait.

With a muttered curse, he drew his service weapon, held the gun out to one side, hauled back, and kicked at the door. Wood cracked and splintered, but it took three kicks before the frame shattered and the door swung in. He rushed into the dimly lit foyer, gun held tightly in both hands now as he swept it around, searching with eyes and weapon both. Just because the sounds of violence had come from above did not mean the place was otherwise empty. Loud voices and the sound of gunfire came to him from a nearby room, but he recognized the flat noise as false immediately. Television.

Another crash came from above, followed by a bestial scream of pain. Castillo raced to the stairs, still alert for signs of anyone else on the first floor. But then the first floor was forgotten. He took the steps two at a time. At the top, in a tastefully decorated hall with antique paintings on the walls and an expensive narrow carpet running the floor beneath him, he spun around again, searching for anyone else.

Nothing.

The sounds came from a room up to his right, the second door. Castillo hustled down the hall, gun held up now. As he reached the room, he put his back to the wall outside the door and paused for a single moment. Then he spun and stepped into the room, taking aim.

A lithe, black-furred female Prowler dressed in tattered clothes faced off against a much larger male. Bloody gashes covered both of their bodies. The male roared and bared his crimson-stained fangs, but he looked tired, unsteady.

The female saw the opening and with a swiftness that belied her injuries, she lunged at the other.

Had they been human, Castillo would have had to call out some warning, to identify himself.

But they weren't human. They were monsters.

He raised the gun in both hands and took aim.

Wary, numb now, Bill knew he was slowing down. He glared at Valerie and waited for an opening. If he could not find one, she would kill him. He was too weak, too tired, and she had the advantage. As they fought he had watched her, seen her savagery, and he thought he knew what it would take. Prowlers they both were, but Valerie was lost in what she was, in claw and fang, and Bill had given himself over to that for a time, but now he knew he needed to think like a man again.

When she lunged for him, she came with both hands up, claws ready to slash, fast and deadly. Bill ducked and turned halfway around, took her attack on his shoulder and back, claws slicing deep. Then he balled his own taloned hands into fists and he struck her across the face hard enough to knock her backward. He moved in and hit her again, fighting like a barroom brawler now instead of one of his kind.

Valerie reeled. She pulled herself up, teeth gnashing, and readied to lunge at him again.

There came a sudden loud report, a gunshot, and a bullet tore through her head, erupting from the side of her skull with a spray of blood and fur. Bill whipped around to see Jace Castillo standing in the doorway of the room, weapon leveled at him. In the bloodlust and heat of the fight he had not caught the man's scent. Now his heart pounded even faster in his chest, and he knew that in an eyeblink the cop would fire again.

Bill dodged.

Castillo fired and the bullet shattered a window behind him.

As Valerie's corpse fell to the ground he caught her, held her up in front of him, a shield of dead flesh.

"Wait!" Bill snarled. "Castillo, don't shoot!"

The detective fired again, the bullet tearing into Valerie's corpse with enough impact that Bill took a step back.

"Wait, dammit!"

Castillo took aim again, but hesitated. "How do you know my name?"

Bill took two long breaths, tried to shake off his pain, and willed the change. Bones shifted painfully, his jaw clicked as it reset itself, fur withdrew into flesh and new skin formed over it.

"Don't shoot," Bill said again, his voice and his face human again.

The detective stared at him, eyes wide and mouth open in astonishment.

"Cantwell," he whispered. "Jesus, you're one of them."

Bill let Valerie's corpse drop to the floor and held his hands up as though he were being arrested.

"It's more complicated than that."

Castillo scowled. "How complicated can it be? That guy in the trunk, all the times you animals tried to kill people at that pub—"

"But they're still alive," Bill argued. "I sleep in Courtney's bed every other night. If I wanted them dead—"

"So, what? You're a *good* monster?" the detective asked, incredulous. His aim never wavered.

"If you want to put it that way. Just think about it. How do you think they've stayed alive this long? They had help, Castillo. We're not all killers. If you shoot me, they're all dead. Courtney, Jack, Molly, who knows how many others at the pub. Look at this!" he said, holding up his left hand to show the detective the shackle still locked around his wrist. "They got the drop on me with a taser, dragged me back here so I'd be out of the way."

"Why didn't they just kill you?" Castillo demanded.

"It's a long story," Bill replied.

He could see the hesitation in the cop's eyes. Castillo thought of him as a monster, a bloodthirsty beast, and he could not blame the man. That was all he had ever known of Prowlers. But there was nothing more to be said. He was either going to shoot or not. Bill waited and held his breath.

After a few moments, Castillo relaxed his grip on the gun and lowered it slightly, though he kept it aimed at Bill.

"I'm listening."

Quickly, Bill told him about Dallas and Valerie, about the contract on Jack and Molly and Courtney. Even as he spoke he could see in the cop's expression that it was making sense to him, pieces of a puzzle falling into place. When he was through, Castillo lowered the gun.

"Courtney called earlier. I went by your place," the detective said. "Maybe I'll pay for it, but I believe you. I'll phone it in, and we'll have a dozen men there in twenty minutes."

"Twenty—"

"It's got to be handled by cops who already know. Those are the orders I've got on this. No one knows about the . . . about you . . . who doesn't have to."

Bill swore. "Not good enough. I can be there myself in twenty minutes. Besides, if you send a bunch of guys in with guns, that won't stop Dallas from doing the job. He's got a reputation he's willing to die for. I'll go. I can do it quieter and faster and maybe keep everyone alive."

Castillo paused a moment, then nodded. "I just hope

you're not too late. I've got to stay until a cleanup team arrives." He pulled out his cellular phone. "Here. Call and warn them. Maybe if they're ready for him he won't do anything."

"I'll call on the way."

As he took the phone and passed by the detective, Castillo flinched.

Bill looked at him. "Thank you."

Castillo nodded. He did not speak until Bill was already in the hall. "Cantwell? You could have rushed me with that dead thing in your hands, used her as a shield, probably killed me, right?"

Bill frowned. "Maybe."

"Why didn't you? I thought you were all . . ."

"Animals," Bill finished for him. "A conversation for another day. I owe you that much."

Then he ran for the stairs. When he rushed through the door and leaped down the front steps to the walk, the sky was fully dark above, the night laden with diamond pinpricks. It was late now. And a tiny part of him knew with utmost certainty that it was *too* late.

Eden was little more than a ghost to him now.

Jack stared at her, this gray silhouette of a person, like a photographic negative. As often as he had shifted his perception to look into the Ghostlands, he doubted he would ever be used to seeing living, breathing people look like this. Like ghosts. When Eden moved there was a kind of blurring effect around her as though he were seeing her through some kind of strobe light.

"Are you all right?" she asked, her voice far away.

"I'm fine," he said. "It's just . . . always a little freaky."

"I believe it," Eden replied.

The kitchen was jammed with phantoms, souls of the dead, mostly victims of the Prowlers, who had come to help if they could. Jack saw them all now, three-dimensional, solid as the chair beneath him. And yet if he tried to touch them . . . nothing but a chill. Somehow, though, that did not happen with the Ravenous. He could touch it, and it could touch him.

Artie stood with Corinne Berdinka, whose ghost wore the nurse's uniform in which she had been murdered. Gray-haired Father Pinsky was behind her, along with an elderly black couple he had also seen before and a dozen others. The only other soul he recognized was that of Alan Vance, a deputy sheriff from Vermont who had been killed by Prowlers there. Jack had tried to speak to Vance's spirit, but the specter had only stared at him and then looked away. He didn't press the issue.

The thing that unnerved Jack the most, though, was Seth. Though Jack had now focused his vision so that he could see into the Ghostlands, as if he himself were dead and lost, Seth looked the same to him. Brilliant, blazing light in the shape of a man. He wanted to ask why that was, if Seth had existed so long that he had forgotten what he looked like, if this was the only image his consciousness could conjure.

But this was not the time for more questions.

The room shimmered with fear and anxiety. The dead were mostly silent, waiting, wary. Artie had told them all what happened in Newburyport, that the Ravenous would be able to sense Jack now. That it would come for him, try to tear his spirit apart, to consume him.

"So . . . what do we do now?" Eden asked. "I . . . I'm kind of afraid, Jack."

He hated hearing that quaver in her voice. The truth was, Eden was only there because where she went, Seth followed, but he probably should have sent her on her way once Seth had shown himself. Not that Eden would have gone even if he suggested it.

"You'll be all right," he told her.

"It isn't me I'm afraid for."

Jealousy.

Molly was horrified to find it in her heart. From the moment she had seen Eden, a tension insinuated itself in her, like violin strings drawn too tightly. As she took orders, went about her work, hustled trays to impatient customers, she felt as though her cheeks were flushed red from embarrassment. Not that anyone would know how she felt, yet still it was as though they could read her mind and see how silly it all was.

Silly. Or is it?

She stopped in the middle of the floor, a tray of drinks for table eighteen in her hands, and sighed. Eden was beautiful, doe-eyed and possessed of a kind of effervescence, an inner glow that radiated from her, marked her as something special.

Molly was jealous.

"Crap," she whispered.

Her gaze ticked toward the stairs leading up to the apartment. She knew that they were up there together, summoning ghosts or whatever, trying to find and deal with the Ravenous. Jack had been more worried than he ought to be, like he was hiding something from her, as though there were some danger to him or to all of them that he did not want to reveal. *And if all of that's going on upstairs,* she wondered, *why am I down here?*

Her eyes drifted across the restaurant and settled upon table eighteen, and she suddenly remembered the tray in her hands. Hurriedly, she brought the women at that table their drinks, a smirk on her face. Not of amusement, but of amazement.

What the hell are you thinking, Molly Hatcher?

As she walked away from the table, she did not head back toward the kitchen, nor did she move to take an order from a party that had been seated a few minutes before. Instead, she walked to the bottom of the steps and started up.

Dallas forked the last bite of his steak into his mouth and watched Molly go up the stairs. With a small grin he lifted the cloth napkin from his lap and wiped his lips, then glanced down at his plate. The vegetables were untouched but he had eaten most of the potatoes that had come with his porterhouse, and the meat had been rare and tender. Exceptional.

It was going to be a shame to slaughter the people who ran this place. Bridget's would likely shut down afterward, and that would be a crime. It wasn't easy to find a place that cooked a porterhouse just the way he liked it.

Dallas took a sip of water and put the glass down on the oak table amid multiple rings of condensation. Ice clinked. He glanced up at the stairs again and saw Molly disappear inside the apartment, shutting the door behind her. Then he stood and walked toward the back of the restaurant without glancing up at the stairs again. He moved as though he were going to the rest room, unwilling to meet anyone's eyes. In that way, he was invisible to them, for most people, he had found, tended not to pay any attention to someone on their way to the rest room, as though it might be rude.

When he came even with the stairs, Dallas shifted direction. Swiftly, but not so much as to draw attention, he started up the steps. He had only made it to the fourth when a voice came from behind him.

"Can I help you with something?"

Curt. Authoritative. He knew before turning that the voice belonged to Courtney Dwyer. When he did spin to look at her, she wore a perturbed, barely polite expression.

Dallas hoped to avoid a scene, but whatever it took was all right with him. He had run out of patience, run out of interest. He did not even really want to be here. With a smile on his face, he moved down two stairs so he stood only slightly above her.

"Actually," he said softly, "I was just looking for a bathroom. I thought—"

"Rest rooms are in the back to the right." Courtney

stared at him, waiting for him to come down off the stairs, almost willing him down with the strength of her gaze.

Ooh, I like her, he thought. *Girl's got backbone.*

He moved down to stand beside her at the bottom of the steps. Though she put some of her weight on the cane, Courtney stood up straight and met him eye to eye.

Dallas grinned amiably, then reached out and took her arm.

"Keep silent and Cantwell stays alive. Maybe you will too, not to mention whoever might get in my way down here."

Her skin became ashen, and she stared at him. With his hand on her bicep he could feel her pulse race in her veins. In the din of the restaurant, a clamor of voices and music, no one could have heard their exchange, but he did not want it to look awkward.

"Smile," he instructed her.

Courtney did.

"Let's go upstairs and talk this over."

Dallas could sense resistance in her, knew that she wanted to scream, to fight him, to call for help, to warn her brother somehow. But he saw the battle of conscience waged in her eyes as she weighed the odds that she would survive, and how many other people might die, and what might happen to Bill, whom she must already know was missing.

After a moment Courtney started up the stairs, using her cane to support her. Somehow she seemed smaller to him now. Dallas followed her closely, as though he were keeping watch in case she should stumble.

When they were nearly at the top, he heard a phone begin to ring downstairs amid the noise of the bar below.

Then they had reached the door and her hand was on the knob.

Somewhere in the kitchen Jack knew the refrigerator hummed and the clock ticked and a night breeze blew in through the window that had not been boarded up. But he could not see or feel any of those things. He had flesh, true, but with his soul focused on the land of the dead, he was barely more than a ghost himself.

"What do we do now," Eden had asked.

"Wait," he said. "Now we wait."

A moment later he heard the sound of a door closing as though from a distance and he turned to see another gray human silhouette. With his visual perceptions attuned to the Ghostlands, she was colorless and without any density, as though he were watching an old black-and-white television, and her features were barely visible. Still, he knew it was Molly.

"Hey," she said, and her voiced was muffled and distant as though she spoke to him through a wall of substance rather than perception.

"Hey."

"Just thought I'd see how it was going."

Jack smiled. "No way to tell yet," he replied. "But pull up a chair if you want. The show's free."

Molly laughed softly and did exactly that, sitting down beside him, right across from Eden. Though Jack could only see them as if through a thick mist, he caught a moment between the two girls as they watched each other, sizing the other up. But Jack did not dwell on it.

His thoughts were only of Molly.

With everything that had happened in the past few days, the space that separated them had been filled with anger and hesitancy and unspoken words. Yet suddenly all that seemed to have dissipated. Despite the tension of the moment, Jack felt a burden lifted from him.

And then a ripple of fear, a murmur, passed through the gathered spirits of the dead and the ghosts began to move about as though jockeying for position. One of them, a thin man with olive skin and glasses, disappeared completely, fear winning out.

Jack glanced quickly at Artie, and then at Seth.

"The Ravenous?" he asked.

Seth's voice was laden with dread. *"It comes."*

Matt Brocklebank poured a Guinness draft from the tap and waited for the head to settle before topping it off. He had been at work since half past ten that morning and exhaustion was setting in. For a while he had been ticked off at Bill Cantwell for not showing, but the more time went by the more worried he had become. It wasn't like Bill, not at all.

So Matt kept working, serving beers and cocktails, wiping down the bar to keep it clean, dishing up bowls of trail mix. It was late enough now that the bar was packed and he barely had time to think about Bill, never mind anything else. The only thing on his mind right about now was quitting time, and whether or not there was some magic spell that could transport him to last call.

"Guinness," he muttered as he slid the pint to a guy with pug features, bright blue eyes, and pepper-gray hair that looked to have set in too early.

The guy raised the glass to Matt and took a swig. He was running a tab, so Matt moved on to a couple of other guys flagging him from the far end of the bar. He grabbed another bowl of trail mix from under the bar and slid it onto the counter in front of a couple of cute blondes who had so far fended off advances from just about every guy in the place.

"What can I get you gents?" Matt asked the two men at the end of the bar.

"Two Rolling Rocks," one of them replied, his wallet open in his hand.

There was a note of apology in his voice as though he thought he ought to be ashamed of ordering such a normal, everyday beer in a place where Sam Adams and Guinness were so prevalent. Matt thought it was silly. If you wanted just plain beer, nothing special, Rolling Rock was smooth and crisp and tasted a lot better than most of the other beers in its class.

"Comin' up," he replied in bartender shorthand. When it got busy, it was almost as though he had only a dozen phrases or so to choose from.

He opened a cooler behind the bar and reached in to retrieve two of the green longneck bottles. As he was popping the caps off, the phone behind the bar began to ring. It was up loud so it could be heard over the roar of the restaurant, but Matt frowned as he looked at it. The main number didn't ring back here. Someone had to either dial in the number for the bar, or be transferred from another phone inside Bridget's.

Bill, he thought, picking it up quickly. "Hello?"

"It's me."

"Hey, Bill," Matt said, relief flooding through him. "Where've you been?"

"Later, Matt. Just listen. Where's Courtney now?"

The bartender frowned, but he glanced around the restaurant to see if he could spot the manager. There were too many people in front of the bar for him to be able to get a good look at the place.

"I think she's on the floor."

"What about Jack and Molly?"

"Molly was working last time I saw her. Jack's upstairs, I think," Matt said slowly. "Bill, what's going on?"

"I'm on my way there now. Just do this for me. When you hang up the phone, get one of the barbacks to cover for you, or a waiter, I don't care. Find all three of them and tell them to sit down and have a drink or something, right in the middle of the place. Tell them there's trouble, and I'm on the way."

"What kind of trouble?" Matt asked, growing nervous now.

"Just do it. I'm going to try to call Jack upstairs."

Matt started to say "All right," but then there was a click and the line went dead. Bill had hung up.

Jack stood quickly, chair scraping on the floor, and he felt his blood rushing, heard it in his ears. Beads of sweat ran down his forehead and yet he felt strangely cold. The Ravenous was coming.

"Be ready," he told Seth.

Before the spirit guide could reply, a scream tore through the apartment.

It was his name.

His sister, Courtney, was screaming his name.

Shift.

Jack spun, the world seemed to invert again and his stomach convulsed with nausea at the instant shift. His perception altered, Molly and Eden and the room around him regained their color, their life, and the ghosts were merely shadows again.

In the corridor outside the kitchen, Courtney stared at him, blue eyes wide with fear and heavy with consequence. Behind her stood a long-haired blond guy with a half-hearted goatee on his chin and wild eyes. Even if it were not for the grip he had on Courtney's arm, Jack would have known, would have seen it in the way he stood, the way he carried himself, the way his body seemed to flow with every motion.

Prowler.

He locked eyes with the beast and he recognized those eyes from the night before, knew this was the one who had tried to kill Molly, maybe kill them all. The one he had shot.

"Hello, Jack," the Prowler said. "You can call me Dallas."

Then Dallas began to change, the animal erupting from within.

And even as he did, the ghosts cried out in alarm.

The Ravenous was here.

CHAPTER 14

Jack froze.Panic surged through him and he was torn. The golden-furred Prowler had changed completely now, his black lips curling back in a disdainful snarl as he clutched at Courtney's arm. The beast—Dallas—had the upper hand and he knew it.

Yet on the opposite side of the room, the lost souls who had come to aid Jack were now crying out in terror. All but a few of the ghosts were dark, faint traces like visual echoes. Some of them, Artie and Corinne Berdinka, and Alan Vance, had more substance, a shimmering, diaphanous mist in the gloom of the kitchen. And Seth was there. Eden's spirit guide shone brightly.

Jack could see them, but without shifting his perceptions to the Ghostlands, he could not see the Ravenous. But he did not have to see it to know it was there. The ghosts cried out in alarm and one of them, a woman he could barely see, began to shriek in agony as the Ravenous tore into her, began to rip at her essence with its snapping jaws.

With Corinne and the others, Artie rushed at the Ravenous. The ghost of Father Pinsky grabbed at the invisible beast, and then he screamed in agony as his arm simply disappeared, trailing misty tendrils like scraps of savaged flesh and muscle.

"Hold it," Seth shouted. *"You must hold it still."*

"What the hell do you think we're trying to do?" Artie retorted.

Jack stared, open-mouthed. He had to help, to do something to stop the Ravenous from destroying all of these souls, including Artie's. His gaze ticked back and forth from the hall where Dallas clutched at his sister, to deeper in the kitchen by the windows where the ghosts cried in panic.

In the hall, his sister with her lips pressed together, refusing to scream or plead. And the Prowler who held her, leering.

"What are you waiting for, a rescue?" Dallas growled. "Cantwell's not coming. He's out of the picture."

Courtney winced, then, and bit her lip. "Oh, Jesus," she whispered.

"He's not coming either," Dallas said with a chuffling sound that might have been its laugh. "What's it gonna be, Jack? I'm supposed to kill you all, but I've decided I'll settle for you. I don't really want to be here anymore, but you shot me. You pissed me off. Come on over here, show me your throat, and I'll let the cripple go."

PROWLERS

His attention still split, the ghosts crying out in anguish and panic behind him, Jack glared at the thing.

"Your timing really sucks."

Courtney gritted her teeth, held her breath, and shot her elbow up and back with all the strength she could muster. It connected with Dallas's throat and the thing grunted in pain and released his grip on her arm. Then she spun, keeping her weight on her good leg. She raised her cane, held it at the bottom, and swung it like a baseball bat, cracking the silver lion's head across the beast's face hard enough that he staggered back. The cane had belonged to her maternal grandfather and it was made of stern stuff. Courtney swung again and this time the lion's head struck Dallas in the left eye, and he cried out and reached his claws up to its face.

"Now who's the cripple?" she screamed, her throat raw with the fear and rage and adrenaline. "Come into *my* place, *my* house, threaten my brother and the people I love!"

She raised the cane again.

Almost more swiftly than she could see, Dallas lunged for her, batted the cane from her hand, and raked his claws up her body from abdomen to throat, tearing her clothes and slashing her skin. Courtney did not even have time to breathe. She went down hard on the ground, legs unable to support her, blood spilling out of the wounds, spreading too quickly across her shirt.

She heard Jack cry her name.

Already numb, her eyes beginning to shift out of

focus, she saw her brother grab up the chair he had been sitting in, raise it up, and rush at Dallas. The beast spun too quickly for him, whipped a hard backhand at his face. His fist connected, and Jack was thrown backward, falling. He struck his head against the edge of the table and when he hit the floor he did not move.

Courtney felt blood pooling beneath her on the floor. She heard Molly and the girl, Eden, screaming for Jack to get up, crying out for help. Deeper in the kitchen, for just a moment, she thought she saw other people, a panicked crowd screaming silently and grappling with some unseen force.

The door in the hall behind her opened and Courtney just managed to turn her head enough to see Matt Brocklebank come into the apartment. He was just a kid, really, a good worker and a sweet guy who almost never noticed the women at the bar hitting on him.

"Bill called and said there was trouble," Matt said hurriedly, glancing around. "What the hell's going on up—" His eyes widened as he stared at the lithe, slavering creature crouched in the darkened kitchen.

Then Courtney's vision began to dim . . . and faded to black.

Molly snatched a butcher knife from the wooden block on the counter. She brushed past Eden, who stood staring in wide-eyed terror, too frightened to move.

"Help or get out of the way!" Molly told her.

Dallas—this Prowler that had been in her bedroom the night before, watching her sleep, hoping to taste her flesh—had his back turned. Matt's arrival had drawn his attention and now it seemed to size him up as the greater threat. *A mistake,* Molly thought. Courtney was on the floor bleeding, maybe dying. Jack had hit his head, was either unconscious or barely so. She had no compunction about attacking Dallas from behind.

With a shriek that tore up from deep within her, Molly gripped the blade of the butcher knife with both hands and rammed it into his back. The beast roared, arched his body, and lashed back at her. Its claws just barely caught her arm but the slash stung even through the fabric of the shirt. Dallas had cut her.

The knife was still embedded in his back. Molly had no weapon.

"Jack!" she screamed. "Get up, Jack! Eden! Matt! For God's sake do something!"

Eden muttered something under her breath, the beautiful girl still frozen, almost as though entranced. Molly could not make out the words, but she thought there was something about *building* in there. And "not now. Not so early." Those words were very clear.

Dallas came at Molly.

"You little fool. Why couldn't you all have just acted like most humans, worry about yourselves instead of the pack? But the cripple hit me, I can barely see out one eye. And you, with the knife? I was going to let you live."

Behind the beast, Molly saw Matt rush at him, silently, terror plain on his face. Yet despite that all-encompassing fear, he leaped at the Prowler, drove him deeper into the kitchen, and they tumbled to the floor together. Matt was fast, his fists pistoned, and he struck the thing three times before it clenched a hand around his throat, then swept the claws of his other hand down and tore his arm off.

Matt screamed. Blood fountained from the ragged stump of his lost limb. Then Dallas shot his snout forward, jaws clenched on Matt's neck, and the beast tore his throat out and swallowed the torn flesh in a single gulp.

Tears sprang to Molly's eyes and they stung even more than the cuts on her arm. *Bill's coming,* she thought. *Matt said he called. He's got to be on the way.*

But she knew that all of this would be over in minutes. Over.

Artie watched the Ravenous tear Corinne Berdinka's soul apart and eat it. Her ghost in tatters, the huge beast gnashed its jaws as it ripped another huge part of her essence off in its maw and consumed it. The thing's eyes glowed yellow, feral . . . evil. Its scorpion tail whipped around, slashed right through the wounded spirit of Father Pinsky.

"You've got to grab it and hold it," Seth instructed.

Artie hated him in that moment, this ancient soul, this supposedly sage being who had all the answers. *Spirit guide,* he thought. *What the hell is that?*

Across the kitchen he saw one of the ghosts—Jimmy something—disappear through the wall. Artie cursed him silently. *Who didn't want to run away?* He wanted to take off himself, but the Ravenous, this huge, maggot-ridden, drooling beast, was not just death. The end it brought was worse than death, it was the end of all consciousness, the destruction of eternity. Artie felt terror in his soul, in all that was left that was still *him*. He had lost his life, his flesh, lost everything that he thought had mattered to him, but now he knew it was not *all*.

He did not want to disappear forever, to truly die. But the Ravenous had to be stopped, and Seth—know-it-all Seth—had a plan.

"Grab it and hold it!" Artie snapped at those who had not yet been consumed, those who had not run despite the fate that awaited in the jaws of the Ravenous. *"If it doesn't work, we run. But we have to try!"*

The ghost of Alan Vance, who had been a policeman in life, met Artie's gaze from across the room and then the two of them, after a moment of silent communication, lunged at the Ravenous. Each of them grabbed an arm, and then other spirits swept in. Two latched onto the monster's tail. Others helped with its arms. They clung to its legs to immobilize it. Artie felt the little bits of tattered soul squirming in the thing's matted, filthy fur as it bucked against them. But for that moment, they held it.

"Seth!" Artie shouted.

The blazing brilliance of the spirit guide's soul drifted forward. He lifted his arms and grasped the sides of the Ravenous's face. Seth dipped his head forward so that he stared eye to eye with the soul-eater.

"Calm yourself," Seth whispered. *"I know you hear me and understand. You do not belong here. There is a place where your kind can hunt forever, where your pack has gone. Look and see what I have to show you, let me guide you there so that you can be at peace."*

Something happened then. The gray, washed-out world of the Ghostlands that was laid over the fleshworld kitchen, just as insubstantial, seemed to fluctuate. In that flux, the wall where the windows were—one boarded up, one open to the night—suddenly disappeared. Beyond it was a place of even deeper darkness, the stars in the sky in that spirit realm were golden as the moon. A harsh wind whipped through trees in the forest there and howls split the night, first only a few, and then more and more joining in.

The Ravenous stopped struggling. It turned to look at that place.

"Go," Seth whispered. *"That is where you belong."*

With a snarl, the beast bucked again. Artie felt his hand slip across one of the horns on its back, and he lost his grip. They all began to. The Ravenous lunged forward, its maw open wide, rows of razor blade teeth gleaming, and it bit Seth's head off.

The spirit guide's decapitated form winked out, gone, like a snuffed candle.

Eden *knew.* She felt as though some tether had broken in her soul and she cried out in sorrow. While Dallas savaged the corpse of the young guy who had tried to help them, Molly tried to help Jack to stand. He seemed disoriented, but he was coming around fast.

Not fast enough.

Eden picked up the chair Jack had tried to attack Dallas with earlier, raised it over her head, barely able to hold it aloft, and then she brought it down with every ounce of strength in her. The chair broke on the Prowler's head and Dallas slumped onto the corpse.

There was a ringing in Jack's ears and he felt as though his equilibrium was completely off. He saw the world around him in a kind of haze, not like looking into the Ghostlands, but as though he were drunk. Then he saw his sister lying on the floor in a pool of blood, saw Eden crash a chair down upon the Prowler, saw the almost unrecognizable corpse of Matt Brocklebank under the monster, the creature that even now was beginning to stir.

Felt Molly shake him.

"Jack!" she said. "Snap out of it. This thing is killing us!"

Almost simultaneously, he heard Artie call out to him. Jack twisted around to see the ghost of his friend thrown across the room. Artie passed through the wall, but a moment later he reappeared, eyes wild with panic, long gashes on his face and chest, some ethereal soul-matter leaking like blood from those wounds.

"Artie!" Jack shouted.

"What?" Molly cried. "What's happening, Jack?!"

His head throbbed as though someone had hammered nails into the back of his skull, but Jack's mind was clear now. He was torn, but he had to act.

"Under my bed! The shotgun. Go!"

Molly took off, running past Eden even as she brought the chair down on the Prowler again. Jack fought the urge to leap on the monster, to pull the knife from his back and stab him again and again. Molly was going for the shotgun. And there were other terrors to be dealt with. Matt was dead. Courtney might be fatally wounded. If he did not stop the Ravenous, their souls, rising from their bodies right here and now, might be torn apart, consumed, destroyed forever.

Damnation, he thought. *That's what it is. The Ravenous is like damnation for them.*

He spun, praying that Molly hurried, and he looked at the ghosts on the other side of the kitchen. Jack lowered his chin and with a thought, his vision shifted, his perception altered.

Shift.

The world swam away into a sea of dull grays but the ghosts were solid again. And he could see the Ravenous. It was thrashing about, tearing into them, its spiked tail shattering souls, claws tearing spirit matter, jaws darting forward to rip and gnaw and swallow them up.

It seemed somehow larger, but he thought that might have been just the room they were in. Its claws lashed out like knives, and with the matted fur and the maggots that squirmed in there, Jack realized now that the thing looked dead. The walking corpse of a monster.

He recalled his first conversation with Seth and immediately wondered again if this was what Prowlers looked like before they had evolved, if this was the primal beast.

The Ravenous sniffed the air, then its head snapped up and its lunatic eyes spotted him. It *saw* him. The wounds on his soul where it had slashed him before seemed to be healed, but still ached.

"Where's Seth?" Jack asked, glancing over at Artie.

The ghost watched the Ravenous warily and did not bother to look at Jack. *"It took him."*

The soul of Alan Vance attacked the Ravenous from behind and the thing shrugged him off, the horns that ran up its back opening long gashes in the specter of the dead officer.

"What the hell do we do now?" Vance asked, staring in horror at the wounds on his soul.

"Run," Jack told them. "Take off."

"No!" Artie shouted. *"We've got to destroy it. It's the only way."*

He looked almost foolish in his torn sweatshirt and untied sneakers, but when Artie rushed the Ravenous, Jack thought he saw something else in his friend, a kind of warrior angel, a blazing being like Seth had been. In that moment, he understood that it was a war indeed, against the Prowlers, and now against the Ravenous as well. Somehow his friendship with Artie, and Artie's murder, had given him this gift, the ability to speak to the dead. This talent gave him a unique advantage in the war with the wild, and Jack realized now that he had to use it, not out of necessity for survival, but simply because it must be done. He had not chosen war, but he would fight it with all his heart.

"Come on, then!" Jack screamed at the Ravenous.

It rushed at him, batted aside the ravaged ghost of Father Pinsky. Artie and Alan chased after it and Jack stood his ground. Just before it reached him, the two ghosts grabbed its arms. Others who had not been eaten or frightened away latched onto it as well and for a moment the Ravenous was off-balance.

Jack could not use weapons from the fleshworld. He had only his hands. He clenched his hands together and brought his joined fists around in an upward arc that hammered at the side of the thing's head. Soul-maggots fell to the ground and disappeared. The Ravenous bucked, but it was weakening and they held it. Jack hammered it again, then he twisted his hand up as though he too had claws and he raked his fingers across its face, across its eyes.

The Ravenous roared.

It shook Alan off, one arm free, and it slashed Jack across the cheek and neck, tearing open new gashes in his spirit. It shot its head forward, its jaws clamped down on his shoulder and it tore a chunk of him away. Not flesh. Worse.

It swallowed a part of his soul.

The shotgun felt heavy in Molly's hands as she ran down the hall toward the kitchen. The light in the hall made her blink as she tried to adjust her eyesight, knowing the kitchen would seem darker to her now. She had checked the shotgun, found it fully loaded, and now her finger was on the trigger as she ran to the kitchen.

Across the room Jack struggled with something unseen, and even as she watched he threw back his head and cried out in pain as though wounded. And yet she could not see any wounds. Still, Molly knew what it was.

By the cabinets to her right, Eden lifted the chair

PROWLERS

again, but too late. Dallas was moving. The Prowler
shook himself as he rose. A clawed hand lashed out and
grabbed the chair, stopped the blow from falling. Then
Dallas snatched up Eden's hair in one fist and rammed
her facefirst into the cabinet. Snarling in fury, given over
completely now to the savage beast, he slashed at the
girl's back.

Molly swung the barrel of the shotgun over and took
aim. For just a moment she hesitated. If she fired now,
some of the spray from the shotgun was sure to hit Eden.
But if she did not, the girl was dead.

Her finger tightened on the trigger. The shotgun
bucked in her hands, jerked back against her shoulder
with jarring force. A huge hole was torn out of Dallas's
lower back, and she cursed loudly that she had missed his
spine. Blood and fur and pieces of his loose clothing spattered Eden and the wall behind her. The gaping wound
laid bare the monster's insides, dark wet organs and
gleaming bone.

Still, Dallas turned and lunged for her, claws raised,
fangs bared.

Molly took aim again, at his face this time.

The Prowler fell at her feet, choking up blood, dying
but not dead. His yellow, feral eyes glared up at her and
he began to crawl toward her, still trying to rip her
apart.

"It was . . . just a job," Dallas snarled. Then he looked
up at her, and his eyes seemed almost human.

Eden stood across from Molly, the monster on the
floor between them. The reincarnated girl screamed at

her to kill it, to destroy the thing, and Molly glanced up to see the tears running down Eden's face.

Jack's soul screamed. The pain was almost blinding, nearly enough to make his mind shut down completely. Again he smashed his joined fists against the monster's head, and again it slashed at him, tore at him, and he knew that he was going to die. Or that it would eat his soul and his body would be left behind, some hollow shell.

The ghosts piled upon the Ravenous again. Artie wrapped his hands around its neck from one side, choking it, while the others tried to hold back its arms. With a single snap of its jaws, the ghost-beast twisted to the left and bit off several of the finger's on Artie's right hand.

Artie screamed, recoiled, fell back in horror, and stared at the place where his fingers had been. Only then did Jack notice what shimmered behind him. It was gray and distant, like the real world was to him now, and so he had not noticed it before. But it was a window into another spiritual realm, just as Seth had described. Something underneath this world, underneath even the Ghostlands. Or perhaps just beside them.

Seth had done what he'd said.

But the Ravenous must have seen it, sensed it, and it was not interested. It was only interested in its hunger.

It's useless, Jack thought. *They've got to go. Got to run. Seth showed it what it needed to see and it doesn't want to go. Like Artie and some of the other lost souls. It doesn't want to go on yet.*

Then, as he staggered back out of range of the thrashing beast's claws, he heard the boom of the shotgun and turned to see Dallas lunge at Molly and then crumble to the ground. He was dying. Molly stood over the twitching Prowler with the shotgun. Eden screamed at her to kill it, but she hesitated. Dallas was going to die in minutes, perhaps seconds, so grievous were his wounds.

Bill had said Prowlers had no afterlife. But now they knew differently. Not only that, but Jack had seen it, right there, a misty gray world of mountains and forests . . . and howling voices.

A chance, he thought. *They had one chance.*

"Molly, shoot it again!" he screamed. "Kill it! Right now! Do it!"

Jack turned back toward the Ravenous just as the spectral thing shattered the hold the ghosts had on it again. It slashed its claws out and tore open the chest of a huge, bald man who had grabbed it and held it from behind. The phantom did not scream or cry out, but merely staggered back and stared in horror at the soul-energy leaking from his chest, and he began to cry.

Then the Ravenous lunged at Jack again. This time it grasped him by the throat and one arm and it lifted him off the ground. He tried to batter it away, but the thing opened its jaws and tore his hand off. Jack cried out in agony again and he could not see or feel his hand. To his eyes, it was gone.

The Ravenous brought him toward its jaws.

The shotgun boomed again.

The beast paused. It turned with Jack still in its grasp, and it stared. Jack hung loose in its grip, not wanting to draw attention back to himself, too weak to fight it. Then he saw what it was looking at.

Though the world was still inverted, still all gray and flat, he saw Molly standing over the Prowler, shotgun drooping in her hands. Dallas was dead, but his spirit, his essence, lingered. He seemed more of an animal now even than before. His snout was longer, eyes brighter, his fur bristling. This new ghost, the ghost of the beast, of the wild, looked around at them all.

His eyes focused on Jack. "Tell Bill . . ." he rasped, an animal growl more than a voice. "Tell him to find Olivia. Tell him to find her and tell her I'm sorry."

Then he moved in a lithe, crouching run toward the far wall, toward that gray misty place beyond the flesh-world, beyond the Ghostlands. That ethereal world crystallized then, and Jack saw that it was not all dark shapes and swirling mists, but a landscape of mountain forests and golden stars. He understood then that this was what the dead Prowlers saw. Somewhere within that other place he heard howling, the voices of the wild.

The Ravenous watched the ghost of its kin retreat into that landscape, and it raised its snout and sniffed the air. Its ears pricked up as though it was hearing the howls for the very first time. Without even looking at him again, the thing dropped Jack to the floor and began to follow its kin, its spirit brother. Jack lay on the floor, his chest and face numb where it had torn at him, his wrist on fire where the hand had been torn away, and he watched them go.

Seth was right, he thought. *When it came right down to it, the Ravenous was just another lost soul.*

Ghosts, spirits, had been destroyed, so many of them consumed or wounded. He himself had perhaps lost part of his soul. But they had held on, they had not given up, they had fought the Ravenous. Yet without the death of Dallas, who had been so intent upon killing them, all would have been for nothing. Jack's own spirit would have been forfeit.

Dallas and the Ravenous, the souls of dead Prowlers, disappeared into that ethereal landscape, yet it still shimmered there, open and yawning, waiting. The howls on the other side of whatever barrier separated those spirit worlds grew louder at first and then they diminished, echoing off into the distance.

Artie's ghost drifted over, mist swirling, leaking from his wounds, and he stared down at Jack.

"You all right?"

Jack scowled. "Do I look all right?"

"You look alive."

"There's that," Jack agreed.

Then he saw the ghosts gathered around, but their eyes were not on him. They were looking beyond him, toward the kitchen door. A fog seemed to lift from Jack's mind, though his pain and numbness remained.

"Jesus, Courtney," he whispered.

Shift.

He struggled to stand, and as he did the world inverted again. His nausea was greater than ever before and bile rose in his throat. He spit on the floor as his spirit left the Ghostlands, and then he could see them. His family. The devastation.

The blood.

Matt was dead. Eden was wounded. Molly had blood on her shoulder from gashes there.

Courtney lay in a pool of her own blood, unmoving. Jack held his breath, and he was sure that his heart stopped. He ran to her, his left hand dangling useless at his side. It was still there, but it was numb and unmoving.

Jack knelt by his sister's side, and he saw that her chest still rose and fell, but her breathing was shallow. He put his fingers to her neck and felt for her pulse. It was slow and weak.

"Call an ambulance," he said. "Call someone!"

"No," rasped a familiar voice.

Jack looked up to see Bill standing in the hall, staring in at the kitchen. He had a cellular phone in one hand and slashes all over him, blood on his face and body, dried dark in his salt and pepper beard.

"She's alive," Jack said quickly. "But she needs help right now, Bill. Right now!"

The big man slapped the cell phone into Jack's right hand and held it for a second. "Call the cops. Talk to Lieutenant Hall Boggs. Tell them it's an emergency related to the case Castillo's working on. Castillo's not there but Boggs can reach him, and he'll know what to do."

Then he knelt and lifted Courtney into his arms. Bill glanced at the girls, focused on Molly. "What about you?" His gaze ticked toward Eden, who had slumped to the ground but was awake, aware. "And you. You need medical attention right now."

PROWLERS

"I can wait," Eden said weakly. "Trust me. I've done this before."

Bill's gaze then went to Matt's corpse. "The cops will help figure out what to do about Matt. But I can't carry her out through the restaurant without having to explain it."

"The fire escape. Right outside my window," Jack said quickly.

Together they rushed down the hall to Jack's room, and Bill lay Courtney gently on the bed while he tore the bars right out of the window frame. He shattered the glass with one kick and knocked out the shards. Jack kissed his sister's forehead, his body still numb, still aching. But he wondered now if that was because of the way the Ravenous had slashed at him, or if it was because of how pale and ashen his sister looked.

"I love you," Jack whispered to her.

Courtney lay still, only her shallow, ragged breathing in response.

"Go," Jack said to Bill. "As fast as you can."

Bill lifted her and then stepped gingerly through the shattered window onto the metal grating of the fire escape. Jack watched him go down, the iron clanging with the weight of his descent, and then Bill was sprinting along the alley with Courtney in his arms, heading for the parking lot, for his car.

"Please, God," Jack whispered as Bill ran out of sight. Then he thought of his mother, Bridget Dwyer, who had died and left them both too young. Somewhere, she watched over him. He knew that she did, believed it now with all his heart.

"Help her, Ma," Jack said into the dark, empty room. "Give her strength. Watch out for her like you always did.

"I can't lose Courtney, too."

But there was no response, not from God or ghost, not from the black night outside the window.

Nothing but the wind.

epilogue

"So, do you hate me?"

The air-conditioning in the hospital room hummed and ticked, a bit too loud. It was a reflection of the age of the facility. Despite crisp linens and new paint, and linoleum floors buffed to a high shine, this entire wing was long past its prime. Not that it mattered. As far as Jack was concerned it was the quality of the staff and equipment that made a hospital. The rest might as well be a circus tent.

Eden lay on the bleached sheets, one light blanket covering her. Her skin was pale, wan, dark circles under her eyes making her look not merely older, but ancient. As though he could see, for the first time, the true soul within her. The spirit who had returned to flesh time and again.

Jack had been thinking about that a lot. With what happened with the Ravenous, and Artie's determination to go on to where he was meant to be, the idea of heaven had been on his mind. Heaven. Paradise. Or, at least, that's what it was supposed to be. He did not know what the afterlife really was. There were clues, and yet he found himself less than enthusiastic about pursuing them further.

The Ghostlands were not heaven, of course. Just someplace in between. But Jack had seen that place, touched it, and it had seemed to touch him as well. He had gotten a glimpse into what might truly be heaven for monsters, for the Prowlers, and he did not know how he felt about that. Creatures like that, predators, killers . . . did they even deserve an eternal rest? Peace?

Paradise?

In the end, Jack had decided that it was not for him to say. But in the process, he became more and more curious about Eden. There were so many questions he wanted to ask her when she was up to it, when she had begun to truly heal.

If she would talk to him.

"Eden?"

Her eyes were heavy, tired. She had been staring for a moment at the television bolted to the wall on the other side of the room. A curtain was drawn to separate her bed from that of the older woman she was sharing the room with. *Betty something,* Jack thought. The woman had had surgery of some kind; she had told them, but he had not been paying much attention.

At the moment, thankfully, Betty was sleeping.

"Hey," Jack prompted again. "Why don't I go? I can come back later."

At last Eden turned her porcelain features toward him, her ancient, wise eyes narrowing as she studied him. The rest of her body stayed absolutely still. She was not even really supposed to be laying on her back, but she refused to be on her stomach all day.

"I don't hate you," she said, as though she had just come to that decision.

Jack glanced at the floor. "So you *were* listening."

"Sorry. I'm in and out. They give me something for the pain. But as long as there's no infection or anything, I should be out in a couple of days, and then maybe we can talk some more."

"And you're sure about that? The not hating me part? 'Cause I wouldn't blame you."

A weak, thin smile blossomed upon her lips. "I'm sure. You couldn't have known what would happen, Jack. I . . . I wish you and Seth had explained things about the Ravenous better to me. What happened to . . . what it did to Seth, that hurts me much worse than my wounds. But Seth would have done it anyway, so I can't blame you. Much as I've wanted to."

Despite her forgiveness, Jack felt a rush of fresh guilt wash over him. "I'm so sorry."

"I know. You're a good guy, Jack. I'm glad I know you. I'd like to know you better. After I've had a chance to recover."

He did not know if she meant physical or emotional recovery, but he did not want to ask. Instead, Jack leaned over the hospital bed and kissed her gently on the forehead.

"Thank you."

As he turned to leave, Eden reached a hand out to touch him on the arm. Jack glanced down at her again and was surprised to find a broader smile on her face, her skin flushed with color as though she were already regaining her strength.

"Artie's really something else, isn't he?"

Jack frowned. "Artie? Well, yeah. He was the sweetest guy I . . . but you can't talk to ghosts. How did you meet Artie?"

"During surgery, while I was unconscious, he came to me. He knew that Seth was special to me and said he could sense my grief. And he wanted me to tell you that he's going to try to stay away for a while, away from you and Molly. But—and he was emphatic about this—he said to tell you he'll be around if you need him." Eden smiled softly. "I'm glad. He's so funny and passionate. I hope I dream of him again."

Jack shook his head in disbelief, pleasantly surprised to know that his friend was not gone forever, and he grinned. "I hope so, too. And, by the way, he said you were a babe."

Eden actually blushed.

He figured maybe she had found herself another spirit guide.

When Jack stepped off the elevator onto the fourth floor he spotted Molly immediately. She stood by a bank of pay phones, one hip cocked out at an angle, her left hand on the back of her head as though upset or bored.

She wore cutoff shorts and a green top with spaghetti straps. Where she had been gashed, her shoulder was wrapped in a thick bandage, and yet she seemed oblivious to any looks she might receive because of it.

"Hey," he said as he approached.

Molly glanced at him, her hair falling over her eyes, and held up one finger to indicate that he should wait.

"All right. Thank you for everything. We'll be in touch later today."

She hung up the phone.

Jack frowned and studied her. "Castillo?"

"Yeah." Her expression turned dark, her eyes distant.

"What did he say?"

"They're taking care of everything," Molly said, voice tinged with wonder, disbelief, and a bit of disdain. "Just like they always do where the Prowlers are concerned. Witnesses in the pub picked out pictures of this Dallas guy as the one who went upstairs with Courtney. They've got a warrant out for him for attacking us all and for murdering Matt. See, according to them, he *escaped*. They've also told the press that he killed that Paul Manning guy, but didn't breathe a word about the body being found in Bill's trunk."

Jack let that all sink in. He thought he ought to be happy. Castillo and his superiors had cleaned up their mess, kept them all out of the media. But then he thought of Matt Brocklebank's parents and his little sister Jeannie, who was still in college, and he could not find it in himself to be happy.

"They'll never know what really happened," he muttered.

"They can't," Molly agreed. "The guy can never be caught because the cops already incinerated his body, just like they do anytime one of the monsters shows up."

Her voice was bitter, angry. Jack wanted to call her on it, but knew he had no right, for he felt the same. Yet the police were doing their best. The conspiracy was understandable. The world would change completely if knowledge of the Prowlers' existence were to become common. And it certainly was convenient for Jack and the people he loved.

After a moment, Molly sighed, her hands fluttering in the air. "I'm sorry. I know we have a lot to be grateful for. The Ravenous is gone. This thing, Dallas, wanted to kill us, and we're all still here. But none of us are walking away without scars, Jack. Courtney especially—"

"And everybody wants to pretend it didn't happen."

She stopped, blinked, and stared at him as though she had only just noticed him standing there. "Yes. That's it exactly."

Jack smiled softly. "Makes you wonder how many other secrets there are, what else they're keeping from us."

"It does. Artie talked about conspiracies all the time. I thought he was just paranoid."

They shared a soft, uneasy laugh.

"How's your hand? Still numb?"

He flexed it, shook it out a little. "Getting better."

"It will," Molly said, pushing her wild red hair behind her ears and gazing at him earnestly. "We'll all get better. The numbness will go away. Then we'll be able to feel again."

Jack smiled softly, not wanting to look away, never wanting to break the connection he felt with her then. The space between them was alive with possibility.

Then they fell in beside each other and began to walk down the hall toward the room where Courtney had been brought after surgery. After he had seen the extent of her injuries, Jack was afraid to even hope his sister would be all right. Instead, he had prayed with all his heart. He knew, after all, that there was *something* out there. Whatever it was. Something that might listen, and might be able to help.

Doctors had been forced to remove a section of her intestine, and it was touch and go for a while because of all the blood she had lost. But in the end they stitched her up, pumped her full of antibiotics to fight potential infection, and announced that as long as she rested, gave herself plenty of time to heal, and there were no further complications, she would be all right.

It would likely be days, perhaps a week, before she could go home, and many more weeks before the wounds would heal. Cosmetic surgery would need to be done in the meanwhile if she did not want the scars to be there forever.

But Courtney was alive.

She had survived.

They all had.

Just outside Courtney's hospital room, Molly hesitated. He thought she might actually be blushing, but did not dare ask her.

"What's wrong?" he asked.

She lifted her chin and met his gaze, her emerald green eyes sparkling. "I just wanted to tell you that I'm staying. I'm not going to Yale."

"What? Oh, Mol, you can't just—"

"Yeah, I can. I might try to get into someplace local for a January admission. Boston College maybe. But Yale is just too far away. With Courtney out of commission for a while, it's going to take all three of us to run the pub, especially if we're really going to try tracking these things."

Jack hesitated. The night before they had stood in Courtney's bedroom and stared at the news clippings on the bulletin board, and they had agreed, in just a few words, that the smartest thing they could possibly do was forget the Prowlers ever existed, keep their heads down, and pray that Jasmine would forget about them as well.

But they had also agreed that they could not do that. The Prowlers were out there, hunting and killing, forming new packs. And Jasmine seemed as though she was intent upon seeing them dead.

The only thing they could do was find her first and destroy her. This war against the Prowlers was no casual thing anymore. It was a mission now, a purpose. No one else was going to take on the responsibility, so it was up to them to hunt the monsters. Jack had wondered how Molly could be so emphatic about that if she was going away, but he had said nothing.

One of the things that they had not yet talked about was Bill's niece, Olivia. According to Dallas, the girl had disappeared. If they were really going to get into this thing, that would certainly be Bill's first order of business, to find that girl and make sure she's alive, find out whose side she was on. And they would have to track down Jasmine as well.

Make the predator the prey.

Molly watched him, waiting for a response.

Jack smiled and shrugged. "If you're waiting for me to talk you out of it, I'm not going to. I think you should go to college. But if you went somewhere nearby . . . that would be better. I feel like we're a part of something. All of us. And . . . and maybe just you and me. It would be a shame not to find out what's meant to happen next."

Molly nodded slowly, gaze earnest. "I couldn't agree more."

Together, they turned to look into the hospital room. Courtney lay in bed, pale and drawn, her hair a mess. But she smiled up at Bill with her eyes aglow, as though he were her lifeline. They talked softly, the big man dwarfing the metal and plastic chair next to the bed, and whatever they whispered about, Jack decided it was not for him to hear.

Beside him, Molly reached out to touch his hand, and their fingers intertwined. He felt the warmth of her skin, the comfort of her touch, and a kind of strength surged up in him. Jack held Molly's hand tightly and watched Bill and Courtney whisper to each other, and he knew that whatever came, whatever monsters stalked the shadows, they would be all right.

They would face the darkness together.

about the author

CHRISTOPHER GOLDEN is the award-winning, *L.A. Times* bestselling author of such novels as *Straight on 'til Morning* and *Strangewood*, and the *Prowlers* and *Body of Evidence* series of teen thrillers.

Golden has also written a great many books and comic books related to the TV series *Buffy the Vampire Slayer* and *Angel*. His other comic book work includes stories featuring such characters as Batman, Wolverine, Spider-Man, The Crow, and Hellboy, among many others.

As a pop culture journalist, he was the editor of the Bram Stoker Award-winning book of criticism, *CUT!: Horror Writers on Horror Film*, and co-author of both *Buffy the Vampire Slayer: The Monster Book* and *The Stephen King Universe*.

Golden was born and raised in Massachusetts, where he still lives with his family. He graduated from Tufts University. He is currently at work on the fourth book in the *Prowlers* series, *Wild Things,* and a new novel for Signet called *The Ferryman*. There are more than four million copies of his books in print. Please visit him at *www.christophergolden.com*.

TURN THE PAGE FOR
A PREVIEW OF
THE NEXT
PROWLERS THRILLER

WILD THINGS

AVAILABLE JANUARY 2003

PROLOGUE

Alone in the dark.

Chet Douglas lay on a bedroll in the cab of his rig and stared up at the ceiling in the dark. Whenever he was on a long haul like this one—the trailer filled with electronic parts on their way from Alabama to Albany, New York— he split the drive up with two and three hour catnaps. It had taken some getting used to, but it got the load there faster, got the pay in the bank sooner. He was young, after all. There would be time to sleep later.

In his mind, all those excuses seemed completely reasonable. But there was another reason Chet tried not to sleep too much on a long haul. Sometimes . . . sometimes the rest areas were empty, the lot abandoned, even the highway quiet. Chet prided himself on his safety record. He was not going to be another one of those long-haul boys who fell asleep at the wheel and took out some grandmother or a couple from Iowa with three kids in the car. So when he was tired, he stopped. He rested. But he never liked those darkened spots, bereft of any life save for whatever rustled in the trees beyond the pavement.

Chet Douglas hated to be alone in the dark.

Of course he never would have admitted that to anyone. He was a grown man, after all. But now, there in the truck, he felt like a child again. He knew, absolutely, that if he dared to look out the windows, he would see things shifting in the shadows, just as he always had as a little boy.

Dawn was hours off and he had to lie there and force himself to close his eyes, try to keep his mind from turning again to the dark. He felt the world slipping away from him, a haze falling over his consciousness. Exhaustion finally catching up with him, and Chet gave himself over to it willingly. He drifted toward oblivion, his chest rising and falling in a soothing rhythm, his breath slowing. Outside, the muffled sound of the wind.

The wind, soothing, gently rocking . . .

Chet opened his eyes, suddenly awake. For a moment he was confused, lost in that realm between sleep and consciousness. Something had roused him, had reached in from the night and touched him. A loud engine passing by on the highway?

Then it came again, distant and muffled as the wind, a shriek of terror and anguish, a desperate cry that made him freeze, eyes wide. His heart began to hammer in his chest and his breathing became ragged.

"Jesus," Chet whispered, there in the dark.

A third time the voice cried out, somewhere in the night beyond the metal cradle of the cab of his semi. This time it was closer and there were smaller sounds accompanying it, little squeals of fear that sounded more than a little like surrender.

A woman. Maybe a girl.

But where had she come from? If a truck had pulled in he would have heard the rumble of the engine, the hiss of hydraulic brakes. Even a car engine coming up that close would have woken him.

From the woods, Chet thought. *She came from the woods.*

Get out of here!

Suddenly he was in motion. He sat up, threw the curtain back and climbed into his seat. Chet scrambled to get the keys out of his pocket. They jangled as he pulled them out, listening hard to for any sound outside the truck that should not have been there.

The engine roared and at last Chet looked out the window to his left, where the sounds had come from. Out there in the darkened lot, by the trees. He saw her then, a dark-haired woman stumbling toward the truck, dark streaks on her face that might have been mascara or dirt or blood, one arm hanging limply at her side.

In that moment, Chet Douglas hated himself.

Coward, he thought.

Here was this woman, maybe barely old enough for him to call her that, injured and in trouble. If she came from the woods, she had likely been camping and gotten lost. He had no idea how she came by her injuries, maybe an angry boyfriend or even a bear. She was running away from something, that much was obvious.

And you were gonna take off on her. What a child, he

scolded himself. *Afraid of the dark.* There would be more recriminations later, more guilt, of that he was sure. But that was for later.

Chet killed the engine and reached behind the seat to grab an aluminum baseball bat he kept back there. Its paint was faded and its surface scarred, not from parking lot scraps but from playing ball with his boys. The metal was cold against his skin and its weight felt good. He hefted the bat, popped the lock on the door and stepped down out of the truck. Chet sucked in a breath of cold October night air and lifted his chin, stood a bit straighter.

The girl—he could see now that she was no more than sixteen or seventeen—ran right at him, staggering the last few feet.

"Oh God, oh Jesus, thank you," she whispered, breath coming in ragged gasps.

Chet could practically smell the blood on her face and clothes. Her eyes were wild with terror, half blind with it as her gaze darted around at the truck, the darkness, at Chet himself, trying to focus, maybe just to make sense of it all.

"What happened to you, honey?" he asked, voice a tired rasp. "Where is the son of a bitch?" He felt braver now. "Come on out, you bastard!" he shouted into the dark, sure now that it must be her husband or boyfriend. "I'll give you a taste of what you did to her!"

The terrified girl began to laugh softly, madly. *Poor thing really has snapped,* Chet thought. He squinted his eyes and thought he saw someone else moving in the trees, in the woods. He was surprised that the guy had the guts to come out now and face him.

"Come on," he muttered to the figure in the woods. "I'll give you a taste."

Then, as Chet watched, the man stepped out of the woods. No, that wasn't right. The man stumbled out. Even in the dark, with only a sliver moon and the stars above, Chet could see that he had been hurt, that his face was ravaged and his clothes hung in strips from his body.

"What the—" Chet began.

The man collapsed in a heap on the tar and did not move.

Beside him, the girl laughed again, a bit louder now, a sharp edge to it. Chet turned to look at her . . . and the girl began to change. As though it had consumed her from within, a monster tore its way out of her skin, a sleek, slavering thing with sable fur and glistening needle teeth. As if the darkness itself had claws, it reached for him.

The beast laughed.

Alone again, alone in the dark, Chet had time only to think that all along he had been right about the night and the shadows and the faces at the window.

Then it was upon him.

The bat clanged to the ground, leaving only the whispers of the wind and the low, contented growling of the darkness.

Red and gold neon lights gleamed off puddles left behind in the road by rain showers that had passed through Boston on and off all day long. But it was night, now, and the rain had passed. A chill wind swept in off the ocean and weaved its way through the streets, even far away from the harbor. Jack Dwyer could taste the tang of salt on the air, the influence of the sea reaching deep into the city to touch him where he walked side by side with Bill Cantwell on a narrow Chinatown street.

Jack shivered and zipped his coat, scuffed and battered black leather. His burly companion had only a light cotton jacket, but did not seem to be bothered by the chilly night at all. Not that Jack was surprised. Bill was far more than he seemed. The big, bearded man was the bartender at Bridget's Irish Rose Pub, which twenty-year-old Jack and his older sister Courtney owned and managed. Bill was also Courtney's boyfriend.

But he wasn't human.

A delivery truck was parked halfway on the sidewalk up ahead, and they had to walk out into the street to go around it. Jack had no idea what was being delivered to a Chinese corner grocery store at ten o'clock on a Wednesday night, but he figure it was useless trying to figure it out. Though the entire neighborhood was only a few short blocks, walking through Chinatown was a journey through another world.

There was something wonderfully exotic about the place, a kind of electrical current that charged the air with mystery. Young Chinese men and women cruised slowly by in their cars, engines growling low and dangerous. A middle-aged man and a white-haired old woman exchanged pleasantries on a corner, angry voices shouted inside a bar, all in a clipped language that seemed more sounds than words, just as when written it seemed more symbols than letters.

Bars and restaurants lined the street, interrupted by a Laundromat, a video store, and a dozen other small businesses, some of which Jack could only guess at because most of the signs were painted in Chinese characters. Most, but not all. Amidst the words he could not read was a single word in English: "Lotus." Even as he and Bill drew closer to the unremarkable brick front of the building, the door opened and a Caucasian man emerged. He was short, yet powerfully built, and his hair was cut to an inch of stubble. Dark glasses wrapped around his eyes, though it was long after dark.

Strange music and unfamiliar odors poured out the door in the moments before it clicked shut again behind the man. He glanced up once at Jack and Bill, nostrils flaring, and then he turned his back to them and started off in the opposite direction. Bill paused a moment outside the door of the Lotus as though waiting for the other man to put some more distance between them. Then he glanced at Jack.

"Remember what I said."

Jack nodded once, more than happy to keep quiet and follow his friend's lead. Bill knew this place. He didn't. That was reason enough. Bill nodded in return, then rapped hard on the thick wooden door of the Lotus Club. A moment later there was a click and the door pushed in several inches. Jack reached for it, but Bill shot him a cold look and he pulled back just as it swung open.

Within there stood an Asian man so large he dwarfed even Bill. His head was shaved bald and the image of a tiger tattooed on the left side of his skull. Beyond him was a stairwell that led down into the cellar club, and it was from there that the odd music thumped. Multi-colored lights strobed the walls.

The huge doorman narrowed his gaze and glanced form Bill to Jack and back again.

"Good evening, Lao. I'm afraid we're a few minutes late," Bill said.

Lao did not take his eyes off Bill again, but he sniffed at the air and his upper lip curled back in distaste. His teeth looked too long, too sharp and even though Jack had expected that, still he shuddered at the sight.

"You brought a new face, Guillaume," the creature known as Lao intoned. "Winter's not going to like that."

"Winter owes me, Lao," Bill replied. "Are you going to turn me away from the Lotus? With all the other threats to our kind, would you make me an enemy?"

Lao lifted his chin and took a long, audible breath. Jack watched the two huge men-who-were-not-men, and he felt the rhythm of the music below pounding into his chest, and he inhaled the rich aromas of mint and cinnamon and coffee and so many other things from below. With eyes narrowed, Lao studied him again.

"What is your name?" the doorman demanded.

If he speaks to you, answer immediately and truthfully, Bill had said. *If you lie, or you become afraid, he'll smell it on you.*

"Jack Dwyer."

Lao leaned forward, practically bending over, to stare

at him eye to eye. "You don't look like much, boy," the doorman grunted. "You know there are those downstairs who'd like to kill you just to prove you're not as dangerous as the whispers say you are."

Jack could not help a tiny flinch, not of fear but of surprise. He had no doubt, any time he was within any real proximity to Prowlers, that they would be happy to kill him. But the idea that he was considered dangerous, that they whispered about him . . . Jack found that he liked that. He liked it a lot. But he did not allow that pleasure to show, did not crack the tiniest smile.

"He wants peace, Lao. Live and let live. Same as you do," Bill explained. "Nobody who comes to the Lotus has anything to fear from Jack, or from me. Come on, old friend. We're not here to start any trouble."

A car passed by with pop music turned up loud, somehow out of place here. A short way up the street, a girl stepped out from the darkness of a recessed doorway and strode toward the car as it pulled to a stop. She wore a white shirt tied at the waist to bare her belly and a plaid skirt that would have looked like a school uniform if it had not been so short. She bent to speak softly to the man in the car and then walked around to climb into the passenger's side.

The distraction caught his attention for mere seconds. When he glanced back at Lao he realized that both the doorman and Bill were staring at him.

"Is he brave or stupid?" Lao asked.

Bill chuckled softly. "A little of both sometimes."

Jack frowned, not liking this turn in the conversation.

"You turned your back on me, boy. I might have had your life just now," Lao told him.

"Not if you wanted to survive the night," Jack replied curtly, remembering too late Bill's admonition to keep silent.

But Lao only smiled and nodded and stepped aside. "Go in, Guillaume. Remember this, though. If there is a mess, you will be the one to clean it up."

"Agreed."

With that, Bill led Jack further inside. The door closed behind them and Lao locked it with a metallic clank. The music grew louder the moment they began to descend the stairs and as they entered the club, the swirl of colored light seemed to mute and diffuse everything so that at first Jack could not see well at all. Slowly his eyes began to adjust.

As they moved through the club, Jack found himself disappointed. Down the center of the club was a long oval bar that appeared to be constructed entirely of stainless steel. On one side was a small dance floor upon which several dozen gyrated slowly to Asian techno-punk—or whatever the music was that pumped from the speakers. On the other, tables and booths where club goers sat and drank, perhaps ate something off what Bill had told him was a very limited menu.

The clientele was mostly Asian, though he saw a lot of faces that were not. And though there was a kind of grinding, insinuating flavor to the place, as Bill led him around tables and past the bar, Jack at first thought that there was nothing really extraordinary about it.

Then his eyes adjusted further and the music seemed to grow louder and the lights blurred into one red haze glittering off the eyes of the clientele in the Lotus Club. As he passed, one by one, they sniffed the air and turned to gaze at him. Some of them reacted physically, crouching just slightly as though on guard. Jack felt the hairs on the back of his head prickle and his breathing slowed. He could practically feel all their eyes on him, all those predators.

And he the prey.

Then he remembered what Lao had said, and he knew that the roles of predator and prey could easily be reversed, and he felt better. Most of the customers in the Lotus were not even people, but Prowlers, members of an ancient race of shape shifting monsters who could look human, but who would never *be* human. Their numbers were comparatively few now, and the great packs of olden times dissipated far and wide, hunting the fringes of human society, many Prowlers hunting alone.

But Bill was proof that there were also those who had given up the old ways, whose only interest was surviving the spread of humanity, living peacefully within that society as best they could. Even for those, however, there was an urge to gather. Perhaps there was no pack for them now, not really, but they felt a desire to draw together, to be amongst their own for a time.

The Lotus Club was the place where they could do precisely that. Jack knew from his friendship with Bill that there were Prowlers who were not savage killers, but he had never imagined there could be so many of them existing beneath the notice of their human counterparts. So many of the Prowlers in the club were Asian that he had to wonder if the Lotus was the only such place in Boston. And what of the other cities in America . . . and around the world? The implications of that line of thought were staggering to him.

Bill led the way to a booth in the rear corner of the club, far from the bar and partially shielded from the swirling lights of the dance floor. A thin black man with a white streak in his hair glanced up at them from the booth as they approached. He clutched a tumbler of whiskey and ice in one hand and rapped the table in time with the music with the other. He wore a dark silk shirt without any visible adornment on his clothes or body. And yet there was something about him, the way the bartender and waiters looked his way and the fact that there was no one seated at the adjacent tables, that spoke volumes about the man's power.

At the edge of the booth, Bill paused and Jack followed his lead. They stood there as the thin man studied them, a slim smile on his face.

"Hello, Guillaume."

"Winter," Bill replied.

The Prowler's dark gaze swung toward Jack. "Why do I think you're Jack Dwyer?"

You already know I am, Jack wanted to say. He could sense it. Someone had told Winter he was there, or the man had seen him before somehow, but it was not a guess. Winter *knew* who he was. But this time Jack remembered Bill's admonition and kept silent.

"Sit," Winter told them, and it was not an invitation.

The skin at the edges of the man's eyes crinkled slightly when he smiled. Winter sat back in the booth, leather sighing as he moved, and he regarded them.

"Thank you for coming," Bill said. "I would not have asked you to look into this if I knew of any other way. It's been nearly two months since Dallas died, and I've tapped all my sources in the underground trying to track Olivia down. She just disappeared, Winter. I couldn't turn to anyone else."

Winter barely acknowledged Bill's words. Instead he focused on Jack, who forced himself not to squirm under the intensity of the creature's scrutiny.

"You really killed Tanzer?"

Tanzer. The leader of a vicious pack that had ranged up and down the eastern seaboard slaughtering humans with abandon. It had been many months ago now, but the memory was still fresh.

Jack nodded. "Not alone, but yeah, I killed him."

"And you took out the sanctuary up in Vermont?"

Again, Jack inclined his head, but more slowly this time, less willing to lay claim to that particular feat.

Winter laughed softly. "I wonder how long your luck is going to hold out, Jack. Jack the Giant-Killer."

The dark-skinned man's eyes were almost mesmerizing. Much as he wanted to tear his gaze away, though, Jack would not. A dozen retorts came to mind but he kept his teeth clamped down on all of them and simply stared back at the beast expectantly.

At last, Winter looked away, turned his focus on Bill.

"Guillaume, I owe you my life," Winter said kindly, almost sadly. "And when I had an opportunity to save your sister's, I failed in that. No matter how far I wander or how many people whisper about me, I will never forget that. You have never called upon me before because you did not want to."

Bill began to protest but Winter waved his words away.

"I understand. Truly, I do. I walk a line between this underground world and the surviving packs and yet somehow I stay alive. Somehow." He smiled, and there were a thousand secrets in the lines of his face. "But you should know that you could call upon me forever and my debt would not be paid. Claudia's death is a dark cloud upon my heart, just as it is upon yours."

Winter paused, glanced at Jack, and then looked to Bill again.

"When her mother died and she realized her father was not going to ever behave toward her the way a father should, Olivia stayed for quite some time with your mother's pack in Quebec. In April of last year she simply left without a word. Weeks later she turned up in New York. She made friends in the underground quickly enough, and word from the wild there is that she wanted to make it in the music business. She played clubs, met all the right people, joined that scene.

"Six months ago she disappeared. Whispers in the wild say something went bad with the music thing, but I think that's just a cover."

Bill stared at Winter as though at a loss for words.

Jack wasn't. "Why?" he asked.

Winter shot him a questioning glance.

"I mean why do you think that?"

The thin Prowler tapped his fingers in time with the music again and when he spoke again, it was to both of them.

"Jasmine," Winter said calmly.

"Shit," Jack whispered. Jasmine had been Tanzer's mate, one of the few survivors from the pack he and his friends had destroyed. She had had a vendetta against them ever since.

"Jasmine has gathered a new pack in Manhattan," Winter continued. "She hired Dallas to kill both of you and your loved ones. Dallas was concerned for Olivia. Jasmine told him she might be able to help him locate the girl. Maybe that was just blowing smoke, hoping to guarantee his allegiance. But what if it wasn't?"

"Then Jasmine knows where she is," Jack replied. "No disrespect intended, but we knew that already. It isn't like Jasmine's just going to tell us."

At his side, Bill shuddered. Jack glanced at his friend and saw that the big man had covered his face with his hands. He ran his fingers through his beard and then turned to Jack.

"You're missing the point. Just like I missed the point. What Winter's saying is that he thinks Jasmine *has* Olivia. Took her on purpose, an insurance against me."

Winter nodded slowly, thoughtfully, fingers still tapping rhythm.

"Either that," he said, "or Jasmine already killed her."